MOONLIGHT WATER

MOONLIGHT WATER

Win Blevins

and

Meredith Blevins

A TOM DOHERTY ASSOCIATES BOOK

NEW YORK

MOONLIGHT WATER

Copyright © 2014 by Win Blevins and Meredith Blevins

All rights reserved.

A Forge Book
Published by Tom Doherty Associates, LLC
175 Fifth Avenue
New York, NY 10010

www.tor-forge.com

Forge® is a registered trademark of Tom Doherty Associates, LLC.

The Library of Congress Cataloging-in-Publication Data
is available upon request.

ISBN 978-0-7653-1994-4 (hardcover)
ISBN 978-1-4668-6980-6 (e-book)

Forge books may be purchased for educational, business, or promotional use. For information on bulk purchases, please contact the Macmillan Corporate and Premium Sales Department at 1-800-221-7945, extension 5442, or write to specialmarkets@macmillan.com.

First Edition: January 2015

Printed in the United States of America

0 9 8 7 6 5 4 3 2 1

*To our family and friends
and everyone walking in* Hózhó

TEACHINGS OF THE NAVAJO BLESSING WAY

Be generous and kind
Haáh wiinit'í

Acknowledge and respect kinship and clanship
K'ézhnidzin

Seek traditional knowledge and traditions
Hane'zhdindzin

Respect values
Hwił iłi

Respect the sacred nature of the self
Ádá hozhdilzin

Have reverence and care of speech
Hazaad baa áhojilyá

Be a careful listener
Hazhó'ó ajíists'áá'

Be appreciative and thankful
Ahééh jinízin

Show positive feelings toward others
Há hózhó

Express appropriate and proper sense of humor
Dłoh hodichí yá'átéhígíí hazhó'ó bee yájíłti'

Maintain a strong reverence of the self
Ádił jídlí

Maintain enthusiasm and motivation for your work
Hanaanish ájíł'íinii bízhneedlí

Have a balanced perspective and mind
Hanítsékees k'ézdongo ájósin

—from a poster
in the elementary school
at Moonlight Water

PART ONE

In Which Robbie Meets Creation

1

A CHOICE OF WORLDS

Roiling and rebellious. Gray water heaving with great white sharks. Ships sailing under the Golden Gate Bridge packed with mysteries from China. Fortunes earned and burned. Writers and millionaires made. Mark Twain and Mark Hopkins. San Francisco has eaten giants and ordinary dreamers alike. It has sculpted them from legends and landfill along the Barbary Coast.

Crushed, reborn, or created. The city does not care. Rock musician or railroad magnate, all the same. San Francisco was built on visions. Dead dreams, shiny ones, those unspoken, and those stillborn. Rob Macgregor was just one more soldier in the city's army of waking dreamers. One night, sleeping in his boat, Robbie was handed a possibility from the city's ancient chest of dreams.

————

Cruising. Dark highway punctuated by the two headlights of his Alfa convertible. In the distance a bridge teetered toward the east side of the bay, a span that always made him edgy.

Up the steep angle toward a summit. He knew perfectly well that from there the bridge simply curved out of sight, downward. But he often imagined, teasing himself, that at the top it ended. Simply ended. And, in this particular dreamscape, his fantasy turned to reality. When he got to the apex, he flew off the end of the bridge into empty air.

Fear bolted through his veins like a psychedelic nightmare. The Alfa hit the water like a missile and slid toward the bottom. Robbie felt the water rise in his body from his feet to his legs to his belly and on up. When it flowed into and out of his nostrils, he knew he was about to die. He was paralyzed.

The convertible bumped onto the sandy bottom nose first, then tail. As it settled to horizontal, the water gushed out his throat, his mouth, and his nose. Rage to live rose with it.

Spasmodically, he tried to jerk in breath, knowing it would drown him, and . . .

The miracle happened. It was air. He was breathing sweet air.

As quickly as a lightning bolt is gone, water was air, and life was death.

Relaxing, he looked around. Sea urchins. Small fish. Off to the left, a bed of kelp. The cells of his body calmed, and he felt welcome here. He opened the door of the car, put his left leg on the bottom of the bay, and stepped deeper into his dream.

He saw himself climb out of the bay on the east side. He was buck-naked. In front of him all the towns of the East Bay had disappeared. In that direction, toward the middle of the America this urban man barely knew, he saw no streets and no houses, only hills cloaked in trees and darkness. He turned, sat, and looked back at the watery grave of his fine car, oddly at peace.

People gathered, walked around the edge of the bay, and

pointed. Their mouths moved, but he heard nothing. They didn't notice the naked Robbie.

A tow truck backed to the water's edge. Cop cars wheeled in. Divers put on wet suits, and still no one noticed the naked Robbie.

Before long the Alfa was cable-hoisted to the bank.

Robbie felt a tremolo. Who or what might be in the driver's seat? Robbie Macgregor, the once-celebrated rock musician, now a corpse?

He couldn't look.

But he did look.

Nothing there. No one. Seat empty.

Robbie felt a pulse of sweet exhilaration. *I am invisible. I am a no-man. I could . . .*

He peered into the waters and wondered. *Never mind. Why examine a miracle? Why try to wrap it in puny words? I am free.*

Photographers showed up, the crowd swelled, and not a soul saw Robbie Macgregor sitting there.

He stood up and held his hands high. He shook his hips. He laughed into the sky. No one heard, and no one noticed.

He turned and looked at the darkened lands, the unknown eastern side of the bay across from the city where he had grown up, become a man, learned music, got rich, and got . . . Never mind.

I could walk over those hills into a new world and do anything.

He started to shiver. Fear? Excitement? Didn't matter.

I could do and be anything, anyone.

When Robbie woke in the middle of the night, he couldn't get back to sleep. He sat on the deck of his sailboat and waited quietly, drank coffee through first light to the dawn, and let images from the dream play in his mind. They faded some and got jumbled in their order. But he held its core in a pocket of his soul. He knew he'd been carrying the shadow of this dream for a long time.

Later that day Robbie walked the shore of a half-moon beach to the south, and then far to the north. He let the dream play like a musical score in rhythm to his steps while he turned his life around and around in his mind.

When he got tired, he sat on a low stone, took off his sneakers, and wriggled salt-sand between his toes. The tide was out, and the anemones on the seaward side of the stone had closed. Wondrous anemones.

He picked up a stick of flotsam and drew in the sand. He loved drawing, and he'd let himself drift away from it. In fact, he'd drifted away from many parts of himself. Fallen into doing music he didn't love, playing it only for other people, living out other people's fantasies. He wasn't sure exactly what his own way *was* anymore. One hell of a predicament.

He rubbed out the drawing and started a new one. After a while it grew, it had life, and he thought it wanted to be a man dancing. Robbie danced a lot onstage. That sketch felt pretty good, but he rubbed it out, too. One day it might be easy again. Could be.

He walked to a beach shack, bought a hero sandwich, found another boulder to sit on, and ate slowly. The tide was starting in now.

What do I know? Nothing.

He ate.

If I knew something, what would it be?

That my dream was about me dying. And an invitation to being born.

He wadded up the sandwich paper and stuffed it into a jeans pocket. Put his shoes back on. Walked again. He walked all afternoon. The incoming waters slushed around his sneakers. He looked at the sun, setting far to the west. Which, he said to himself, thinking of Japan and red paper fans, was also the East. He smiled at how many possibilities each direction held.

He took a few steps onto drier sand and walked toward the parked Alfa.

What do I know?

I want to walk over those East Bay hills, low and curved like lion paws. I will go as a new person, a blank slate, waiting for a life to be written.

As he walked, he carried that knowledge in each step, and he knew it in his flesh. Felt it the way a man feels his desire to meld himself heart and soul with a particular woman. Knew.

2

STANDING IN THE DOOR
TO HELL

*Several weeks earlier, just north of
San Francisco*

Denial. Robbie had been fending off reality for years, and he never needed his denial fix more than now.

So there he was, sitting at the kitchen counter of his fancy house, Anchor Steam at hand before breakfast, toying with the break in a new song. "You'll come," he said. "Just one simple break, why are you holding out on me?" He could have been talking to his wife. Music was like that sometimes.

Robbie often talked to his songs as he wrote them, especially now when it was getting harder to bring them into the world. Frustration ate at him as lyrics and melodies hid in the shadows. Sometimes he whipped his songs into being, his words a charging team of horses. Other times he seduced them into life. Performing under the name Rob Roy, he threw his tall, burly body around the stage with the madness of a Scot warrior going berserk, and he belted out songs like battle cries.

Robbie played half the musical instruments known to man, sang choruses with the brassiness of a trombone, and wrote every kind of music imaginable and some that wasn't. *Rolling Stone* once wrote that his songs resembled classical music gone Grateful Dead. Robbie thought they meant something positive, though he didn't know what.

So get at it.

His band, the Elegant Demons, had to have a new song for its upcoming tour. If personal life was hellish for Robbie right then, so what?

The guitar break was coming. He could feel it now, a gentle interlude before a pagan-blast chorus. At the end of the second line, where the verse made mention of the lost lover, he tried a B minor in place of the D major. "Nice," he said. He crossed out "D" on the lead sheet and wrote "Bm." Tried it again— "Grabs the ear." This didn't feel like a great song, but when the band had it going on, when the moment and the music fused with the energy of a huge crowd, any of his songs could turn magical. They were a jam band, not known for their studio recordings but for their break-down-the-wall improvisations.

He took a deep breath and let the tune run through his bones. He coaxed the first phrase along, it was just about there.

The phone outclanged the music. "Shit!" he snapped. But he flipped the damn thing open. Only his wife, the band members, and his manager's office had this number.

"Speak," said Robbie, the greeting he always used.

"It's Nora."

"Yes."

"Georgia and I are on the way. We'll be there in ten minutes."

———

He put his guitar in its case, thumped back onto the stool at the counter, and pulled on the beer. This was wrong, all wrong, more of the hell he was denying.

Two days ago his wife, Georgia, had lost the baby—three times they'd tried now, three miscarriages. He'd first gotten the call about the baby catastrophe from Nora: "Get down to the hospital. Georgia's lost the baby, and she wants you."

He spent the short drive furious at Nora. His wife was in deep trouble. Why hadn't anyone, why hadn't Nora, called him until it was over?

He brushed by Nora toward the hospital bed, ready to yell back at that damned woman, but—

One look at his wife's face stopped all words. He felt like he was inside a walk-in freezer. Her pallid cheeks, her hands lifeless on the sterile white sheets, the chrome IV stand, the tubes, the needle—the thought of the dead child—this region of grief struck Robbie dumb. He had no words for anything as brutal as the life the gods threw at human beings.

Dr. Packard talked to him. He explained. When the doctor discovered that the baby in Georgia's belly, their baby, had no heartbeat, he gave her a shot that forced her to issue forth a dead thing. You couldn't call it a birth. Robbie had no energy for questioning anything. The sorrow, the bitterness, the weariness gonged in his head. Three tries, three miscarriages.

Dr. Packard threw Robbie and Nora out. "There's more bleeding than I'd like. I've sedated her heavily. Go home and let her sleep."

Robbie gave his wife's hand a squeeze. Though the grief belonged to both of them, they were ice cubes in separate trays. Even her closed eyelids seemed to shut him out.

"Robbie," Nora whispered, as if to tell him everything would be all right. He shook his head and barged out of the room. He couldn't bring himself to talk. Nora had been their business manager for a decade, and the band's accountant. Robbie liked her fine but had never felt as if he knew her, not really. Georgia's best buddy or not, he couldn't get close enough to hear her rhythm. And recently things with Nora were off, way off.

The next day at Georgia's bedside was a jumble of half-toned memories. Their decade together, Georgia all scarves and bangles and bracelets and gaiety. Georgia the explorer, meditator, practitioner of feng shui, devotee of Pilates and yoga, connoisseur of fine wines. Georgia, who loved to dance, Georgia the whirligig of fun. For years they had everything but the children they wanted. In the last year or so, less fun, but he didn't know why. Hadn't asked, either.

The second half of the day was a shuffle of comings and goings of people who called themselves helpers when their world was beyond help, actions that were useless, occasional words from Georgia. He sat numbly in his bedside chair, unable to talk to anyone, unable to talk to Nora. He felt like he was wandering through endless corridors looking, looking for something he would never find. And the corridors meandered on.

Dr. Packard put an end to it. "Clear out, both of you. Tomorrow after I've checked on her, maybe ten o'clock, I'll call and you'll probably be able to take her home."

Now the heavy front door of their house opened and broke his reverie. He swigged on the beer. *I'm drinking too much, but fuck it.*

3

DESTRUCTION

From the front archway, one set of high heels clicked their way, and one pair of slippers shushed, across acres of Mexican tile. Robbie set the bottle on the counter and waited. Two days ago the death of their child. Yesterday silence. What now?

They stopped ten steps away, Nora a step in front of Georgia. "We're in love," Nora said. "Georgia and me. We want to get married." She looked hard into Robbie's eyes, Georgia looked at Nora.

Those words stopped his breath and his heart. Robbie couldn't open his mind or his throat.

She went on. "You two . . . It's been over for a long time." She waited, as though he might say something. "Things like this happen, you understand."

He was going to suffocate.

Nora went on and on in a businesslike tone, drivel about financial and legal work to be done—truckloads of it—how her office and their lawyers could work it out.

Robbie couldn't listen. He was fighting for breath. He wanted to charge into battle with Nora, or Georgia, or himself, but he couldn't even move.

He looked into Georgia's eyes and saw grief. She looked down. He forced his body to pull over a chair for Georgia, then took her hand and helped her sit. Nora stood still, watching, but only for a moment.

"Naturally, Georgia wants the house," droned Nora.

"House is mine," Rob mumbled.

In California a spouse could keep the wealth he came into the marriage with.

"The lawyers will work it out. There's no reason things can't be settled quickly and amicably."

Breath finally came in a heaving gasp, as after a blow to the diaphragm.

Robbie willed himself to be quiet inside, and looked around his house, what was in sight and what wasn't. Odd things, the over-sized shower with twin showerheads, the bamboo garden and koi pond. His state-of-the-art recording studio. Georgia's collection of contemporary art, odd, sterile stuff. Except for his studio, Georgia had made the house her own. With his money.

"We think a week is a reasonable amount of time for you to get out of the house. Meanwhile, Georgia will stay with me."

Robbie realized they were waiting for him to say something.

He looked from the face of his wife to the face of her lover. But his throat wouldn't make words. His mind slashed with violent answers, which fit Rob Roy of the Elegant Demons but were wet noodles in the hands of Robbie Macgregor, husband.

No goddamn words were right. He squatted in front of his wife. She closed the blinds on all feeling and shut him out.

He looked up and tried to peer inside the heart of the woman who was stealing his wife. Nora stood behind brick walls.

"One minute," he finally muttered.

He held his wife's chin. He felt her head sink onto his hand, but she kept her eyes down. Georgia was no Julee, his first wife of long ago. Julee walked through the world chirping, chatting, and popping her gum. Georgia was a good woman, intelligent, spiritually aware, and maybe the best-looking almost-forty woman in Marin County. So she'd explored herself and found she preferred women. *My fury is stupid.*

Robbie prodded himself to full height and shot a look down at Nora. Homely, tough, middle-aged, armored in classy suits and iron-gray hair. Outspoken, honest, hard-nosed. At this moment he hated her. At any time he would refuse to negotiate with her. That's what he had a lawyer for, his best friend, Gianni Montella.

Robbie hurled the words he spoke like boulders. "I'll be gone day after tomorrow." He let them feel the weight of the boulders. "Anything to say, say it to Gianni."

Georgia blinked tears downward.

Robbie clenched his stomach to keep from throwing up. He turned and slammed his back to them.

As their shoes clicked and padded away, they sounded out Robbie's silent words all the way to the front door. *I despise you. I despise this house. I despise this too-too Marin County. I despise the music business.* And, even more mutely, *I despise myself as a fool.*

At the heavy, carved door Georgia turned. "Robbie?" She waited until he looked around. "It's not just about Nora. It's about you. I can't find you. I lost us."

He ignored the words. Though she shut the door gently, he heard a slam, one that sounded like it was inside him.

4

HOW DO WE GET THERE
FROM HERE?

Robbie sat at his own bar, drank two Anchor Steams, and put the third back. He knew what to do—go ask the one person who always had wise words for him. Robbie needed his grandfather, and he needed him big-time. Top of his car down, time for a visit.

In his Alfa he zipped through the tunnel just north of the city and cruised into the world's finest vista—the Golden Gate Bridge, San Francisco Bay. The city's spires caught light and held it. To the west stretched the vast Pacific. It was a perfect day with the kind of clarity that comes rarely, an extraordinary gift. He could have seen, maybe, a hundred miles out to sea, but he didn't glance that way. He listened to his own heartbeat. That was surprising. The double thump drummed *freedom, freedom, freedom.*

Grandpa, here I come.

Robbie's only relative now lived in the Columbarium, a sanctum of the deified dead in the middle of Pacific Heights.

Like a grand old dowager, the Columbarium faced the world in the style of her youth, Beaux Arts, a high-flown elegance.

Her function was simple: She housed the ashes of San Francisco's finest and quirkiest. Here they rested forever, in a fairyland that fulfilled their mannered or freakish dreams.

Grandfather Angus Stuart first brought Robbie here, just after he came home from his stint in the army. Though the Columbarium had a caretaker and guide, Grandfather Angus conducted his own tour. "This is the end you come to," he said, "when you waste your life on society." Grandfather Angus was a lifelong socialist and had started as an IWW man, one of Harry Bridges's stevedores during the days when unions ruled the docks.

"Look here now. Here's a man gone to his rest, and on his urn are two martini shakers. Sums up his life, don't it, and a wasted life it was. Here's another'n, gone to his grave with a big cigar and a highball glass for a memorial." Grandpa snorted in disgust.

"Now this lady, per'aps she wasn't such a wastrel." Her niche featured a big ceramic baseball in front of a painted backdrop and tiny players surrounding it. "Loved the game, she did, and the Giants. A magnetic key turns on that little light, and the robotic players make motions of throwing, catching, and hitting. Those grown-ups and kids in the bleachers there, they cheer for the team. Nothing beats passion. It's the only reason for being.

"Look here, now, at this niche." It bore two tobacco canisters behind a glass wall, Balkan Sobranie brand, but no legend bearing the name of the deceased. Robbie was antsy—the place would give anyone the creeps. "Pay attention! I want you to put me to rest here."

"Grandpa?"

"Yes, right here. When I was a young man, I had two friends, names of Brian Connery and Hamish McDougal. Real mates we was, did everything together. One night we pooled our cash and made the bet of our lives. The headlines had been beating the drums for the big fight between the new heavyweight champion of the world, Joe Louis, and Max Schmeling. Everyone knew a war was coming, and this was America versus Germany, freedom versus fascism, our way versus theirs. Note, Robbie, that it was the first time a black man carried the flag of American ideals.

"It was the purest patriotism to place a bet, and we won a bundle. We celebrated with Laphroaig, and decided to go afloat on that prince of Scotch whisky for a month. Then Brian, he was the thinker, had a different idea. "Two bottles, then let's go buy a spot in the Columbarium.""

"Says I, 'There's only rich stiffs in that place.'

"'Exactly,' says Brian. 'That place needs a workingman to pollute the cologne of the swells.'

"Hamish and me, stinking drunk, we laughed and come down here with Brian and bought this niche. We drew straws for which of us should rest forever among the bleeding rich. I lost." He fixed Robbie with his eyes. "So you will put me right here," said Grandfather Angus. "Swear it."

When Grandfather Angus went to his reward in great age, Robbie dutifully deposited the ashes inside the two tobacco canisters.

Now he stood spread legged before the man who felt like his real father. There were no benches or other seats in the Columbarium, which was a nuisance. Robbie shifted his weight from foot to foot and read the words engraved on the plate below the canisters:

ANGUS STUART, 1910–1995
WARRIOR FOR HIS PEOPLE
DEFENDER OF THE POOR
REST IN PEACE

Robbie had been an agnostic for twenty years, or what he sometimes called a Seventh-Day Absentist. Nevertheless, he said a prayer. Then he held a Sobranie out toward the canister, a toast to the old man. If Grandfather Angus was hovering nearby, nothing he'd like better than a puff of strong Turkish tobacco. But a hint was all Angus would get—no smoking allowed inside the Palace of the Dead.

"Light it," said a sepulchral voice. Robbie turned toward a head of frizzy hair at the level of his chest. A bony face gazed up at Robbie, skeletal except for the eyes, which were mad, lit with the avidity of the devotee. "It's all right. I have the honor of being the caretaker here. Light it."

Robbie did, took a deep drag, and blew the smoke toward Grandfather Angus's ashes. He offered a cigarette to the caretaker but got a smiling shake of the head.

"Does he ever speak to you?"

Robbie stubbed out the cigarette, thinking. Somewhere in this caretaker of the dead burned an ancient and mystic flame twisted wrong. "Not directly. No. But right now he'd probably like a little piping."

"The bagpipes?" asked the caretaker. "I don't know much about them."

Robbie said, "Perhaps you could read a Robbie Burns poem for him. He loved Robbie Burns. Don't all Scots?" He heard the skepticism in his own voice.

The caretaker whisked Robbie's comment aside. "I know. Some people think I'm crazy. But I've found that if I'm to spend my days among these dead, I must befriend them. Maybe it keeps me sane. And it seems essential. Their lives continue through me, through my stories of them. I yearn to pass them along to other pilgrims who come here."

Those eyes gave Robbie the willies.

"You said he's your grandfather. Were you close?"

Robbie took in a deep breath and let it out. "Lived with him when I was a teenager. My mother's father. Grandfather Angus."

"You don't say now."

What the hell! The weirdo was doing a bad Scots' brogue.

They looked into each other, one man a hungry skeleton, the other a car wreck and wandering soul.

"My grandma," Robbie said, "she died early on. Then it was just me and Grandpa Angus—my mother was off chasing romance. Pretty soon she married an accountant and moved to Ohio. Me and Grandpa, we lived in the old apartment, rented out the downstairs for a shop, made ends meet. We were the gravity of each other's lives. When I think of him, I start striding big, like him. Scots all the way, he was, with a fighting spirit."

Somehow Robbie wanted to talk about his family, and this man had the need to taste these lives and swallow them whole. Robbie looked at the caretaker and understood. The man was less a guardian of the dead than a spirit cannibal.

"I'm a musician," Robbie said, as if that were a shield. Looked at the strange man once more. "Think I'd better go now."

"Glad to hear your stories, Mr. Macgregor."

Robbie's stomach went into a double knot. How'd this ghoul know his name? "I won't be seeing you again," Robbie said.

"Everyone comes back, sooner or later."

Robbie leveled him with a gaze. "Give me a moment alone with him, will you?"

"Certainly." He wafted away.

Robbie turned back to the canisters.

Deep breath. He relit the Balkan Sobranie and blew smoke toward the canisters. "So long, Grandpa." Robbie kissed his fingers, touched them to the glass, and strode out. There was a friend to see, things to do.

Revulsion. Walking into Gianni's law office, Robbie realized he couldn't talk with his friend here. Deep rugs, polished wood, gleaming metal, a receptionist decked out for show—the room oozed glitter and luxury. Gianni owned this law business with a single partner, and they specialized in keeping tax money out of the hands of the government by setting up living trusts.

They had two young lawyers who did most of the actual work. A wealthy man's enclave. The ambience writhed around Robbie like a serpent.

Gianni strode into the outer office, steps long, arms wide. For a little guy he acted big. "Hey, *paisan*." His Italian ancestry served him well in San Francisco. He'd been born Johnny Montella to the only Catholic family in a tiny Mormon town, but now he called the upper echelon of a great city *paisan*. And he was Robbie's oldest friend. They grabbed each other in a bear hug. Gianni's head came up to the middle of Robbie's big chest.

"What brings you to the city?"

Robbie let out a big breath. "I need to borrow your cabin for a few days, maybe a few weeks."

It was a big request. Gianni had a one-room house on a hill above Stinson Beach. He called it his cabin, perhaps to minimize its luxury. On weekends he used it as his personal refuge from the world. He invited almost no one there, and even Robbie had never stayed overnight.

"I'll need to hang out alone, except for tonight. Tonight we need to talk."

"What's going on?"

"Too big. I'll tell you when you get there."

Gianni handed over the keys. "I'll bring cartons of Thai."

He was the best of friends.

Robbie spent the rest of the afternoon in a chaise longue on Gianni's deck, looking out at the Pacific and toward the Farallon Islands, just beyond the horizon. As a devoted weekend sailor Robbie knew those waters well. But he didn't think about sailing. He didn't think about anything at all. He was not an analytical man. His way was to sit with something, whether a new song or a personal problem, and just keep it company until he had a feeling about what to do.

So now he lay back and sucked the ocean into his lungs. He felt the sun on his skin and the wind in his long, thick red hair, now streaked with gray. He deliberately left his mind a blank. There were some comings and goings inside there, faces, remembered bits of talk, and wisps of music, some of it his own, some that belonged to other people, some he'd never heard before. But he let it all come and go.

When the sun went down, he went inside and wandered around the single, open octagonal room of the cabin. Funny, he'd never realized how many beautiful objects Gianni had gathered here. He had Navajo rugs, probably because his hometown was mostly Navajo, right on the border of the rez. The rugs were large and, now that Robbie looked, extraordinarily beautiful. There were baskets, woven with motifs similar to the rugs. There were wood carvings of dancing figures that must be mythological. For whatever reason, all of it pleased Robbie. He felt no need to know what it was, who made it, or what the various designs might symbolize. He stretched out on an eight-foot leather sofa and let his mind roam.

In good time Gianni arrived with the Thai.

Over full plates, Gianni went right to it. "Give. What's going on?"

Robbie told him. First, and in full, about Georgia losing the baby. Then, bluntly and briefly, about Georgia and Nora kicking him out.

He let the information sit between them, no comment. He didn't know any more about what it meant for his future than his buddy did.

Gianni got up and brought them snifters of an Armagnac that probably cost a hundred bucks a bottle. "Where now?"

"Gianni, I have no idea." He wanted company but wasn't ready to bat ideas around. He turned away from Gianni and pretended to study the room. "Would you tell me something about this collection of art? I've never really paid attention. Extraordinary stuff."

Gianni led him from piece to piece. Later Robbie half-remembered terms like *eye-dazzler* and *Two Gray Hills* for the rugs and *ceremonial* for the baskets, but not much more. He fingered a basket woven of sumac and sealed with pine pitch so it would hold water. Robbie listened as Gianni explained that he tried to support young artists doing traditional Navajo art in new materials, letting the art change with the times while paying tribute to the past.

Making conversation, Robbie asked about Hopi art.

"I love the Navajo people, because I grew up among them. I don't do other Native art, not Pueblo, not Anasazi, nothing."

Robbie suppressed a yawn.

"Friend, you need some sleep."

"Gianni, I see a bit of the way ahead. Tomorrow I go to the house, get my clothes and a few instruments. Then I need to hide out here until I can see things clearer, figure out what I want to do."

"What do you need to do in this world, except play music, make a little art?"

Robbie held his friend's eyes. "I don't know. Everything. Something. I'm in the dark here, Gianni. That's why I need time. Time to be alone long enough to figure it out."

In other words, I need to take over your private space. It was a lot to ask.

"Anything I have, anything I can do, it's yours." Gianni walked to the door and turned back. "Meanwhile, I'm still protecting your ass. Georgia and Nora can get half your money, but not the house. It was bought with your money before you met Georgia, payments came out of your money, so it's yours."

"I don't want to talk to them."

"That's what you have me for."

Robbie made two last trips to the house that was now a stranger to him, carefully avoiding Georgia and Nora. He slipped away with his favorite instruments—the Fender Stratocaster, an old Martin D-28, his accordion, and two harmonicas. His collection was a lot bigger, but these he wouldn't do without. Then he got his keyboard. Final thought, urgent, he remembered both laptops. His music-writing programs, the digital versions of all his lead sheets. Someday, maybe, he'd want to write music again. And what about the years of sketch pads stacked in his office, fewer filled as time had passed? He took one that had only a few drawings in it and shoved a Rapidograph pen in his pocket, fine point. Black ink.

Back at the cabin he lounged through the evening, thoughts drifting by, big and small. He decided to quit drinking for a while. The next day he mostly walked the beach. Thoughts came to him like driftwood, the same way his music came. On the second day he discovered that mixing a little jazzy movement in his steps across the sand fertilized his imagination and fed his body. Nothing like the athletic moves he made with the band, but it didn't matter why dancing helped—you don't take a cardiogram of the heart and soul of music, art, or dance. A sign above his desk back in the old house quoted Nietzsche, something like, "Those who can't hear the music think the dancers are crazy." True.

So he walked and napped and remembered and dreamed, and every once in a while he pulled out his pen and sketch pad. Didn't flow like it used to, but it pleased him. Letting his hand do the drawing, he tossed around what had gone right and wrong for twenty years, and the many times he had been sound asleep during his waking life.

Gianni. How clueless and how wonderful we were.

Robbie threw himself into a deck chair and ticked back over their friendship—right now it was an anchor. They'd enlisted, met in the army, one city kid and one country kid, working-class young men, gung ho to help their country in the first Gulf War. By the time they finished basic training, the war was over, and the army assigned them to duty on Okinawa. Turned out the Okinawan occupation was the embodiment of the Japanese government's pretense at complying with the World War II treaty granting America a military presence in Japan—the island was nowhere near the real Japan. They spent their enlistments doing drills, and all they learned, really, was bar fighting.

Except one other thing—they played a lot of music. Robbie scrounged up a guitar and a harmonica and created nice backups for Gianni's lyric tenor—he had a fine voice and an encyclopedic memory for lyrics. They got back to the States ravenous to become big-deal musicians.

They put together several Bay Area bands. They tried everything they thought might sell, and some of the music sounded pretty good. But Robbie wasn't comfortable. He started writing songs for his own big voice and acoustic guitar. He drove up the coast highway to Tomales and sat with Ramblin' Jack Elliott, wanting to learn folk, but that didn't work for Robbie, either.

Then the Elegant Demons came into his life. When the lead guitarist and keyboard player of the Demons got sick before a concert, Robbie sat in for him. The gig was simple—play in Golden Gate Park on a midsummer Sunday afternoon and do old Grateful Dead songs, nothing else, just covers of the Dead.

They only had two days to rehearse, and what they got into surprised them all. The Dead, known for its long jams, hooked into a current and explored it, exploited it. The crowds rode the wave. A Dead concert was a journey into far-flung musical galaxies.

Robbie and Kell had that kind of rapport from the first chord. The Dead songs were great, but they wanted to try their own stuff. During rehearsal, their lyrical tunes turned into dervishes. They took phrases from each other, transformed them, and shaped them into new verses and choruses.

Kell was a special performer, slender and pretty, a gravelly tenor who reminded people of a male Janis Joplin in the rawness and pathos of his expression. Onstage he was pure emotion, and a perfect partner. At the end of the last rehearsal, he said to Robbie, "We're in the *center* of it!"

In person Kell was entirely different. He had almost nothing to say to anyone, just packed up his guitar and left after rehearsals and concerts. He came for the music—he lived to sing—and he gave nothing of himself anywhere else. In some odd way Robbie understood, though he couldn't have explained it. Couldn't have lived it.

When they played live that first time, instead of pulling back to the straightforward renditions on Dead albums, Robbie and Kell let it fly, filled their musical sails, and followed wherever the winds blew. The crowd went with them. Wild, crazed, happy, all good things.

At the end of that concert Gianni said to Robbie, "Hey, I can't do what you guys do. Haven't got the juice for it." Gianni liked to sing music that was written down and stick with it. "You guys are tight, though. Go for it."

Robbie had looked at the hastily printed program sheet Gianni had put together. "This calls the band the Elegant Demons and me Rob Roy." He pursed his mouth. "Are we stuck with those names?"

Gianni gestured at the crowd, still milling around, no one ready to leave. "I wouldn't exactly call this being stuck."

Soon they had all the Bay Area gigs they wanted. They added songs Robbie or Kell wrote, improvising, dancing with their skewed joint muse in epic jams. *Rolling Stone* took notice: "Kell sings lead vocals that break your heart wide open, and Rob Roy puts his soul into everything—composing, playing, and madman crash-dancing. The Elegant Demons are riding the edge of something brand-new."

A record company amped up the roller coaster, the band made the charts, and the cash registers went ching-a-ching-ching-ching. The musicians took in so much they hired accountants to keep track. The band simply enjoyed themselves and spent the dough buying million-dollar houses, fast cars, classic motorcycles, sleek boats, and leaving twenty-dollar tips for thirty-dollar beer tabs. Kell's handsome face made the front pages of magazines, and the music world knew Rob Roy was the pulse of the Elegant Demons.

Through the years, Gianni was there with encouragement and solid sense. He'd long since gone his own way. He went to law school, straight into a posh firm, and then formed his own business handling trusts. In other words, handling a lot of money.

"How can you give up music?" Robbie had asked him.

Gianni answered, "I'm good, but I'm not in your league." Still, he went to almost every one of the band's concerts within five hundred miles, popped in on studio sessions, stood as best man at both of Robbie's weddings, and was ready to go for a sail almost any time. Then Gianni would take a trip back home, disappear into the quiet, and get grounded.

When Robbie asked if he wished things had shaken out differently for him with the music, Gianni said he liked his work, the money, and collecting Navajo art. "Robbie," he'd said, "I love my life."

Now Robbie Macgregor sat in Gianni's cabin and thought, *I damn well do not love mine.* He shook his head, smiled, and looked at the eye-dazzler weaving on the wall next to him.

He had relived his dream a hundred times since it had visited him. He pictured the high flight off the bridge, enjoyed the splash, felt the slow drift to the bottom, and saw himself standing buck naked on the shore. He looked again at the wooded hills to the east, rolling in shadow. What was out there?

He still knew what he knew that night. Because of the divorce, even more so. Time to go. Where to go? He didn't know.

Here's what he knew: It would be hard. Painful. Wrenching. A whole life gone. Money gone. Audiences gone. Thrills gone.

And what might he find to take their place in his heart?

What awaited, far out in the somewhere? Maybe nothing. He had to look that one square in the face.

Well, he thought there would be music of some kind, anywhere. But maybe music alone. Loneliness, that's what might be out there. He refused to let himself get away with not looking at the emptiness. But he also refused to linger there.

Yes, yes, what he sought was there—possibility. A big word with a big reach, it might include anything. Possibility was just that, and that was plenty.

He got out his pen, pulled paper from Gianni's printer, and began. The first part was basic. He needed a new name. The surname was clear—he would take Grandfather Angus's, Stuart, a clan as fine as Macgregor. Robbie had the first name, too, slapping him in the face, and it was a chuckle. The nickname of the infamous Rob Roy Macgregor had been Red. Hi, Red Stuart.

Suddenly he thought of what he had to do, right off, as Red Stuart. He went to the bathroom, got out his electric razor, and gave himself a buzz cut. Looked at himself. Strange. Hadn't looked like this since the army. He'd have to grow a beard to keep from looking like a suit.

He looked at the long, shaggy, frizzy locks in the wastebasket. Good-bye, Rob Macgregor.

He ran his hands all over his head. Felt strange.

He slipped off the plastic attachment and shaved his face clean.

Wow, the mirror said. Odd, very odd.

Who are you, Red Stuart?

He sat back down as the new guy and began to list the hundred details that guy needed taken care of.

Georgia? Nora? The band? He would do nothing. They didn't exist. They weren't real. Same for the divorce, the house, the settlement, everything.

Money? Tricky. A new life wouldn't be free. Nora handled

all his accounts, so he couldn't filch any funds without her knowing. If he took his half, or if he even took a couple of million, even a few hundred thousand, she would know, and he couldn't . . . Do what? He hadn't worked it out.

He pondered long and fell asleep without a solution.

And he woke up with one. Grandfather Angus's money. Grandpa had willed Robbie the equity in his duplex, less than a hundred grand. Robbie had said nothing about it to Georgia or Nora, having been burned in one divorce already. He'd let Gianni put the money in some Silicon Valley stocks for him, and it had more than doubled over the years. Just enough for a fresh start.

Robbie was missing one thing. A gesture. He needed a gesture to Georgia, to the band, mostly to himself.

Back to walking the beach. He was squatting in a tide pool poking an anemone and watching it spout when the idea came to him.

He spent a day thinking it through. This gesture was right. The next morning he made a phone call. Gianni sounded relieved to hear from him, and promised to be at the cabin by seven that evening, this time with cartons of Indian food. Where he was heading, Robbie didn't expect to find much of that.

5

THE LIGHTBULB BLOWS

"First, here's my new cell phone number." Robbie laid a small piece of paper next to Gianni's plate. "You're the only person in the world who has it. Keep it that way."

"Sure." Gianni grinned. He tucked the paper into his wallet and looked back at Red's face. "I'll never get used to seeing you like that."

"Let's not live in the past."

"Whatever you say, Rob."

"Another big favor," he said.

"No problem. Don't you love this curry?"

"You've always said that I should come in on one of your big enterprises. That I'm too conservative, yada yada. Now I'm on board. Sell my stocks and give me seventy-five grand. Cash. Put the rest into something good."

"This doesn't sound like you."

"Just do it, please."

"You sure?"

Robbie set his chin on his hand, looked at Gianni, and said, "As sure as I can be about anything."

Gianni perked up. "Actually, this is perfect timing. I'd like one more person for a joint venture, and it'd be good to have you. Come into the office and I'll go over the details with you. It's a sweet deal."

"I don't want to come to the office. I trust you. But, Gianni, make it come together. It'll be all the money I have in the world."

"Wait a minute. Your boring portfolio, music royalties, the house, the money Nora has invested for both you and Georgia?"

"I kiss it all good-bye."

Long pause.

"I'm keeping enough to live on reasonably for one year."

"You? Seventy-five grand? What's happening here? Really happening?"

"Let's walk." These days Robbie could barely think unless he was walking.

Gianni left his custom-made Italian shoes behind and hopped barefoot through the weeds. The air was still, thick, salty. Robbie felt like he was breathing an essential transfusion of blood and funky new life. They crossed onto the packed, damp shoreline sand.

"Gianni, I'm gone. It's for certain they've looked for me at my boat, and that they'll never look here. Nora and Georgia's attorneys are probably writing me piles of notices, but they don't know where to send them. And with your help, they never will."

"You're not . . ."

Robbie let a beat pass. "The band will find a way to manufacture money without me."

"This isn't funny, Robbie. We're talking your life, your career, your money down the toilet. Why are you grinning? I'm worried about you, and probably not as worried as I should be."

"Hey, we Scots don't weep, we battle-cry," Robbie said.

"Robbie? Enough."

"Here's the bottom line: Everyone wants something from me, and they'll look for me. I have a counter-move." He stopped and took his friend by the shoulders. "I say, 'Rob Roy, who's that? Robbie Macgregor, who's that?' With one gesture, I slip off the world."

"What has possessed you?"

Robbie let go of Gianni and strode on. "I'm wild with ideas. The first is Start Over."

"You've lost your marbles."

"No, I have a new set of them. Gianni, I had one twenty-year adult life. It was good, it was bad, it was juicy, and then it was . . . It's stretched out in front of me now in a casket. I see a bloodless face and eyes that are open but see nothing. But me? I'm alive, and I'm going for it."

"Going for what?"

"That's the best part. *I have no idea.*"

"Maybe if you made this into a song you'd have another big hit."

Robbie laughed, shoved his friend a little, and then grabbed his hand before he could fall on the sand. "Enough of the long face and sweaty forehead. It's going to be okay."

They walked on.

"And, Gianni? No kidding, I'm counting on you."

"What do you want?"

"First say, 'We're old pals. I'm with you all the way.'"

Hesitation. "I'm with you all the way. Jeez, do I have a choice?" He tried out a smile.

Another bear hug and slap on the back. "So, it's simple. Keep telling everyone that you have no idea where I am. Sell the stocks and invest the money. Give me a couple of weeks to get new ID, and when I say, 'Meet me in the dark of night at Point Reyes,' be there for me."

There went Gianni's small smile. "What the fuck?"

Robbie sat on a boulder and looked out on the slate-shake sea, moonlight rippling on its surface. After a moment Gianni joined him. Robbie lit a Balkan Sobranie, inhaled deeply, and handed it to his friend. "Gianni, I'm getting rid of Rob Roy. I'm changing Robbie Macgregor's name. From now on I'm Red Stuart." He paused. "Truly."

Gianni said, "Okay, okay. But what's this melodrama about the dark of night and Point Reyes?"

"After business is finished with the fake ID gypsies, I'm going to trade in the Alfa, buy a van, put a bed in the back, and I'm asking you to bring the van to me at Point Reyes. At night."

Gianni looked at him quizzically.

"Right now it doesn't matter why Point Reyes, okay? Then I'm going to drive into the parts of America I don't know, which is most of it. Walk woods, look at new night skies. Visit national parks." Robbie blew smoke toward the ocean. "You think anyone ever gets laid in a national park?"

"Yeah, bears and other creatures you don't want to get near."

"Gad, you can be a cynical sort. Anyway, I'm going to eat in diners, find the best meat loaf anywhere, and check out whatever folk art is around. Sketch some. I'm hoping every state has something as mind-boggling as Carhenge. Do you know about Carhenge?"

"No."

Didn't sound like he wanted to know either, but Robbie pitched in. "Gianni, in Alliance, Nebraska—get that, Nebraska!—a guy has built a memorial to his father called Carhenge. It's thirty-eight vintage automobiles arranged to look like, you know, Stonehenge in England. The circle is a hundred feet across. Some of the cars have been halfway buried with the grill end up, and others are welded onto them to create the arches.

"Gianni, imagine the dedication, the time, the love, the art. . . .

I want to discover something like that in every state. Art everywhere! Art of the people."

"Watts Towers didn't do it for you?"

A moment of silence.

"Gianni, I don't know who or what I'll find. But I want to explore. That's why I'm going."

"Will you do music anymore?"

Robbie shrugged. "Can't imagine being without it, but can't imagine what to do with it right now."

"What the hell," said Gianni, shaking his head. Gianni took in Rob with his eyes all the way. Then, suddenly, he said, "I'm calling you out. This is shit. I'm asking you, aren't you scared? Don't you know you're scared?"

Rob breathed in and out. "Yeah." Another breath in and out. "Yeah." A third breath. "I'm real scared. I wake up feeling like I'm stiff as a steel beam in a freezing wind and I can't move.

"Maybe there's nothing out there. Nothing that matters to me. Maybe I'm running away to an empty, miserable life."

Gianni nodded at him, a *thank-god* expression on his face.

Robbie went on thoughtfully, his eyes reaching far out to the black sea. "But there are two things. I've driven my life into a brick wall, and it's not running anymore. Nothing to do but walk away from the wreck."

Now he almost waited too long, and Gianni started to speak.

"The other thing," Robbie lurched on, "is a big one. I'm excited. For the first time in probably ten years I'm juiced. I want to know what *can* be out there for me. I want to find a life for me, not for my persona, Rob Roy. Me. And the idea makes my blood rush."

Gianni waited and then said, "So the bottom line is?"

"I'm outta here. Like Lazarus, I'm gonna stand up and walk again."

Gianni stood up and faced his friend. "All right, I'll save your ass. When you run out of money in a year, I'll give you back double what I'm investing for you."

"Bravo."

"But I want you to do two things for me as a friend. And for yourself."

"Name it."

"Stay in touch. I'm the only person with your phone number. The only person from your old life."

"Done."

"I still think it's crazy, but I also know you. When your mind is set, there's no changing it."

"Damn straight."

They sat together companionably and watched the ripples dance, listened to them lap the shore like whispered promises.

Gianni turned to Robbie. "Done any drawing while you've been in the cabin?"

"A little. The patterns in the Navajo weavings, the hand-prints . . . I can feel them in every piece of pottery. Powerful stuff."

"You love it."

"No, I wouldn't say that. It's more like it amazes me. The pieces feel like they're from a different place altogether, from a different time."

"A month after you leave the Bay, why don't you meet me in Moonlight Water? It's past time for me to visit family and old friends, been a while, and Moonlight Water is where the artists are. Who knows what you might get out of it?" Gianni looked at the shades of gray, exquisite chunks of real estate, crawling up the hills of Mill Valley, and the amber lights filling those homes. Across the Bay, towers shone with the fluorescent lights of people still at work, but the lower levels, including the houses, were below his line of sight.

"Moonlight Water is the most beautiful place on the planet," Gianni told Robbie.

Red suddenly understood something real about his friend, something he'd missed all these years. Gianni was truly an expatriate. Never truly at home in San Francisco, and when he was in Moonlight Water he probably missed the energy and the river of money flowing through the Financial District. Maybe Rob was an expatriate, but from where?

He'd meet Gianni, no question about it. Being alone, Robbie needed that. After a month his friend would be a great gift. And, Gianni might like to see both of his own worlds come together. "Done deal," Robbie said.

They smoked a little and walked back to the cabin together.

Gianni stopped at his Mercedes in the driveway and fished for his keys. "Don't forget. One month after you leave, you meet me."

"Don't you forget, when I get things taken care of, meet me at Point Reyes with my new van."

"You got it."

Robbie looked to the west over Gianni's head. Patches of fog obscured the infinite ocean.

6

FUNERAL ARRANGEMENTS

After Robbie set a course and got the boat on autopilot, he carefully set the gas leaking into the bilge. There his perpetrators were, two bare wires pointing toward each other like the fingers of God and Adam in the Sistine Chapel. The wires were ready to launch the apocalypse. He took several deep breaths.

Before reaching the Golden Gate Bridge, he took the tiller again. Robbie intended to enjoy his last sail. She went sweet but not easy, and he arrived shortly before dark. Approaching the Farallons, he pulled himself into a matter-of-fact mood. Things to do.

Then he saw another boat at the moorage, and he held the *Elegant Demon* a quarter mile or more offshore. There was enough light for some sailor to see the shape of Robbie's boat, but not to guess its name or see the man on board. He dropped his sails, as if he meant to motor to the moorage. It would look like he'd started the engine in the usual way, seeing no need to vent the bilges first, forgetting he might have a leak. A spark between those bare wires, bilges sloshing with gas and fumes—the big bang.

After what was going to happen to the *Demon*, no one would be able to tell whether she had been running under sail or power. Nor would anyone be able to tell what had happened to the parts of her. Or him. Some bits would sink, shoved by currents and tides. Some would float away. And most of the fleshy human parts would be scooped up by great white sharks, top of the heap in the ocean's food chain. Simple as that.

A fine gesture.

For sure, whoever was moored at the island would hear the blast and see the flames, and another cautionary tale of a sailor's carelessness would write itself in the annals of recreational boating.

Robbie worked with deliberate, efficient movements, black in his wet suit, an onyx shadow in the fading light. He bolted the big outboard onto the stern and slid the inflatable into the rocking sea. He clambered up and down, stowing food, water, a spare set of oars, mask and fins, and other supplies for his escape. He took a last look around with a practical eye, jumped into the raft, untied, pushed off, fired up the raft's engine, and motored a hundred yards away.

He wanted to do it in the first moments of absolute darkness. With his heart's eye he looked back at her, cradled on the sea like a lover asleep.

Sweetness, sadness, eagerness, fear. All stirred within him.

He lifted a black plastic garage-door opener high. He heard the blast before he saw it.

Elegance and beauty turned to charred chaos. The cockpit belched flame like a bomb hit her. Pieces of the *Demon* arched up like rockets. The sails held her at the surface for a moment, and then she slid to the bottom of the sea.

When the last echoes of destruction had floated away, he said quietly in a tone that was almost steady, "The old me is dead. Long live Red Stuart."

———

Red shook all the way to Drake's Beach. It wasn't the wind and the water. It was the heady cocktail he'd downed, destruction and creation.

It was a clear night, and he picked up the Point Reyes Lighthouse from well out. Nearing it, he turned east and cut around the point into Drake's Bay. Easy going. Headlights beckoned to him from the beach—his one friend, Gianni. Red got on his mask and fins. He slashed each compartment of the inflatable raft with gaping rips. Instantly, he was in the water and the inflatable was ghosting to the bottom of the sea. He started swimming.

About five minutes later he emerged from the water, baptized and arisen. "Hi, Red," he said to himself, by way of introduction.

Gianni shook his hand and cried, "A toast!"

They traded high fives. They drank from Gianni's flask. They crooned in turn, "To a new life."

Gianni looked at the wet suit, fins, and mask. Deep gray smoke, acrid, wove with the fog. He shook his head. "You sure go in for the dramatic."

"A necessary statement."

Red checked that everything was in order, registration, cash, clothes, a cooler. Then he checked his other necessities—his few musical instruments, his computers, sketch pads, and good pens—all that he wanted to keep from his old life tucked into drawers beneath his mattress. He could part with everything else.

Near midnight he dropped Gianni off at his house. Red handed Gianni a handwritten note. Gianni understood— tomorrow he would call Kell and Kell would hold a press conference with the tragic announcement. Robbie's final note for the world would read: "Sorry. I just can't do it anymore."

He stepped out and gave his only friend a hug.

"By the way," Gianni said. He opened the glove box. "I put in a book you'll want to read before you meet me at Moonlight Water. Lots to discover before you get there."

Red glanced at the paperback, *Desert Solitaire,* written by someone named Edward Abbey. But Red had no interest in finding out *about* things. He wanted to suck life deep inside his lungs, and pump every molecule of the journey into his heart.

Red got in the van and started it up. He thought, *Before me lies the adventure.* The first spin of the wheels waved good-bye to his old world.

When he was a kid, Grandpa Angus always bought him bottles of goop and loops to blow bubbles. Right now he felt as bright and fragile as those rising, bright-colored bubbles on vagrant winds.

PART TWO

———•———

In Which Red Arrives. Somewhere.

7

LOST OR FOUND?

Don't eat without feeding something to the fire, or you'll never be rich.

—Navajo saying

A thousand miles and one universe from San Francisco

In the darkness Winsonfred Manygoats had a seeing. It was a flash of light, and he saw it not with his ordinary eyes but with his spirit eyes. A flash of light and parts of a boat flying into the sky, like birds flushed up by gunshot. Strange.

He was 103 years old, and in this last decade he'd gotten used to drifting from one world to another. Sometimes, as now, he also saw things. He knew when they came from another place.

He shivered, not from the evening cold. *Something is going to happen.* He knew that much. He settled back on the bench, closed his eyes, and let his mind wander. After two or three minutes he opened them again. Nothing came to him. Sometimes, along with a seeing, there were clues. None tonight.

His thoughts turned to the taste of tapioca pudding. The

cook prepared it for the old folks—Winsonfred loved tapioca. In his mind he pictured his great-granddaughter Zahnie, who had a good heart but spent her life fretting. He wondered if the seeing had to do with her. She was a good granddaughter, but she lived in a shell, hurt by life, feeling guilty and sometimes afraid.

He was sorry about that foolishness, but she was still his favorite. Zahnie had moved into a cabin in back of the care center so he wouldn't be alone there. He appreciated that, but he wished she had a man. A good man, not like the few she had let peek inside her shell.

Then he pictured Neville the patriarch in the house, glaring down from his portrait on the landing above Winsonfred's recliner. Neville was the bishop of the Mormons who founded this desert town on the edge of the Navajo reservation 103 years ago. It was the summer Winsonfred was born. The two of them had struggled for decades about what this little community would become. He sought out Neville in his heart, for Neville was long gone from the earth. *What are you up to this time?* But Winsonfred came up blank. Maybe Neville was about to make something bad happen again, another disharmony. That was his nature.

Winsonfred looked to the south, where the river ran, and sent out a wordless call to Ed, a call that would wobble his question across the indigo-domed sky to the cottonwoods along the stream. Winsonfred wasn't great with this gift of seeing. His gift was as a singer for the ceremonies, leader of the Blessing Way and Enemy Way and other paths to healing. Only in this last decade, living half in this world and half on the other side, did he begin to develop second sight, and he didn't understand most of what he saw. It was really kind of a nuisance. Maybe Ed would know something.

Ed was a buzzard now. Twenty years ago he'd been a man, a friend of Winsonfred's. He was a writer of books, but Winsonfred had never read any of Ed's books, couldn't read much of anything beyond street signs and the signs that marked Walmart, Safeway, and the like.

Ed had always said he wanted to return to earth, after his human cycle, as a buzzard. He wanted to ring up the sky in great circles on the warm, rising air, behold the deserts and mountains in every direction, get a little to eat every day, and spend evenings roosting in the big trees along the river with his buzzard buddies. Ed had gotten what he wanted, and the two were still friends.

Ed lit on a big branch in the top of the cottonwood by the driveway. Winsonfred sent his silent message upward: *I saw a big flash of light and parts of a boat being flung up into the sky. Then I got a feeling, a strong feeling, something's going to happen.*

Ed cocked his head at Winsonfred, waiting for more details. There weren't any.

You seen anything, Ed? You know anything?

Ed cocked his head the other way and held it, listening, looking thoughtful.

This thing that's coming, is it good or bad?

Ed lifted one wing, then the other. That message was: *I don't know. Good and bad are the way you humans see things.*

Out loud Winsonfred said, "Keep your eyes open, will you?"

Ed lifted his wings, coasted off the branch, and wheeled toward the Old Age River. Keeping his eyes open, that was what Ed did. He spotted water pockets in dry stone and meals that hadn't had time to cool off.

When the time came, and it would, he would tell Winsonfred all that he saw.

Zahnie sensed the music, but she didn't hear it. Always when it came, this was the way, feeling without hearing. It was soft and languid and delicious and it stroked her hair, silk-scarf smooth. Orchid petals, soft and shuddering, a pulse of purple.

The pulse was not silk or orchids but the music itself. She could feel it clearly now, a soprano sax gliding over her skin. Why could she never hear it? Swirling from the sax, it was a gentle waterfall gliding note by note down her shoulders. Floating sound-feeling sensuality.

Zahnie startled awake. She searched inside the half-dark room. She shook her head, realized she'd been dozing in the recliner where her great-grandfather Winsonfred always sat. Where was Grandfather? Must be outside. He would be getting chilled in the cool evening. She stood up, scraped the door of the assisted living center open, and saw the old man on his bench. "You'll be getting cold, Grandfather," she said in Navajo.

She helped him stand and held his elbow as he climbed the few steps to the front door.

"I saved you some tapioca pudding, Grandfather."

He smiled at her. Then he said gently, "I saw something."

She didn't exactly let her eyes roll, but she knew his mind.

Winsonfred told her, "Something's going to happen." And she thought maybe he looked a little afraid.

8

ADVENTURE AND CATASTROPHE

Don't stand on high rocks. They will grow into the sky with
you.

—Navajo saying

Now, by God, now, today. Moonlight Water late this afternoon.
Weeks of wandering, of wondering, weeks of strangers, today
all that would end when he met up with Gianni. A friend to
hear his stories. A friend to report what was happening back
in San Francisco, if Red decided to go into that at all. A friend.

What a month. That first night, when he blew up his life,
Red pointed his van east with no idea where to go in the vast
hinterlands of America, which to him meant anywhere outside
the Bay Area. True, he had touched down in this or that town
on tour, but in those alien spaces he'd experienced almost
nothing. The band had a big tour bus with the rear half cleared
out for a rehearsal area, and Red (well, Robbie) spent all his
time in the bus asleep in a reclining seat, never taking in the
scenery that whizzed by at seventy miles an hour. In the cities
they toured he saw the faces of thousands of fans, backstage
areas, the walls of hotel suites, and, when he wasn't married,
the geography of some female bodies. His knowledge of the

interior of his country was less than what anyone might get out of the Sunday travel section.

On that night he'd pointed the bumper of the van along Interstate 80 toward the deserts of Nevada and—he felt a trill of fear—maybe deserts of the spirit. *But I'm going to explore. . . .*

All past now. Red was one entire month old and had spent those weeks on the road soaking up experiences. He'd visited national parks (without getting laid). He'd burrowed into diners with heavy white china cups and waitresses who called him Hon. He'd stopped by Carhenge—a tribute not to the old Celtic gods but the modern American ones—and it dazzled him. He also made a point of visiting Cadillac Ranch, a line of old luxury sedans buried nose down in the flat Texas prairie outside Amarillo and angled like the Great Pyramid of Giza. Aside from the originality of what could be done with rusted auto hulls, Red's mind was pinwheeled by the way visitors had spray-painted the cars into a graffiti co-op, leaving spray cans around for the next people who made the pilgrimage.

Occasional days were as flat and featureless as the bed of a dry lake. He deliberately refused to spice them up by writing music, playing music, or even listening to music on the radio or CD player. He gabbed with truckers at truck stops on interstates and heard, sometimes, the inner emotions of their lives. He sat in barbershops and pretended to read magazines while listening to the chat of ordinary folk and sketching profiles, holding his pad inside a *Field & Stream* magazine. He lounged on park benches in small towns and talked to anyone who stopped. Gradually, he picked up bits and pieces of something else, a sense of people that didn't yet add up to anything but felt good. He expected the yearning to write music to rush into his blood and muscles and start dancing. That didn't happen, not yet.

In the van, alone, it was harder. He was quiet, or he carried on long conversations with Georgia or his grandfather. He and Grandpa just talked, and if Grandpa had any wisdom about what Red should do with his life, he never passed it along. The conversations made Red think of one of Grandpa's favorite songs, "Tain't What You Do (It's the Way That You Do It)." At night sometimes, sitting at a park picnic table, Red blew tunes on his harmonica and remembered how Grandpa's raspy voice brought a full feeling to it. When Red was a kid, he'd asked Grandpa what it meant, "the way that you do it." Grandpa just said, "The way that feels right to you." He was a grandpa, not an oracle.

While he watched the miles and towns and cars crammed with families roll by, Red's mind ran along the tracks and sometimes clear off the tracks. Uneasy, afraid, itchy as an ingrown hair, crazy as a bedbug, forlorn, and wildly exuberant— he'd felt it all. He'd spent days fighting off tears, because he had—quote-unquote—lost everything. (*Buck up,* he told himself. *You haven't lost it. You left it. By bold choice. Except the marriage.* That helped him some.) He'd surrendered to tears because the world was graceful, beautiful, and sublime. Some days Red was so grumpy that waitresses skirted around him to avoid pouring a second cup of coffee. On bad days he was haunted by Georgia, and their inner talks didn't go so well. She and her lover and the guys in the band would all appear until he shouted at them, "Beat it!"

Lighthearted and giddy, my ass. Most of the time he was scared and pretending not to be.

Was Georgia right that he'd lost his connection to himself? He said out loud, "Red, know thyself." *How can I know someone fresh-born?*

Seeking wisdom, he made the first of two signs that he taped to his dashboard:

AN ADVENTURE

IS A CATASTROPHE

RIGHTLY CONSTRUED

Oklahoma, Kansas, Missouri, Arkansas, and Texas, rolling headlong through the Bible Belt, billboards preached at him. A couple of those signs he liked:

"DON'T MAKE ME COME DOWN THERE!"
—SIGNED GOD

And fifty miles farther on:

"THAT PART ABOUT LOVING YOUR NEIGHBOR?
I MEANT IT."

—again the divine signature.

Then he saw a bumper sticker that summed up his response to the Bible Belt:

"LORD, PROTECT ME FROM YOUR FOLLOWERS."

That became his second hand-printed dashboard sign.

In Nacogdoches, Texas, he read this enticement on a marquee:

MUD-WRESTLING
GIRLS, GIRLS, GIRLS
ALL NUDE ALL THE TIME
NONE UNDER TWO HUNDRED POUNDS

He felt a twinge of temptation, gave in to a big grin, and drove on.

Looking at the word *Lord* day after day on his dashboard started to wear on him. When he was a kid, they'd gone to Mass every Sunday, but by the time he was sixteen, he'd found the whole thing hard to swallow. He decided from now on to give Him or Her a new name. Red changed his dashboard sign to:

ANONYMOUS SOURCE, PROTECT ME FROM YOUR FOLLOWERS.

That felt good, even though he wasn't a praying man unless he was feeling very desperate.

But today would feel good. Very. Moonlight Water. Gianni. An adventure!

Ahead Red could see the desert country, red and buff-colored, rippled into ridges, mesas, buttes, spires, and towers. Gianni had described this place as the epicenter of nowhere, maybe what Red needed. And with Gianni it would be full.

9

MOONLIGHT WATER,
A FEATHERED SPY,
AND THE LAW

Don't throw rocks at a whirlwind. It will chase you.

—Navajo saying

There it was down below, a single man-creature.

"Something's going to happen." That's what Winsonfred told Ed, and he'd asked Ed to watch for the something, maybe for trouble. It was the something, all right, but Ed couldn't tell if it was trouble. Not yet.

Ed wheeled out of the thermal, adjusting his wingtips, and made a wide circle clockwise. He took in the dried-blood color of the sun on the huge, red-rock monoliths of Mythic Valley to the southwest. That red was his favorite color, low-pitched and primal, the fundamental color of this country. He looked at the river that oozed like a glorious green snake across the desert floor. Then he felt the cool air rising from the water and used it to lose a little altitude. He eyed and sniffed Moonlight Water Canyon, the ancients' highway to the Azure Mountains in the north. Ed's eyes and nose were primo.

He angled easily downward toward the strip of concrete through the slender green canyon that sloped into the village.

Ed kept everything in his life easy. It wasn't smart to work hard in the heat of the desert, and besides, ease was his style. He feathered his wingtips just right and cruised toward the man-creature.

He was standing in the graveled area alongside one of the automobiles that human beings traveled in, taking a piss and looking at the cliff drawings. That was okay with Ed. He understood pissing just fine, along with all other means of getting rid of unwanted baggage—he didn't carry any extra weight himself. Ed didn't care for the contraptions people traveled in. Why not get rid of them and walk, so you can see and smell and touch the *whole* country? Now, cliff drawings, Ed had never figured out what people wanted with them. The creatures in those weren't merely dead, which would suit Ed's appetite, they were way, way dead.

The creature lifted a soda pop can, and Ed feared he would give it a heave. But the creature drank and held on. *Good.* Of all the humans' bad habits, Ed had the least tolerance for littering. He often passed judgment on litterers from above with a glob of guano. His aim was excellent.

Ed passed over the creature and banked into a turn for another gander and a good whiff. In Ed's previous life he'd been a human being, more or less like the creature down there, and a lover of the Canyonlands of the Four Corners region. This had given him a good beak for trouble. Ed was the self-appointed guardian angel of this piece of the gods' good earth.

He swooped over the creature's head. The creature walked toward the drawings, and in a flash Ed knew. This was a lost soul tinged with a hint of desperation and a wild spirit. Well, he'd be right at home in Moonlight Water. The place was full of souls searching for something. Some of them felt the call of the Four Corners and stayed. After a few months they got their rhythm back—the country had something good for them.

The creature tilted the soda pop and drank deep. Ed himself had loved such cans, his were full of beer, but now he preferred the taste of water and judged that no drink was worth the trouble of bottles and cans.

Ed watched. Scores of man-creatures and woman-creatures turned their mechanical contraptions into this spot every day and got out, and Ed felt zilch about most of them. Some, mostly locals, gave him a good feeling. A few troubled him. This one felt like Winsonfred's something, maybe good, maybe trouble. Ed would tell the old man about it tonight.

The stranger was still staring at the wall of cliff drawings.

Ed watched and waited. Of course, he didn't have any word like *love* to describe what he felt for this piece of earth. He didn't need words to have awareness. Not needing words, he would have thought that was funny if he'd remembered that in his human form he'd been a man of many words—books full of them, good books that people still read. The local trader had made more money off *Desert Solitaire* than Ed ever had.

All that was gone. He was 100 percent buzzard and crazy about being one. The best views going. Big wings that carried you miles and miles real easy. Never a need to buy gas. You could ride the thermals up high and beat the heat. Eyes so gonzo you could see flies from five thousand feet up. A nose that led you to hidden flesh. Because of that nose, you could get your dinner fresh and your water cool. Plus, you always had friends to cruise with.

Never mind being human—this incarnation was the gift. The universe thought he'd been a good man and had brought him back in a higher form.

The buzzard made Red want to climb into the van. The bird gave him the willies, flying low over him, like it was watching him, waiting for him to croak.

Red spent a last moment with the carvings. They were the damnedest things. He'd read the sign a couple of times and got the facts, how they were made nine hundred to one thousand years ago by the Ancestral Puebloans, whoever they were. But what intrigued Red had nothing to do with facts. What were the carvings trying to say? Some were chipped into the rock, some painted in color. Human handprints, hundreds of them, large and small. Animals, maybe deer or antelope or bighorn sheep. Spirals. A hunched god playing a flute and dancing. And still more shapes that felt like bursts of unconsidered creation from a place far distant.

It was okay with him if people got messages from another world. He'd gotten his music from the sub-conscious world, hadn't he? He'd learned during the last month that new tunes didn't just jump into your body and dance you around when you asked for them. They snuck up on you, as if from a time-warp galaxy.

One set of carvings really grabbed him. In the center was a spiral. On each side of the spiral was a line of people, dancing slowly toward the center. Or were they dancing out from the circle? He looked and looked and wasn't sure. He was damn sorry they were frozen in stone. He'd like to have swayed their thousand-year-old dance inside his bones.

He started to get out his sketch pad but looked up.

That damn buzzard was still there, circling.

Red slid into the van and looked at his watch. For the first time in a month he needed to think about clock time. Half an hour to meet Gianni, buzzard in tow.

The predator followed Red through the canyon. He ignored the bird, concentrating on the world around him. Surreal. The curving canyon was sweet and fine, red bluffs harmonizing with fluttering green leaves on the trees. He rolled down his window, half-expecting to hear the melody of the leaves, but it was drowned out by the whir-wind of the van.

When the canyon opened wide, the world was huge and mind-blowing. He'd seen shots of this desertscape in dozens of TV commercials and movies. The place where Forrest Gump stopped running. The cliffs where Thelma and Louise sailed their convertible into that huge chasm. A land Anglos found awesome and Native people revered.

After another mile, he entered the town of Moonlight Water. He remembered what Gianni had told him. "My friend, it is the edge of the epicenter of nowhere and everywhere. No doctor, no drugstore, no bar—hell, no grocery store. The nearest movie's over a hundred miles away. Hippies, *hosteens,* rez dogs, sagebrush, and sand. The clock ticks Navajo time, which is mañana land only more so. For all that, it's the most solid place in the world—as long as your definition of *solid* includes impossible shapes in stone and a strong creative vibe. Oh, and these people, half of them Navajos and half Anglos, call themselves Moonlighters."

"What?"

"They call themselves Moonlighters, after the town of the first trading post. Translation from Navajo: Moonlight Reflected on the Water. So pretty Mormons kept the name when they got here."

What Red saw first was a filling station–convenience store–restaurant named the Squash Blossom. Beyond that was a run-down Laundromat with an army of kids milling around middle-aged women who looked like Navajo grandmas. They were dark-skinned and gray-haired, talking and laughing, keeping the kids together like hens with their chicks. Some wore velveteen blouses, huge turquoise necklaces, and full skirts above pink Walmart sneakers. Way down was a bridge, then supposedly a café called the Locomotive Rock Café and Trading Post, the place he was meeting Gianni.

Red stuck his head out the window and gawked upward. Damn buzzard was still circling overhead. Red muttered, "Probably the state bird."

He drained the rest of the can of soda pop and threw it on the floor of the passenger seat. He kept a can of Foster's in the cup holder, unopened, to remind himself that he'd banned booze from his life.

Instantly, he heard a siren. A county sheriff's car in the other lane swung into a U-turn. Red and blue lights flashed in Red's rearview mirror.

Red slammed his fist against the steering wheel. He'd flashed the pop can. *Damn it, pop's legal. And I can't chance getting busted.*

Red angled into the parking lot of the convenience store, his stomach roiling, and opened the door of the van.

The cop had the bulk of Arnold Schwarzenegger squeezed onto a frame maybe five and a half feet high, a comical effect, like a clothes dryer with wooden posts for legs.

As Red stepped out, the cop stopped and shot him the standard cop look: *Who the hell are you and are you gonna make trouble in my jurisdiction?*

The cop's mouth snap-crackle-popped out words: *"Get back in your vehicle, sir."*

Red felt himself flush. Dumb to get out. Cops were big on the drill. *Really* dumb to have a van with California plates.

This cop, his nameplate said Officer Lyman, moved upward straight into Red's face. Red put his hands up defensively, and—whooee, the cop was fast for a man built like an appliance. Lyman stepped quick to the side, boosted Red's arm behind him with one hand, and shoved him ferociously on the back with the other. His face crashed onto the hot hood of the cop's car.

Lyman whumped the other arm way up behind Red and clamped his wrists together hard with a sinister *snick*.

The officer tightened the cuffs enough to make them hurt. Letting go, he stood back and smirked at Red.

"Show me some ID—now!"

Red's brain sprang to life: *Get smart. This guy would love an excuse to beat the shit out of you and take you to jail.*

Trembling with fury, fumbling, hurting his own wrists with the cuffs, Red fished out his wallet and fake driver's license.

The cop snatched it. "Red Stuart," he said. He strutted in a tight circle, a banty rooster with too many hens. "Mr. Stuart, we have a fine list of charges here. Speeding, open container, DUI, failure to obey the direct order of an officer, and attempted assault on an officer."

Red squeezed out his protest. "I wasn't speeding, I wasn't drinking alcohol, and you assaulted me."

The cop slammed Red's head back down onto the hood.

Rage. Red reminded himself of what mattered: *Don't let them make you.*

"Charlie, what the hell are you doing?"

Gianni's voice. Running footsteps.

Then a female voice. "Charlie, back off! I mean it. Now!"

Red craned his head to the side. Gianni and a uniformed woman, a Native American cop.

Officer Lyman answered her with a tone of disdain. "Zahnie, you back off. I have a prisoner in custody. We're taking a little trip to jail."

The Indian woman said sharply, "What are the charges? We saw everything that happened."

"Speeding, open container, DUI, failure to obey the direct order of an officer, attempted assault on an officer."

Gianni said, "Picking on a white man this time? This guy's my friend."

The woman jumped back in. "You haven't done a field test, and we both saw you assault him." She looked in the window of the van and grabbed the Foster's can and pop can and held them up. "Not even open. You saw this empty pop can. Throw out the container charge. Both of us will testify to your assault."

She gave him a satisfied, twisted grin.

"Charlie, I've known you as a liar for thirty years," said Gianni, "and a bad cop for twenty."

Charlie gave him a look that could chop the head off a snake. "I'm giving him a field sobriety test."

Charlie Lyman gave her a long look, took Red's cuffs off,

and then Red went through the routine, demonstrating—nine steps forward, heel to toe, thirty seconds standing on one leg, the whole shebang—that he was sober.

Red hadn't touched booze in a month, and he could have passed the test drunk. Born agile. When he finished, he grinned at Officer Lyman.

"No probable cause to hold him," the woman said. "You're lucky this wasn't another Navajo woman. I'd have you doing time."

"You lousy bitch!" snapped Lyman. "I'm sick to death of you."

"Consider me a permanent boil on your behind," said the woman officer. "Get out of here."

Lyman did.

Gianni bear-hugged Red. "Some welcome to Moonlight Water," he said, grinning. "Zahnie, this is my best buddy, Red Stuart. Red, Officer Zahnie Kee."

"Glad to meet you," said Red. "You guys came along just at the right time."

"Watching for you," said Gianni.

Officer Kee didn't say anything, didn't smile, didn't offer her hand. Her eyes were on Officer Lyman's cruiser, speeding up Moonlight Canyon. Red noticed that her shirt patch read: Bureau of Land Management.

Suddenly, she remembered her manners. "Glad to meet you."

"You saved my ass."

"Sorry, but I'm not interested in your ass. I'm after Charlie Lyman's."

Gianni said, "He stops Navajo women for traffic violations and gives them a choice—get a ticket or service him in the bushes."

"His father did the same thing," said Zahnie Kee. "The two sons of bitches did half the Navajo women in this county."

"Zahnie went to college," said Gianni, "and picked up bad Anglo habits like cussing."

"Nobody but Charlie Lyman can make me cuss."

Gianni said, "Let's get out of the east side of town. It can get a little edgy around here."

Red gave Gianni a quizzical look.

"Moonlight Water is divided by a wash," said Gianni, nodding toward the bridge. "East half is all Mormon, west half is Navajos and misfit whites. *Paisan,* give us a ride to the Locomotive Café."

Red drove them across the wash in his van.

"All of Redrock County," Zahnie said, "is officially ten thousand Navajo people, five thousand Anglos, and only half a dozen federal officers to police the biggest county in the U.S."

A vigorous-looking blond fellow about nineteen or twenty came out of the café, stripping off his shirt as he walked. He looked at Red, registered surprise, gave him a big grin, and said, "Yo, dude! What's it like to be dead?"

Red quelled his panic and brushed the kid off with a wave. The kid waved back and moved on.

"What was that about?" asked Zahnie.

"Don't know," said Red. "He's probably stoned."

"Eric doesn't get stoned," she said.

Red watched the young blond. He talked like a cool kid, but with his hair cut into a burr and his toned body, he could have been an advertisement for "our finest Mormon youth." Red just hoped the guy wouldn't come back and call him Rob Roy.

On the porch of the Locomotive Café they found a comfy table outside with iron seats painted dark green. After a moment he realized Zahnie was studying his face instead of the menu. She was wearing a cop look. "Why is your face familiar? You're not tacked on the post office wall, are you?"

He lied with perfect glibness, "I am Red Stuart, late of California, now a wanderer and seeker."

She ordered a Dr Pepper, and so did the other two. "I think you're full of it." Her dark eyes nailed him to a cross of cuckoo truth.

"You got that right." Red grinned at her.

Gianni squirmed and made a worried face.

She said to Red, "You've spent the last month, according to your buddy, wandering from state to state, looking for something. Find out what you want?"

"To live my life large, very large."

"Oh my." Zahnie kept her eyes on him and sucked on her straw until the last sip of Dr Pepper was gone. "Well, this place has enough room, and it's a magnet for lost souls." One last slurp of bubbles made enough noise to turn the heads of the people at the next table.

Red turned his head away and grinned. "Might be a good place for me to spend a little time," he said.

"Amendment: lost souls who are honest," she said.

"I vouch for him," said Gianni, easing the conversation into a different parking spot. "Red, this is the only place in town you want to eat. It's also the trading post, where Navajos go to pawn stuff, the general store, and the post office."

"Not to mention," said Zahnie, "where my vehicle is." She motioned to the stone and beam building behind the trading post. "The far end is the BLM office, where I work. It used to be the jail." The other buildings were a string of railroad cars set on uneven foundations, like tumbled dominos.

"The café is named after that huge rock." Gianni pointed at a formation about a half mile away. "See that monument charging out of the rock wall, sort of the shape of a locomotive with an engineer at the controls? It's speeding forward at ten feet per eon. The trader here is the owner of the restaurant and the river ranger. I mean, the other ranger, along with Zahnie."

"Let's go," Zahnie said. "It's getting toward dark and we're having supper at home."

Red walked with Zahnie to her BLM Bronco, opened the door for her, enjoyed the rear view of her bottom, and then climbed into his van. Zahnie stuck her head out the window and said with a grin, "By the way, Red, you're in luck. Because you're Gianni's pal, you have a free hotel—the old folks' home."

Red raised an eyebrow.

"Consider this treat a preview of hospitality to come," she said. "Follow me."

"I'll ride with the lost soul," said Gianni, and he climbed in next to Red.

10

MADHOUSE AND REFUGE

Don't look into a mirror at night. Your shadow might leave you
and you'll die.

—Navajo saying

Zahnie's Bronco spat gravel. Red and Gianni trailed her in the
van, north out of town and onto a dirt road leading up a wash.
Red had already learned that a wash was a wide creek bed
without a creek when he'd blown a tire exploring New Mexico.

"I haven't slipped up and called you Robbie once."

"You better not." They bumped along. The road was probably no smoother than the creek bed. "So this is the loneliest,
most remote place in the lower foty-eight."

"You better believe it."

"Looks like the freaking edge of the planet. The creeks aren't
even on speaking terms with water."

"The water speaks in the spring, when the snow melts."
Granni pointed to the mountains spiking high at the head of
the wash.

Red looked down at Zahnie Kee's taillights and had a vivid
thought—maybe he'd give up intriguing women. He'd learned

long ago that the interesting ones were a lot of work and the uncomplicated ones bored him.

She made a hard, skidding right turn onto a dirt road, and they bounced along for a while. "So what's this old folks' home?"

"Assisted living center, and they've got a room set up for you there. I help support them."

"What about staying at your place? A motel? Gianni, this is pretty weird, and that woman doesn't like me at all."

Gianni unclenched his teeth and took a deep breath. "This *is* my place. You wanted adventure. Open your door to this part of it."

Red felt like a kid being dropped off for the first day of school.

"Zahnie's good people, a little rough around the edges, but we've all got edges." Gianni looked sideways at Red, smiled like the Cheshire Cat, and thonked him on the knee. "This is Moonlight Water Canyon we're driving through. Stick your head out the window and smell the desert."

Red did. The evening air was full of hints he couldn't catch. His eyes gave him rimrock walls on either side of the dirt road, the last of the sunlight making them glow red, the treed tops of the bluffs high and dark. On the canyon floor were the voodoo shapes of desert plants and rock formations, each one a goblin or leprechaun or space alien. The quiet was steep and layered, just like the ancient canyon walls. Dense, dark folds of silence held unknown civilizations and strange worlds of time, frightening, enchanting, enticing. *Eerie,* he thought, *maybe okay, maybe not. Adventure, I guess.*

They pulled into a dirt driveway that circled in front of a big stone-masoned building, almost a mansion. Zahnie beat them up the stairs and shouldered open the sticky front door, its solid wood warped by time and solitude. They stood in an anteroom. The air swirled around Red, carrying a flood of memories and feelings.

He shuddered. There was a two-story living room, Victorian in style, with a balcony. Smells drew him to, to . . .

"*Ya-teh-eh,*" said a whispery voice behind them. Red jumped and whirled to meet the voice. A very old Navajo man sat in the shadows, deep in a battered recliner.

"*Ya-teh-eh,*" the old man repeated. His smile was Buddha with a pinch of chile.

Winsonfred crooked his finger at Red. The younger man bent down and put an ear near the elderly mouth.

"*Ya-teh-eh* means 'hello'!" His smile was big and his cloudy eyes sparkled with delight. "You're supposed to answer, '*Ya-teh-eh, hosteen,*' which is a term of respect, such as you owe your elders." He pronounced it more like *hah-steen.*

"I'm sorry, *hosteen.*"

"Grandfather," said Zahnie, "this is Red. A longtime friend of Gianni's." The old man extended a hand. When Red took it, the man gave him the faintest touch. "Red, this is Hosteen Winsonfred Manygoats, my great-grandfather."

The old man added formally, "Welcome, friend of my friend. If you were a Navajo, I would tell you that I am born to the Folded Arms People and born for the Red Running into Water People, and from my grandparents the Bitter Water People and the Badlands People."

"He always does that," Zahnie said, "in his dotage."

"Zahnie!" This was a musical baritone from beyond the living room, perhaps the kitchen. A potato-bodied Indian man of about forty came bouncing toward them.

"Tony," Zahnie said, "this is Red."

"We've been expecting you. You're welcome here as long as you want to stay."

"Thanks."

"My cousin, Tony Begay," Zahnie finished.

Right off the bat, Red liked Tony. Judging from his body language, the name Begay suited him. Almost made Red homesick for the Bay Area.

Tony led Red by the elbow into the living room, Zahnie and Gianni alongside and . . . Winsonfred? . . . trailing behind.

"This house," Tony spat, playacting disgust. "It was built— can you believe this?—by the town's patriarch, the leader of the Mormon pioneers, also the first bishop and first local polygamist. Which is the reason we have a big upstairs and so many bedrooms."

"Neville, my enemy," said Winsonfred in his papery voice.

"My ancestor on my Anglo side," Tony plunged ahead. "Thank God I'm not all Anglo. This house, it still feels like his—so masculine it makes me wiggy. Look at that fireplace, petrified logs. Like this was a hunting lodge or something! I want more color and light in here, but we don't have the time or the money."

"What's that?" Red nodded toward a wall hanging.

Tony smiled. "A rubbing of some rock art—Kokopelli, a big-time god of fertility. You see his back? That's not a hump, it's a sack. He travels from village to village carrying seeds for plants and babies. Unmarried women, like Zahnie here, are afraid of him because he'll plant a baby inside them."

"Cool it, Tony," said Zahnie. Clearly he was enjoying his role as tour guide.

"And he plays the flute," said Red.

"Dancing and playing the flute, that's how he comes to the village. He's also a god of music."

Right below the flute-playing god stood a baby grand piano that seemed to be in good shape—hey, a Steinway, no less. Red chuckled. Strange world here.

"That rubbing shouldn't have been made," said Tony. "That's what the archeologists say now, but it belongs to Miss Clarita and she's going to keep it. It's her personal angel, and she is ours."

In the dining room, Red recognized the smells that had hit him when he walked in the front door. His grandparents' house was filled with scents like this, decades of beeswax rubbed on furniture, rosewater, the satisfying odor of frying foods, hot bread with butter. Tony led them through the wide entrance to the kitchen, where two women worked, one very young and white, the other very old and red.

"*Ya-teh-eh,* Zahnie," sang the ancient woman. She came toward them with a spry step, then quickly hid something behind her back.

"It's okay, Clarita," said Zahnie.

Clarita drew her hand into view. Red recognized the aroma, even among the delicious kitchen smells. The old lady held a fat joint. She outwrinkled Methuselah, and under a big apron she wore the traditional purple velveteen skirt and plum blouse, plus a load of turquoise jewelry.

"Clarita Begay-Shumway," said Tony, "Red Stuart."

"*Ya-teh-eh,*" said Clarita. Without repeating the "born to, born for" ritual, she offered him the hand without the joint. Red considered kissing it but shook it instead. Close up, she smelled like Pond's cream and Pears soap, just like Red's grandmother.

"Red is Gianni's friend," Tony went on, "and he'll be staying with us, too."

"Don't worry about the joint," Tony said to Red. "We use it medicinally. Only thing that helps certain kinds of pain."

Red put his hands up. "Hey, it's cool."

Tony led him to the young white woman. "Jolo, this is Red Stuart."

She stuck out a hand before she realized it held a serving spoon gobbed with mashed potatoes. She laughed at herself and drew it back. She was about nineteen or twenty and looked sweet as creamed corn.

"Clarita instructs, Jolo cooks," Tony added. "Especially when Clarita's having pain, like tonight, until she got that toke. She's a ninety-year-old miracle."

"Sit down," rang Clarita's voice, a soft, clear bell. "We're about to serve."

People flocked toward a huge, circular oak dining table, a handsome antique.

"Virgil, come to dinner!" Tony called toward the living room.

A wavering shape, made ghost-like by the blue light of the TV, began to rise. Very slowly, as Clarita and Jolo put big bowls and platters on the table, Virgil shuffled forward and materialized from shadow into a bathrobed figure encased in a walker.

Tony pointed with his lips, Navajo-style. "This is Virgil Rats. He always watches the old programs, especially *I Love Lucy,* no sound. He is well down the road of Alzheimer's, but he recognizes Lucy and Ricky. Maybe he thinks they're his kids." Tony put a hand on the old man's shoulder. "Virgil, this is Gianni's friend, Red."

Virgil roared at Red, "Lucy, you got some 'splainin' to do!"

Red smiled politely and sat at the table. Winsonfred eased back toward his recliner.

"Virgil eats like an elephant, Winsonfred seldom eats," Tony said, "and our other permanent guests take their meals in bed, two upstairs, two down." Jolo was going in and out of bedrooms off the kitchen. "Those ladies back there, every day Virgil plunks his walker up to each of their doors, looks in, and starts cackling, 'Sex-sex-sex-sex-sex. *Sex*-sex-sex-sex-sex.' The ladies are used to it, but we have to move him along."

Clarita passed the food. Red discovered that, after four weeks of coffee shop meals, he was starved for real food.

"Harmony House is an unconventional society," Tony said. "Grandmother Clarita came from Navajo Mountain, over to the west. She was raised traditional and later she added Mormon to her mix. Us kids were raised traditional Navajo and Mormon, going to squaw dances and getting our endowment ceremonies, both."

Since he had been a casual agnostic for twenty years, Red shunned all forms of religion. But Navajo combined with Mormon? The thought pained him, and that must have shown on his face.

"A problem in your mind but not in mine, I assure you," said Clarita. She flashed a radiant smile.

My grandmother would have looked so beautiful, thought Red, *if she'd lived to great age.*

"I live in two cultures," Clarita went on. She held herself like a Navajo Katharine Hepburn with a scepter of cannabis.

"Would you care to hear the story of my family and the Mormons in Moonlight Water?" Clarita asked. She lit her joint again. Apparently it was her custom to toke at the table.

Red would have listened to any story the queen wanted to tell.

"I am, as Tony said, two creatures in one, a Mormon and a traditional Navajo. The Mormons colonized Moonlight Water in 1900 exactly. Neville the patriarch was the bishop. There's a big portrait of him hanging above the landing on the stairs. In those days the LDS Church had a policy called placement. It was to help the Indians, they thought, by adopting them right into Mormon families and teaching them white ways. As a matter of fact, the Church still does placement. Tony's great-grandfather on the other side, Albert Begay, was adopted by Neville. I was adopted by the Allreds, but that's another story.

"This house"—she gestured broadly with gracious ninety-year-old energy—"is where I raised my family. I married Brigham Neville Shumway, who inherited the house when the patriarch died. The family attitude was that Brigham was a wild hair—and a wild heir—marrying a Navajo." She smiled faintly at her own pun. "Our children are gone, so I gave the house to the foundation that Tony created to give old people a home. Tony has a big, big heart."

"A disgrace," said Tony, wiping his mouth on a linen napkin, "to send old folks up to the nursing home in Montezuma City. I can't stand how this country treats its elderly."

Clarita proceeded to her conclusion. "So, I created a haven for my own old age, and a few other guests. Their monthly Social Security checks help us all."

"The state didn't like licensing Navajos," Tony said, "but I dotted all the i's and crossed all the t's in a stack of papers three inches thick. They were afraid of a lawsuit if they turned us down."

"Dessert," said Jolo, sliding dishes in front us. It was tapioca pudding. Red hadn't seen that in years. When he was a kid, he loved it.

"I want chocolate pudding," Virgil demanded of the world.

Jolo looked chagrined.

"Chocolate pudding one night," Clarita reminded him, "and tapioca the next."

"I want chocolate pudding."

Virgil kept his tone exactly the same, like a movie actor doing take after take after take. "I want chocolate pudding."

Tony looked at Clarita, who looked at Gianni. They rolled their eyes in unison.

Virgil changed his line. "You people are mean. I'm getting outta here." He rose and leaned heavily on a chair while he inched into his walker.

He piddled his walker toward the kitchen door that led outside. No one made a move to stop him.

"You people are mean."

Red watched from somewhere between horror and fascination. After three or four more choruses of *mean* and *outta here,* Virgil reached the kitchen door.

To Red's astonishment, Zahnie got up and opened the door for him with a flourish. Old Virgil bumped his walker over the sill and disappeared into the night.

Zahnie closed the door and sat down, smiling.

Clarita looked equally amused.

"Watch," said Tony. "He does this every time."

"Every night that we don't fix chocolate pudding," Jolo corrected.

Tony led the way into the living room, and they circled the piano to the bay window.

Red felt, hell, he didn't know what. *Here at the end of the earth they let old people walk off the edge!*

Outside, under the exterior floodlights, old Virgil pushed his walker along a cement walkway with rabid determination, one inch at a time. Pipe railings kept him in line.

Jolo crossed to Winsonfred's recliner and put a dish of tapioca in the old man's hands. He made no move to eat it, but stared up at the portrait hanging above the landing on the stairs.

"Winsonfred," said Clarita, "was actually born the same year the Mormons came to Moonlight Water, 1900, or believes he was. If it's true, he's a hundred and three years old. Winsonfred thinks the whole history of Moonlight Water is the story of a spiritual struggle between him and Neville."

Red's mind was fixed on Virgil. The old guy could take a left turn and roam out among the spiky cactus and hungry coyotes. God knows what else.

"Winsonfred doesn't talk much," said Tony, "but he's perfectly lucid."

Red looked hard out the side and front windows, but he saw no Virgil.

"Don't worry," said Zahnie.

The doorbell rang. "Come on," said Tony. As they gathered in Winsonfred's foyer, Jolo waltzed forward and opened the door.

Outside stood Virgil. "Them people were *mean*," he said.

"Hello, Virgil," Jolo said. "Would you like to come in?"

"I ain't staying over there anymore," he rasped at her, bumping his walker over the doorsill.

"We'd be happy for you to stay with us," she said, a sweet melody in her voice. Tony and Zahnie beamed at Red. Gianni kept a straight face.

Virgil moved slow and stately, like an ocean liner.

"Here's a nice sofa to sit on," said Tony. "Look, *I Love Lucy*'s on TV."

"I like *I Love Lucy*."

Virgil crept sofa-ward.

"You heard that joke," said Zahnie, "one of the benefits of Alzheimer's is that you meet new people every day. Virgil really takes it to the limit."

"I love it," said Tony, "every single time. I love it."

Virgil plopped onto the sofa, happy and safe among his new friends.

"We'd better arrange the sleeping," said Zahnie. "Red, you get Winsonfred's room."

Red looked down at the Ancient One, and noticed that he was following their conversation with glittering eyes. "Don't you need your room?"

"I like this recliner."

To Zahnie: "What about Gianni?"

"He has a semi-permanent bedroom upstairs."

"And you?"

"I live out back, in what we call the Granary."

"You live in a grain shed?" His voice suppressed laughter.

"It's got plumbing and electricity and it's mine." She hesitated and said, "Winsonfred's room is free and available for as long as you want it."

She did an about-face and headed into the kitchen. Thinking delightful thoughts, he watched her move. They were only somewhat spoiled by the hard edge of the reality of Zahnie.

The Ancient One grinned at him.

Mumbled words.

Red started awake on the sofa. He looked around the room, dark except for the faint glare of a muted TV. Everyone seemed to be in bed. Even the house felt as if it were asleep

"I want to talk to you," came the words again.

"Who's that?" Red craned his head around and fingered his head. Damn, that new buzz cut still didn't feel right.

An arm waved, lit eerily by a boob tube. Hosteen Winsonfred, sitting in his recliner.

"Let's go outside and talk," said the Ancient One. His slow speech didn't seem like feebleness, rather a high degree of attention. He polished the words and set them out one by one.

Red offered Winsonfred a hand, suspecting what the old fellow really wanted was help walking outside.

He stood sturdily without help. "I want to talk to Ed, too, while we're out there." he said. He scooped up his dish of pudding with one hand. They walked to the back door and into the pleasant, shimmery night air. The old man went down the back porch stairs nimbly enough and sat on a wooden bench.

"Here will be fine," said Winsonfred.

"Who's Ed?" Red blurted out.

"I sent him a message. He'll come in a minute or so," said Winsonfred. He spoke softly and precisely, like a precocious child. "Ed is a buzzard."

Red thought, *Oh, shit.*

"You don't have to hide words like that from me," said Winsonfred. "I know what they mean. Like most Navajos, I just choose not to say them."

Jeez, thought Red, then corrected himself. *Anonymous Source, he even knows my thoughts.*

"Who is Anonymous Source?" said Winsonfred.

"The Big Man Upstairs I don't believe in."

"Odd that you're talking to Him, then." Winsonfred set down his pudding carefully, reached into his shirt pocket, and drew out the makings.

Red watched fascinated as a single 103-year-old hand-rolled a cigarette, flipped a Bic, and lit up. The younger man wondered why the Ancient One didn't use both hands.

He drew deep on the cigarette, holding it between thumb and forefinger. "Tony doesn't let me smoke in the house," said Winsonfred. "He's so modern he acts like tobacco isn't sacred. If you'd like a cigarette, help yourself."

Red wanted to try to roll a smoke with one hand. He licked the edge of the Zig-Zag paper, and tobacco fell into his lap. Winsonfred smiled. Red fumbled. He fumbled some more. Finally, he gave up, rolling it badly with two hands, and he flicked Winsonfred's Bic.

"I saw you," said Winsonfred. "Not you, but what you did. I knew something was going to happen. You, you're bringing it, whatever it is."

Red dropped the burning cigarette and had to pick it up. "What did you see that I did?"

Winsonfred let smoke spiral from his mouth into the night sky. "A big flash of light and an explosion of water. Parts of a boat whirling into the air, and the main part sinking. It was chaos."

Oh man, Red thought. Nothing he could say to that. He felt short of breath.

He matched the Ancient One's plumes of smoke, rising like clouds in front of the moon. It seemed like ordinary, secular tobacco to Red. Without appearing to, he scanned the dark skies for buzzards. The one he'd seen today was enough.

Again without appearing to, Red edged his attention sideways at the old man. Winsonfred gazed at the moon with unaltered raptness.

"Here's Ed," said the Ancient One. "I'm going away for a little while."

Red felt very alone. He smoked and fidgeted and smoked and wondered where Winsonfred was, if he'd actually gone somewhere, but there he was, right beside him. Red fidgeted for a very long time.

Winsonfred took a deep breath and gave a little sigh. "Okay, I'm back."

Red leaned forward to make sure Winsonfred was all right. "You're back?"

"I went off to talk to Ed." The old man began to eat the tapioca pudding with his free hand, scooping it up with his index finger.

Red looked him in the eyes now, and for the first time they seemed unnaturally bright.

"You're a lost soul," said the Ancient One. He licked pudding off his fingers slowly and delicately.

Seemed like Red was transparent to everyone. What he didn't say was that he'd lost his soul years ago.

"Ed watched you out at the petroglyphs this afternoon."

Another one Red had no words for.

"He flew over your van in the canyon, followed you into town, and saw that cop stop you."

Red felt his eyes do a whirligig, but he held his tongue.

"Ed said you're a seeker. Moonlight Water is full of those. I told Ed, 'Something else, too. Something's gonna happen 'cause he came here.' Ed and I, we don't know what that is, yet.

"Ed said, 'This country will heal the man.' It doesn't do that for everybody."

Red gazed into the desert darkness, scared and excited and wanting to run as fast and far as he could. *I didn't come to the end of the earth to sit outside with a 103-year-old man who's half in this world and half in the next, blow smoke at the moon, and talk to buzzards. Especially if he sees my past and future.*

"Yes," said Winsonfred, "you did."

A long shiver ran up Red's spine, and then it tiptoed back down.

"There are good things for you here, very good," Winsonfred said. "If you open your heart." He patted Red's knee.

Right. A woman who thinks I'm a clown, a buzzard who spies on me, an old man who reads my thoughts, and a cop who hates me—maybe not such a brilliant adventure. Red could not imagine what Gianni had been thinking, setting him up to stay here.

"Ed said you'll be okay here, even good, but I'm a little worried about whatever's going to happen. Anyway," Winsonfred said, "you'll see Ed hanging around, watching over you, just to make sure."

Red held the old man's eyes. They were brown, friendly, clear, simple. Questions spun Red's mind dizzy.

"If you want to ask me something, anything, go ahead."

Why the hell do you think you can talk to buzzards? How'd you see me blow up my boat? Are you a psychic?

Winsonfred grinned at him.

Red settled on something other than anything that had to do with himself. "Why did you call Neville the patriarch your enemy?"

Winsonfred laughed. "I guess a man's got to have a few enemies to feel alive. Navajos and the Mormons came to Moonlight Water the same spring. People doubt, but that's the way it was. Came here with different ideas, real different, ideas that have been fighting since human beings first came onto the earth. Sad to say, Neville's spirit still inhabits this country, partly through his descendants, and they strengthen the evil.

"I walk with the forces of harmony and peace with other people, other creatures, and the world—I know these are stronger than all the striving and greed that oppose them. The harmony Clarita spoke of, Red, is harmony within yourself— walking in the right way with your own nature, with your family, with other people, the right way with the earth. If you do that, you walk in beauty. That's what the medicine man sings in a ceremony. Remember, I used to be a singer. 'May you walk in beauty.' It means inner beauty, rightness."

Red didn't know what to think. About any of it.

Winsonfred said, "I'd like to go back inside now. I just needed a little visit with Ed, and with you."

Red marveled at the old man's spryness, standing up, climbing the stairs.

At the landing Winsonfred turned back and dove into Red's eyes. "How you heal, young man, you go out around the country, breathe the air, see everything, feel everything. Also, you listen to the stories. All the stories, from people here hundreds of years ago and people here now. Four-legged people, rooted people, winged, all. And the river, too—we call it Old Age River—it knows many stories and murmurs them along its way. For the old stories, listen to the rock and to the waters."

Red had heard every New Age phrase that washed into the Bay. He couldn't help it—his knee-jerk response was a cynical grin.

Winsonfred said, "That's not good for you. And, Red, however many years you've lived? I've lived more than twice that long. That's a good reason to listen to me." He gave Red an endearing smile.

Winsonfred leaned on the door and pushed it open. Red stayed a moment, listening for the sound of the river, wherever it was. Nothing. He followed Winsonfred inside.

11

THE LONELY RANGER
AND TONTO

Don't watch a river flowing swiftly. You'll get dizzy and fall in.
—Navajo saying

Ri-i-i-in-ng! Ri-i-i-in-ng!

The shrill phone and thundering footsteps woke Red up.

Tony's sharp voice snapped, "Leeja?!" Said in the tone of, *Why the hell are you calling at this hour?*

Silence. "Okay." He pressed a button on an intercom. "Zahnie, come in and talk to Leeja." He looked at Red and said, "No surprise, right? We don't have cell phone service in Moonlight Water."

Tony started the coffee and put something in the oven to heat. Zahnie banged through the screen door into the kitchen and grabbed the phone. "Yeah."

Red sat up and got his bearings. TV playing on mute, walk-in closet beneath a set of stairs, full-length beveled mirror, baby grand. Yeah, he remembered, he was in the old polygamist's house in Moonlight Water. Never made it upstairs to bed.

"Leeja, I don't care what Sallyfene and Wandafene do with the Jensen boys."

The woman was *muy guapa* but mouthy.

"Oh." Silence as she listened. "Jeez."

Red wanted to go back to sleep.

"I'll go get them."

Tony brought Red a cup of black coffee and a cinnamon roll right out of the oven. Then he brought the same for Zahnie and himself and plopped down on a corner of the couch. The cinnamon roll was delicious, the real thing.

"What's up?" That was Gianni, coming down from upstairs, his silk pajamas a maze of wrinkles.

Tony said softly, "Leeja." To Red he added, "Zahnie's sister, a nurse." Gianni got himself a cinnamon roll.

Zahnie held up a hand for silence. "I'll take care of it right now."

Pause.

"No, I'll kick their asses today. Bye."

Zahnie turned to face them. "Leeja's daughters are loose on the river with the Jensen boys. Evidently rowed to Serpent House yesterday to camp out. They so-called *borrowed* a BLM boat to go."

Tony laughed.

"Okay." Zahnie spoke like a command officer. "I'm going after them."

Tony said, "Zahnie, so they might get pregnant. So they stole one of your boats. So what?"

Zahnie gave him a look of disgust. "My nieces do *not* take advantage of me being a ranger to steal from the BLM. Second, the rapids at Echo Canyon are really dangerous at this water level. Even the river guides are lining the boats through it. The Jensen boys won't have that much sense. Which means," she finished, "this is how I spend my day off."

"The way she spends most workdays," Tony told Red.

"Take our new guest with you," said Winsonfred. He was buttering his own cinnamon roll very slowly.

Zahnie glared at him.

"Our new guest," said Winsonfred. "Good for him to see the river, hear it. Good for you."

Zahnie said to Red, "Want to take a ride down the river?"

Gianni said, "The guides charge big for that."

"Okay," said Red, sounding half-okay.

"I want you around here awhile anyway," said Gianni. "Something special to show you."

Red raised an eyebrow at him.

"You're gonna love it, but it's not ready yet."

"Gianni, help us with the boat," said Zahnie.

"I'm on it," he answered.

Zahnie flew into motion, stuffing gear into a pack. Then she hustled back to her house and came back wearing her uniform, with some kind of radio or phone on her belt. A little more work and she flew out the door, Red and Gianni trailing.

"Jolo, we'll need two lunches," she called back.

"Make that lunch for seven," Red yelled. You could never have too much real food.

"Let's move!" Zahnie barked to Gianni and Red. "Gimme your keys."

She drove like a madwoman. When they started bouncing all over the dirt road, she hit a rut so hard that Red whacked his head on the roof. "I'm just along for the ride," he murmured, "but I'd like to keep a few of my brain cells."

"That Jensen kid Hal, he gets crazy when he drinks beer," Zahnie said. "When they go into those rapids, I hate to think." She slammed to a stop at a big garage or barn with no walls.

In a jiffy Gianni was pumping up a huge rubber raft with a machine that made a piercing whine. Obviously, he knew the drill. Zahnie grabbed a laminated sheet with an equipment list and began to call out items and hand things over to Red. "In my

Bronco! Sleeping bags, thermal pads, tent. Five-gallon water bag, two big wet bags, two small wet bags, two water bottles . . ."

Red packed it all in, including extra batteries for the flashlights, and Gianni pulled the boat trailer toward the government truck.

They connected the hitch together. Red kept thinking, *Don't say a word or she'll change her mind.*

Jolo showed up with a cooler of food and gave Gianni a ride back to Harmony House.

Zahnie's foot was heavy-plus. They slid onto the highway too fast, drove west too fast, skidded around a corner onto a dirt road too fast, and bounced their way toward the river. The best thing that happened to Red was when she skidded the Bronco to a stop.

She did the work so fast he had almost no chance to help. Trailer backed to the water, boat into the river, tied to the rail of the trailer, gear into one end of the boat, net snapped over it to keep it in, big water bag snapped to a D ring, everything shipshape right quick.

"Sit on the back tube," she instructed.

She untied, waded in knee deep, boarded, got into position, and hoisted the big oars. As she took the first stroke, he wondered, not for the first of many times, what she was really thinking.

Three hard pulls toward the far bank, where the current was.

Zahnie was irritated. Damn her nieces for their carelessness. And damn herself bringing someone along.

She looked at the stranger on the rear tube. Why had she brought him? Because he was well built and good-looking? And where had that gotten her in the past?

She thought of the flotsam her love affairs had washed into her life through the years.

And she was irritated about something else: Why had she brought *anyone* on a river trip? She knew better. She liked being alone with all that she loved on the river, the great blue herons, the bighorn sheep, the vultures, and most of all the ever-pulsing current. Taking passengers along violated her personal code. She didn't think the Old Age River was crazy about it, either.

Across at last, she felt the pull of the river, rested her oars, and just let them float. She drew a deep breath and let it out, took another, and told herself to let her irritation go. She wasn't going to let anything spoil this moment. She always loved to feel the current take hold and sweep them into the rhythm that went on forever, downstream, downstream, downstream, drawing these waters everlastingly to the salt sea. Even now, maybe her thousandth time of paying attention to this unappreciated energy, she was delighted to feel the irresistible current. Deep red canyons, swift green river, a slot of blue sky—this was Zahnie's world.

It was also her beat. She checked boaters on the river, making sure they had permits, the right equipment, fire pans, legal potties, and followed the rules. She floated the river and gave them tickets when they got out of line, cleaning up campsites as she went. She'd worked this job for nine years. Yes, it was untraditional for a Navajo to work the river. But she'd been fascinated by the river as a kid—she never believed that old-time story about Water Boy lurking in the waters, waiting to grab you—and after nine years she felt like the river returned her love and made her whole. It gave her more love than any man ever had, or her kid either.

She turned her face into the sun—another thing she loved about the river, hot sun and cool water, rays and waves.

She cocked an oar, whacked the water, and splashed Red.

He gasped from the sudden cold, then stuck his tongue out at her.

A perfect start. "Lay back," she said. "Enjoy."

He started singing a song in a haunting minor key:

"My heart goes where the river flows—
I gotta go-oh, where the river flows—
Rolling river wild and free—
The restless ones are you and me."

Her heart pinged when she heard the line about "the restless ones . . ."

"New lines to 'Cry of the Wild Goose,'" she said. "Where did they come from?"

"River guides I talked to. I always imagined floating down a river and singing that song. Never thought I'd really do it. But here I am."

What a strange guy! She looked at him. *What the hell am I doing? Something's not right with him.*

She stroked back into the strong part of the current and rested the oars. No point in doing the river's work. "Why did you leave California?"

He smiled and tossed out, "In search of America."

"Don't take anything seriously," Zahnie jabbed. "It would spoil your act." She let it rest.

"Will the rapids be dangerous?"

"Not for us."

"And the rescue?"

"Let's not think about that." She watched him take a couple deep breaths.

"This all seems so, *real,* compared to the way I was living in San Francisco."

"Real is good."

"I needed something new."

She decided to trust her cop instinct. "New name too?" she ventured.

He didn't want to tell her, she could see. Maybe he was on the lam. She weighed that. Well, Grandfather Winsonfred liked him. She took a stroke, easing them away from an eddy line, giving him a chance to decide what to say.

"Yeah, new name. I used to be Robert. I'd rather not say the last name. I haven't done anything illegal."

She wondered what he was sidestepping. "You still look familiar."

"I guess I've just got one of those faces."

"Well, Red, what kind of guy was Robert?"

He looked at that question like maybe he didn't want to know. "Robert had some dumb luck, was in the right place at the right time, and came by some money. Had two wives. The first one ran off with his business manager, a guy named Alvin Friedman. Alvin knew where every dime was. At the time Robert had to admire her style."

"Then years of the single life," Zahnie guessed. "In anything-goes San Francisco."

"Yeah. And I got a *female* business manager, just in case I ever got married again. Matter of fact, I got Nora Friedman, the daughter of my very first business manager, Alvin. Then I met Georgia and married her three months later."

"Let me guess. Twenty-two. Gorgeous, blonde, and what you might call untroubled by deep thoughts."

"That can be appealing in a woman, but it wasn't Georgia. Thirtyish, seriously spiritual, a seeker. Well, a couple of months ago Georgia and Nora confront me. They're having an affair—they want to get married."

Zahnie whooped. "This is too good."

He clenched his fists.

"Sorry." It wasn't friendly to whoop at a guy's catastrophes. And she knew the story had to be true. Only real life could throw you that kind of curveball. Your business manager steals your wife, and then his daughter, your next business manager, steals your next wife. Winsonfred would question Red's harmony.

"Of course, no one needed to tell me Nora had been burning the midnight oil, arranging my finances so Georgia's name was on absolutely everything. Wouldn't want to miss a dime in the property settlement."

Zahnie lolled her head and crooned, "Even *The Enquirer* wouldn't believe this."

"Some guys blow theirs on cocaine. I blew mine on business managers who stole my wives."

She concentrated, rowed them into the tongue of a riffle, and they splashed through.

"So, Red Stuart, who's this new guy going to be?"

"I don't know yet. He's set out to make a new life."

"With the safety net of a nice nest egg."

"Very small nest egg. The money's gone. I walked out on the whole shebang. No more Robert, just Red. Just me."

"Whoever you are."

"When I hatch, we'll see."

Time not to tease. "That takes guts. To start all over and figure it'll be okay."

"To tell you the truth, I've been listening for the rhythm, you know, *the* rhythm. I haven't caught it yet."

Nizhoni, Zahnie thought, what her people called walking in harmony with yourself, your family, and the world. Though in some ways she wasn't a traditional Navajo, she paid attention to Nizhoni in herself.

Suddenly she saw it and pointed the Navajo way, a kissing motion. A giant blue bird floated gracefully across the river, neck and head curved back on its own body. At the far bank it spread its wings to slow down, landed, and perched at the water's edge. Suddenly it was as still as an aged cottonwood branch, a time-shaped sculpture of the eternal winds.

"Great blue heron," she said.

The expression on his face said he'd never seen one before, and now he was in love with great blue herons.

Strange man, who are you?

He moved his eyes away from the heron to her. "You have kids?"

Sneak attack. She felt wary again. "One boy, Damon, seventeen." She didn't want to talk about Damon.

"He doesn't live at home?"

She shook her head. "He lives in Santa Fe, doesn't do much but a few drugs and play music day and night." She tried not to let her bitterness show, couldn't quite pull it off. "I screwed up."

"Never been lucky enough to be a parent, but I have plenty of friends who are. Sometimes hard things just happen. No matter what you do as a parent."

"Nice of you to say, but no, I screwed up mothering royally."

She knew what Damon was doing was commonplace, but that didn't make it easier to swallow.

She looked across to where Wilcox Wash came in. She shipped the oars and checked out the petroglyphs, barely visible in the desert varnish from this distance—and no time to stop today. "There's a special panel of rock art over there. Make this trip when you can take time to really look at all the nooks and crannies along the river. You could spend a lifetime doing that, actually, and it would be worth it."

The current took them close to the far bank. She eased her mind by taking a couple of unnecessary strokes. This was the Navajo side of the river, her side. Now she worked for the U.S. government and enforced its laws. She'd learned white people's customs—not only their spoken language but their body language and their social ways. Give people a peppy hello (which feels like an assault to Navajos), look them right in the eye (which feels like an invasion of privacy), worry a lot about whether things are getting done fast enough, do that paperwork, meet those deadlines. She'd spent her teenage years in Albuquerque and then spent more years going to their university. She'd even learned to push like a white person—mouthy as a Jewish American princess, her boss called her.

It's a disguise, a white mask. If you don't see through it, that's your problem. I am Navajo.

She wondered how much this man in the stern of her raft knew, what he understood. She decided to speak up. "Red Stuart, the big reason we're going to this effort, trying to protect my nieces and maybe help them grow up, too, is that we're all a big family, us human beings. You understand that?" She didn't look him in the eye when she said it. Just let her words float above the water. Her eyes followed a lovely green dragonfly, floating above her voice.

Red looked at her. "I don't have family anywhere, and I sure don't feel related to everyone in the great big world. Whatever connections I had like that, I've lost them. I've almost forgotten how they work."

He reached for a reed floating on the surface, picked it up high, and let the sun make the drops sparkle. Red-brown water ran down to his wrist and off onto his lap.

"How come you live here in the boonies? Must get pretty lonely."

"Albuquerque didn't cut it for me. More lonely in a big city than here. I came back home. My family's from across the river, Mythic Valley."

Red cast his eyes around. "And then there is all this. . . ."

"Red-rock country? Yes, born to the Red House Clan, born for the Bitter Water Clan. My ancestors were born here. I'm Navajo." She wondered what that meant to him. Who could blame him? Sometimes she wondered what it meant to her. Exactly.

Just then she looked up, and Red followed her eyes. High, high, two of them cruised.

"Buzzards?"

"Just one of them is," she said. "Unusual. One buzzard, they're common as fleas, and a golden eagle—they're not so common. They're circling in different arcs, but this angle makes it look like they're actually together."

Red grunted, and squirmed a little.

Zahnie asked herself, *Did Grandfather Winsonfred fill Red with stories of Ed last night, make him wonder if he was under a buzzard's watchful eye?*

"What're you thinking about?" she asked.

"Hosteen Winsonfred. The Ancient One told me to breathe this country and feel it. I'm trying." She saw him let his eyes roam the skies again.

He's thinking about Ed, all right.

She turned the boat fast, the current picked up, the roar started, and big waves rocked the boat. "Sand waves," she called out. A whole row of them lined up. She hit them head-on.

"Ride 'em, cowboy," Red hooted.

They both got soaked.

She slewed sideways and splashed him. They laughed and laughed more. Then the boat shooshed out into easy water.

"Why don't you take a swim? Just float along in your life jacket?"

Up, a quick cannonball, a big splash, and she was alone. She rowed hard, picked up the thrust of the current, got ahead of him, beached on a sandbar, got out a couple of sandwiches and two bottles of frozen water, and took a seat under a big cottonwood.

He dripped his way toward her and they ate in silence, a good-enough silence.

"Okay, enough. Time to get back on the water and find those nieces of mine. We can only go as fast as the river flows."

When he pushed them off and clambered from the river into the boat, he took a risk. "You mind if I ask you some personal questions? I don't want to get in the way of finding the girls."

"Depends on the questions. Talk won't slow us down."

"Winsonfred is a traditional Navajo, right? Clarita is Navajo and Mormon. Are you a traditional Navajo?"

He watched her hesitate, but her words were firm. "My people don't consider me traditional. I think some of the old stuff is just superstition. Watch out for the river—Water Boy is down there and will get you. Don't go near a dead body, or a place of death, or say a dead person's name—their spirits may be hanging around and jump inside you. That one would keep me from going into the Anasazi ruins, which is part of my job, and I like it. I don't like the traditional white stuff either.

"There's a lot about Anglo culture that I'm not crazy about, mainly the rush, the push, the greed, not caring about other people, forgetting about your relatives. Sure, I've adjusted to it—I operate on the Anglo system of time, which Navajos don't take to at all—but I don't get swept up in it."

She took three big pulls on the oars. He waited.

"Navajo tradition for me is believing in *Nizhoni*. Harmony. I like the inner beauty of the path better than Anglo technology."

She studied the current a moment and took one stroke across.

"Relatives," he went on, pushing. "You mentioned your son. I met Winsonfred and Clarita. We're going after your nieces." His eyebrows made question marks.

"Lots more. Other sisters, other nieces and nephews, my whole clan—"

She interrupted herself. "Look!" Red followed her eyes.

At the bottom of the sheer red face of the cliff, in white rock, stood what looked like an apartment building that had been pushed forward or backward in time from some other world.

"*Whoa!*"

"Leaning Bird Ruin," she said.

"Ruin? I'd give a million bucks for that place."

"Except you no longer have big bucks."

"It's probably not for sale, anyway." He laughed.

It made a long, curving line against the cliff wall. In some places the ancient architecture stood twice the height of a man's head, and in others the stone walls had crumbled to knee-high. The sun lit the stone bright and made deep shadows inside, shadows where human beings once made their lives.

He made a strange sound in his chest, and he felt as if the air was being sucked out of him.

"It's a nice one, Leaning Bird," she said.

She could see that her words jolted him. He inhaled deeply and let his breath out. It sounded like years of breath and secrets withheld.

She went on impersonally, "Leaning Bird. Single family, dating from about eleven hundred A.D., lots of potsherds and corncobs still in it because it's on the Navajo side and it's hard to land there. If you take the time . . ."

He struggled not to get sucked into the magnetism that sang to him from Leaning Bird. He grabbed Zahnie's words as a lifeline to the present and held on.

"I mentioned time. You've heard about Navajo time?"

"Kind of, yes."

"It's similar to what Anglos call mañana land—it'll get done when it gets done. Maybe. Makes them very impatient. Navajos, we think it's what whites don't know, what they don't hear. Leaning Bird reminds people of that rhythm. That things happen when they happen, no rush, give everything the attention it needs, get to the next thing whenever you get there. Which will piss off an employer who is expecting you at nine o'clock."

He paid attention to the ebb and flow of her words.

She said, "This is amazing country, ruins and rivers and redrock walls. You want the short, white-man version of where you are?"

"Sure."

"These rock walls date to more than two hundred million years ago, when dinosaurs were roaming around. Further downriver, the walls rise higher. The whole area was pushed up by a collision between oceanic and continental plates. When they collided, the rock layers were folded up, just like when you push on a rug. The river has since cut its way down the crevices into the fold.

"This place is a map of time on the earth, geologic time. The river cuts a giant slice and lays it bare so you can see it, where the ocean once was, where all the layers were formed, fossils from sea creatures. A million years here, a million there. You understand time passing, shaping the earth, how things changed and how they keep changing, going on forever. You don't feel it with head knowledge. It's bone knowledge."

"And there were people here."

"Lots of them, Desert Archaic, then Basket Makers, then Anasazi. The rock art is their message, what they wrote down, not for us, but for themselves and their children, to describe their world. We're part of that chain going back in time, forward in time, one link as important as another."

"I saw rock art yesterday. It vibrated."

He saw her look at him strangely, and felt a little embarrassed. "I'm not sure what the Anasazi story is," she went on, "the real story, beyond the facts. New Agers imagine them as an ideal society, farmers who lived in tune with the earth.

"Some archeological evidence says the Anasazi had the same troubles we have, including war.

"Whatever we can know of the truth, it's in the rocks. Rock is what lasts, so that's where the story is told, the rock of the cliffs and the rock of the ruins."

Red gazed down into the water as it rolled by. *I'm doing it, Winsonfred,* he thought. *I'm listening to the stories.*

He grinned to himself.

"What are you thinking?"

"It's smart-ass."

"Just like you. What are you thinking?"

"About that old Bill Haley and the Comets song, 'Rock Around the Clock.'" He sang out the first line smart and sassy.

"I give you all that great stuff, hand you mysteries, and you're reeling old rock and roll through your head!"

He shrugged. "It's a funny head."

First he heard it. A blast of sound loud as a Tchaikovsky symphony with all 120 instruments blaring full bore, except that this sound was chaos—slams, sucks, swooshes, gushes, every sound water makes, fighting its way between boulders.

She pulled for the left bank, where the current was strong. "Echo Rapids is just around that bend. Serpent House is right there beyond those tammies, in the cliff face," she said, "but you can't see it from here." She worked hard for several strokes.

"They've gone on," she said, a little breathless. "If they were at the ruin, the boat would be tied somewhere right along there." It looked like just another stretch of bushes to Red. "Let's get into the eddy."

She muscled them there, and the eddy actually eased them back upstream. Zahnie jumped out, painter in hand. "Help me!"

He plunged in and helped pull the boat most of the way out of the water. Grabbing the painter, he threw a clove hitch around a stub on a downed cottonwood, grinned, and said nothing about being a sailor.

They climbed a sandy hillock and she glassed the rapids with her binocs. A hundred fifty to two hundred feet long, he guessed. She took her time, sliding the binocs slowly downriver. "They're not here. Not at the ruin." Her voice was tight, low. "They made it downriver."

"Easy from here?"

"Easy enough." Her voice relaxed a little. "C'mon, let's scrub our way through these tammies, see Serpent House. Just a couple of hundred yards."

"Tammies?"

"Tamarisks, those big bushes that line the bank."

In a couple of minutes they were bushwhacking across a flat.

"Up there is Neville Canyon," she said, pointing off to the right to a break in the rock wall.

They hand-fought their way through tammies. Suddenly they were in a clearing and the ancient Serpent House ruin gazed down upon them.

12

SERPENT HOUSE MAGIC

Don't cross a snake's path unless you slide or shuffle your feet.
—Navajo saying

In one breath he lost his heart.

He gasped, drawing his life back in.

It was higher up the wall than the other ruin, and bigger, maybe three stories high. It had a couple of round towers that blew harmonicas through his skin. From the high buildings in the center small structures rambled sideways along the cliff, like flowering vines. It had the magic of paintings in fairy-tale books.

Then he saw. A huge snake was painted bloodred on the wall above the ruin.

He wandered forward, toward Serpent House, enchanted, and came to the base of the rock. Odd steps led upward, cut into the stone, now smoothed by wind, water, and time.

"Forget it," she said. "Higher up they're worn too smooth. You have to be a daredevil or use a rope." She handed him the binoculars. "These aren't the same as being there, but they're better than nothing."

Red glassed from building to building like a sleepwalker. He knew he could make it up there, touch the rock, smell the musty air.

"Check out that snake," she said softly.

He trained the glasses on it. Spectacular, as thick as a man's thigh and undulating about twenty-five feet across the wall above the buildings. The color was a red that probably was once bold, but now faded with age. In form it was a wave, perfectly regular in the way of no earth-born snake. Mysteriously, it had neither head nor tail.

He noticed Zahnie eyeing him peculiarly, but he had no time for that, only for the strange new feelings lifting his chest and spinning his head.

Red felt her touch his shoulder. "Let's have another swig," she said. "You're probably dehydrated."

They sat on a rock in the shade of a giant sagebrush. Red pulled deep on the water bottle.

"The big snake," she said to him, "how do we know it's not a painting of the river?"

"Don't know. How do we?"

"We ask the descendants of the Anasazi, the modern pueblo people, the Hopi, the Laguna, all those tribes."

"And what do they say?"

"That's the problem. One tribe says snake. Another may say river, another maybe something else."

Red gazed up at the big . . . whatever it was . . . and wondered whether it mattered to him what it was supposed to represent. He couldn't decide.

"Look over there."

A low boulder ten feet away was covered with shards of pottery, arrow points, and miniature corncobs.

"Those were found in the ruin," Zahnie said. "Normally we ask people to leave them where they lay, but these had already been moved."

He turned the ancient pot pieces over on his palm, traced

their designs with his finger. He especially fingered a big piece with a smooth rim and a handsome geometrical design.

"Black on red, the Moonlight Water style." She looked on the ground next to the rock. "Oh hell!"

Zahnie held out a plastic barrette decorated with pink and blue flowers, baby colors. "This belongs to Wandafene."

Red chuckled. "A brand-new relic to add to the old." He stepped to the far side of the sagebrush and gingerly lifted a small bra up by one strap half-buried in the sand. "Seems the shade looked good to them, too."

Zahnie's expression said she wanted to do anything but think about her niece's underwear. She snatched the bra and shoved it in her jeans pocket. "We try to keep telling them 'graduation before pregnancy.' I'm going to look around. You stay here."

Good. Red wanted to be alone in this place. He could feel the low drum of the ancient earth.

Red held the glasses on the ruin. Everything was different here, wavy-lighted, as if he might catch something out of the corner of his eye, something from another dimension. Grandpa had believed in other worlds and said pookahs opened the doors between them. Didn't seem a likely place for a Celtic pookah, but Red was beginning to realize that the more he knew the less he understood. Another prism of freedom revealed itself to him.

He remembered dioramas from a museum in Los Angeles. Women using handheld rocks to grind wild seeds. Men shaping arrowheads. Children playing with rattles made of dewclaws. Women making sandals from strands of yucca, others building a wall from stone and mud. One man pecking at the cliff with an antler, drawing a deer. Meat drying on a rack.

Those people might be around the next corner. He tossed thoughts away, spun reason out into space, and ate the ruin with his eyes. The people became a swing of pictures, like music, people dancing life here, dancing eternally.

Red smiled, and again he sucked air so deep inside his lungs, it was like drinking it, like having a transfusion of it. He let all words go and tasted the briney lick of time.

"I didn't find anything else," she said.

Red snapped out of it. *Was I asleep?*

"The people who lived here are fascinating." Again, her voice had the ring of a tour guide's. Red looked at Zahnie, thought of asking her not to tell him about them. He wanted to keep his own impressions, which felt misty and too big for words.

She plunged in. "This region has been inhabited for at least two thousand years, starting with Anasazi. Ancestral Puebloans, to be PC."

Her words hung like strands in front of Red, but he paid them no attention. Colored motes in his eyes, they were pretty, but they made it harder to see. He kept staring at the ruin, like opening a hungry maw. Half-willingly, he began to come back to the ordinary world.

She said, "There are ruins all over this country."

"Like this? Incredible."

"Some much bigger, more complex. Most smaller. Maybe most of them still under the ground. The thought of how many are undiscovered is mind-boggling."

"Way too much to get my head around."

"Red, I see this place speaks to you. That's really good. Spend some time here alone." She chuckled. "You might even get over yourself."

Hey, lady, I left myself floating with the great white sharks. But Red couldn't help grinning. She was more right than she knew. He still had plenty of his old self to shed.

"Find a place that calls you and just hang out there. The way I see it, the Ancient Ones welcome us."

He felt close to her. He wanted to say thank you for the gift of this place (or something like that but not quite so sappy), maybe tell her about the advice from Winsonfred.

"It's ruins like this where looters come and steal things."

He snapped his head toward her, and his words came out with a bite. "You don't mean *here*?"

"No, not such public spots. The looters do their dirty work in out-of-the-way places." She let that sit a moment. "I would like to flay them and nail their hides on the barn to dry."

She cocked her head.

"You hear something?"

"Slam. Car door."

"Me too." She clicked her head in several directions, holding still at each, like a bird. She grinned. "Want to do a little cop work?"

Red had no idea what she had in mind. "Why not?"

13

TONTO TO THE RESCUE

Don't open your mouth when you see a snake. It will jump in.
—Navajo saying

Ed watched the slate-colored Suburban proceed in a stately manner down the wash, almost to the river. He turned the other way on the thermal so he could keep an eye on it. His buzzard brain was pulsing, *Trouble, trouble, trouble, in the form of the Emperor and Empress.*

He knew these two. Even the way the Emperor steered his car down the faint track annoyed Ed—only the Emperor could bump down a dirt track pretending to be a road and make it look like an imperial procession. *Bleck.*

The Suburban stopped at a washout, and the Emperor and Empress exited. Ed felt a nasty spasm in his gut. The rotund man and skinny woman started unloading. Ed's buzzard brain didn't need to know their names to be angry. Ed noticed that everywhere the Emperor and Empress traveled in the wilds the trees, the grass and cactuses, even the animals seemed more dried up after they left. It was like they sucked the vitality out of everyone and everything around them. The Navajos would say they were stealing a creature's life force. Hosteen Many-goats said you couldn't catch a coyote, for instance, unless you got the tip of his nose and the tip of his tail, both, because that's where he hid his life force. And hiding your life force is a smart thing to do.

One of Ed's duties was to clean up dead things. He circled for one more look. The Emperor and Empress were shouldering their backpacks and picking up their gear. Unfortunately, they looked perfectly healthy. Okay, today probably wasn't the day, but Ed could wait them out. Cleaning up the carcasses of the Emperor and Empress—Ed's tongue told him how savory that would be. He yearned for the day.

"I have no idea what we're dealing with," whispered Zahnie, "but this close to the river, it can't be much, at the worst petty vandals."

They kept to the soft sand of the wash and trod in silence. Five minutes, nothing. They crossed a broken-down barbed-wire fence. Ten minutes, Red could see motion. He put his hand on Zahnie's shoulder. She stopped, nodded, and used the binocs. Finally, she said, "The Nielsens again." Without explanation she strode quickly toward the two figures.

The woman squeaked out a noise when she saw Red and Zahnie. The man dropped his tools and looked ready for who knew what.

Zahnie advanced, and Red followed warily. The bad guys were an obese, sixtyish fellow and a woman with a fierce and wrinkle-ravaged face. He would be cast as a rotund Lex Luthor and she as Lady Macbeth on a bad day. They wore huge gold wedding rings, and it was painful to imagine them in bed together. They carried shovels and other heavy-looking tools.

"Hello, Dr. Nielsen, Mrs. Nielsen."

"Zahnie, you know you may call me James."

"That's more intimacy than I want," Zahnie said.

"Good morning, Ms. Kee," said the woman. "My, but law enforcement is everywhere these days."

"This is my friend Red Stuart."

The doctor's hand was tiny for a man his size, and cold.

"Dr. and Mrs. Nielsen are pot hunters," Zahnie said.

"Actually, I'm just a chiropractor," said the doctor.

Zahnie went on. "They loot ruins like this one. They especially love to get into the kivas." She inclined her head toward the buildings in front of them.

"What's a kiva?" said Red.

"A chamber sunk into the earth," said Nielsen. "Tall, narrow, and circular. Like a water glass."

"Where they performed their sacred ceremonies," said Zahnie, "and left some of their best relics. Which is why the doctor and his wife would love to dig illegally there."

Red could see the remnants of the kiva, two rooms to one side of it, and what looked like a storeroom on the left.

"Zahnie, you know it's legal. We restrict our collecting to private land where we have the owner's permission."

"Unless you dig in grave sites." She said aside to Red, "NAGPA—that's the Native American Graves Protection Act. Which the Nielsens probably intended to do right here."

"Ms. Kee," said Mrs. Nielsen, "we stick to the law. We keep in mind James's license to practice, and our relationship with our God."

"Your God has probably seen you on public land, but I haven't. Yet." She turned to Red. "They steal pots and other artifacts from the ruins. Then they show them off in their fancy collection or sell them for bundles of bucks."

"We use them to beautify our house," Mrs. Nielsen said.

"Their mansion," Zahnie said, "and chiropractors don't make that much. Especially around here."

"When we're gone," said Dr. Nielsen, "our collection will go to the local museum."

"And what do you plan to do here today?"

"Do you know we're on Kravin land here?"

"Probably are."

"I will show you by GPS."

"No, that's okay."

"You may watch us work if you want."

"I intend to, just to make sure you don't dig in the midden." She glanced at Red.

"Mr. Stuart, would you like to see how collecting is done?"

"Sure."

"Excavating for artifacts is a fascinating hobby." The doctor did all the talking, his wife all the glowering.

"Will you come into the ruin, Zahnie, or are you traditional?"

"I'm not worried about *chindi*," she said, and came close. Later Red found out *chindi* were spirits to avoid, the residue of disharmony and evil left behind by the dead. "My job is protecting ruins, and especially grave sites." Zahnie's expression could have nailed boards to a fence post.

"What do you think?" Dr. Nielsen asked his wife.

"Front wall of that room," she said, pointing to the largest one.

Red pulled Zahnie aside. "What's the story here?"

Zahnie stepped to an area directly in front of the ruin. "This," she said, "on the south side, is probably the trash midden. That's where the goodies usually are, and where they'd dig if we weren't here. The Anasazi buried their trash and their dead in the middens, and nice belongings were interred with the dead. It's illegal. NAGPA says one bone and you're out."

"Zahnie," said the doctor with his amused smile, "your tongue spoils your beautiful face."

"The men in my life, past and present, would agree with you."

Mrs. Nielsen snorted.

Red hid his grin.

Dr. Nielsen ducked through the low portal into the room and stomped his feet. The rest of them peered over the half-wall. The corner where roof and walls once met was missing. "This is going to be hard work." He peered out at Red. "Mr. Stuart, you look fit. Feel up to digging?"

"Not unless you want to walk home," said Zahnie to Red. "Without any water and weighted down by the curses of the ranger."

"Look here." The doctor rose to hand Red a miniature corncob. In coming up, he cracked his head.

"You're going to knock Wayne Kravin's ruin down with that hard skull of yours," Zahnie said.

Dr. Nielsen rubbed the spot, regarded a little blood on his hand, and spoke softly. "The Puebloans farmed for most of their food. Cobs like this are emblems."

"Don't pretend you respect these people and what they've left. Not in front of me."

"Listen up," said Red.

Zahnie looked at him sharply. She'd been talking, but now she heard it, they all heard it, the throb of an engine.

"Who's coming?" said Zahnie.

"Probably Wayne Kravin," said the doctor. "He said he'd come by."

Zahnie made a disgusted face.

An ATV came into sight, driven by a man shaped narrow and hard, like a tree trunk. Garishly painted purple and white, it passed the Suburban, jumped the low bank into the gully that had blocked the Nielsen vehicle, and putt-putted on to the bottom of the slope. The wiry man moved up toward them fast. It was an uneven slope, with dirt and rock jutting out, but he bounced up with a mountain goat's agility. *Strong,* thought Red. They all moved out of the ruin to meet him.

"What are you doing here?" he said, glaring at Zahnie.

"Checking out a potential violation of the law," she answered calmly.

"It's all right, Wayne," from the chiropractor.

Wayne gave Dr. Nielsen a look that could have set his hair on fire. If Red had seen Wayne drunk in a bar, he would have grabbed a cue stick as a weapon, knowing trouble was brewing.

"Get off my property," growled Kravin, his furious eyes aimed squarely at Zahnie.

Everyone froze. Mrs. Nielsen was eyeballing Kravin with an avid expression, like lust, or thirst for blood or money, or all of that mixed up. Her husband didn't seem to notice. Red reached down behind and got the handle of Nielsen's spade.

"Get off my property," repeated Kravin, "you and your boyfriend."

"Wayne, NAGPA has holds on private property just like public. Native American Graves Pro—"

"I know your talk and your laws and they don't mean squat to me. I want you moving out before I count to three. One!"

Red flicked his eyes briefly at Zahnie. Looked like she intended to stay.

"Two!" Kravin moved a few steps in Zahnie's direction.

Red watched Kravin. Timing, timing. The man was a half-dozen steps downhill, well out of reach of Zahnie. Red stood two steps up and sideways from Kravin, and was half again as big.

Kravin reached for his hip, raised a .45 toward Zahnie.

Red took one step, swung the blade, and whacked the gun hand. The .45 flew half a dozen feet.

Kravin collapsed to one knee, holding his hand.

Red bulled into him full force.

Kravin fell backward on a yucca, which stabbed him in tender flesh somewhere near the crotch of his jeans. He howled and rolled onto his back.

Red slugged the big man in the solar plexus. *Whumpf!* exploded from his throat. Kravin gasped desperately for air.

"Help him!" cried Mrs. Nielsen. "He's dying."

"I hit him in the diaphragm," Red said calmly. "He'll start breathing in less than a minute."

Red grabbed the .45, flipped Kravin over, and sat on his butt. Then Red waited for the breathing to start. The moment it did, Red stuck the barrel of the .45 against the bastard's temple. He worked the action, so the man would know a shell was in the chamber. "Kravin, you feel that muzzle?"

Kravin nodded.

"I'm going to stand up and back away. If you try to get up, I'll shoot. What do you think, Officer Kee?"

"That would be murder!" cried Mrs. Nielsen.

"Self-defense," corrected Zahnie. "He tried to assault an officer of the law with a deadly weapon." She paused. "And reporting crimes is what the satellite phone is for." She reached for her belt, pulled out the phone, and started punching buttons.

"You going to be still?" said Red to Kravin.

Kravin nodded.

"Reach in your pocket and give me the keys to that ATV."

Hesitation.

"Now."

Kravin fumbled around and dropped a key ring onto the sand. Red picked it up, slid backward off Kravin, and carefully, not letting the barrel waver, stood up.

"Yazzie?" said Zahnie. "Yazzie?"

Impatiently, she punched more buttons. "Dispatch? Dispatch? Dispatch?"

She put the satellite phone back on her belt. "No angle on the satellite, the canyon's too narrow," she said to Red. She got out her GPS, tried it, and gave Red a strange look. A pale look.

"That's all right," Red said. "Mr. Kravin's not going to make any trouble. Are you?"

Kravin tried to manage an evil eye, prone, with his head pointed down the slope. "When I get loose, I'm going to cut off your balls and feed them to my dogs."

"You have quite an imagination, Mr. Kravin."

Red backed up, pistol still on its target, until he stood beside Zahnie and the Nielsens.

Zahnie said, "Mrs. Nielsen, give me your purse."

With baboon fury on her face, the woman did.

"Dr. Nielsen, give me your truck keys."

The doctor did.

"Any other keys, the three of you, on you or in your vehicles?"

Silence.

"I'll take that for a no."

Red put in, "If it turns out that you're able to drive away, I will become your personal nemesis." He glared at each of them, one at a time.

Zahnie said, "Mr. Stuart and I are going to walk back to the river and to satellite reception. Then I will call my superior. They'll send a helicopter to pick up you perps."

"We didn't do anything!" shouted Mrs. Nielsen. She pointed at Kravin. "It was all him."

"Your testimony may affirm that," said Zahnie. "In the meantime, sit nicely and wait for the helicopters to arrive. You'll probably post bail tomorrow."

"Tomorrow!" protested Mrs. Nielsen.

"Enjoy the ruin!" Red said.

14

CELEBRATING

Don't shake hands with a stranger. He might witch you.

—Navajo saying

"You were fantastic!" said Zahnie. They were out of earshot, a hundred yards down the wash, odd-footing their way along.

"Got to be some good come from a life spent in beer joints," Red answered. "What's with Kravin anyway?"

"I put his father in jail." The glee rang in her voice.

"No wonder he's so fond of you."

"I caught the old man looting, called for help, testified against him, and he went to federal prison."

"Federal?"

"Your government is tough on looters."

"Oh, jeez. Well, Kravin *really* loves you now."

"He and his family, old-timers here, they've been looting ruins for a hundred years, just like some of the other longtime Mormon families. Anyway, I caught Travis Kravin on public land bulldozing a kiva."

"What?"

"Just what you heard. Knocking down a kiva with a skid loader. You saw how narrow and deep those ruins are in the canyon. Now they're filled with blowing sand thanks to Travis. He wanted to get in the easy way—anything of value would be in the ground on the bottom—so he was taking the whole kiva out. He had to bring the skid loader in on a flatbed."

"What are those kivas for?"

"Two things: men's clubs and ceremonies. If I hadn't already gotten past the Navajo taboo about going into ruins, kivas would have done it. Shadows of people past, sounds, intimations . . . never mind. Trouble is, pot hunters love them, too. Besides middens, kivas are where you'll find the fanciest, most decorative stuff. If you found a whole pot in an ordinary ruin, it might be worth a thousand bucks. In a kiva you'd find a very unique pot, worth a lot more."

"How much?"

"Depends on the quality and age. Through a New York auction house? You could be talking six figures."

"It's legal to sell it openly?"

"If it's acquired legally on private property. Most of us find looting kivas even more disgusting than looting dwellings. Kravin totally destroyed the site and destroyed the chain of people past and future along with it."

Red snorted. "There's no end to where greed will lead a man, and that's the truth of it." He could almost hear his grandfather's voice, and for a moment he imagined Angus and Winsonfred having a smoke together on the back porch, bemoaning the loss of civilized ways.

Red and Zahnie came to the river, and she tapped at her phone again. Same routine. "No answer at my office, no answer at the sheriff's office. Those are emergency numbers, manned twenty-four/seven. Something's really wrong."

She tapped another number. Zahnie identified herself to

someone who obviously didn't know her. She asked them to pick up three perps and got into an argument. Exclamations of surprise. Words of annoyance. Finally an abrupt hang-up.

She grinned at Red. "That was the sheriff in the next county, San Juan. They have no jurisdiction to pick up anyone out here, and they can't raise anyone at the office in Moonlight Water on the phone, either, no one in Redrock County. So . . ."

She thought a moment. "They'll send a squad car down there and deliver my message and the GPS coordinates. Maybe this evening or maybe not." She smiled. "If Mrs. Nielsen doesn't get to spend the night in jail, she'll spend it sleeping with snakes and scorpions."

Red guffawed and untied the boat.

The rest of the way down the river Red and Zahnie whooped and hollered and splashed. They sang old songs. When they couldn't remember the words, they made up new ones that were gross and funny. They recalled awful titles for country songs. She started with "My Head Hurts, My Feet Stink, and I Don't Love You."

Red answered, " 'My Wife Ran Off with My Best Friend, and I Sure Do Miss Him.' "

" 'Please Bypass This Heart.' "

" 'She Got the Ring and I Got the Finger.' "

" 'If I'd a Shot You When I Wanted To, I'd Be Out by Now.' "

Red upped the ante. " 'I Got Tears in My Ears Laying on My Back Cryin' over You.' "

Zahnie grinned and said, " 'If I've Been on Your Mind, Please Jerk Me Off.' "

Red bent over laughing, tears running down his face. "That's it. I know when I've been topped."

They saw lots of cave swallows, a couple of blue herons,

way too many buzzards, and four bighorn sheep bearing huge curls of horn.

Red said, "Those sheep seem like magical creatures."

"They're always on the Navajo side," Zahnie said. "Don't know why."

"Sure you do," said Red.

15

NIGHT WATER

Don't stare at the moon. It will follow you.

—Navajo saying

Two hours downstream, they pulled into the hamlet of Splendora. Zahnie got a kick out of watching Red take in what the town was—a single enterprise combining gas station, motel, and café. No houses. Then she used the pay phone. When Leeja picked up her sister's call, Zahnie listened hard and her heart slowed. When she hung up, she told Red, "Leeja's got the girls. They're across."

"Across?"

"It means 'across the river,' on the rez. Anyway, they're safe home with Leeja in Mythic Valley."

Zahnie dialed another number and spoke to someone at Harmony House.

"Gianni will come right now with my Bronco to pick us up, and the boat. Half an hour. Want to eat?"

"Always."

In the restaurant they were greeted by a middle-aged woman in a pioneer-style dress, high at the neck and skirt to the ankles.

She bore three visible burdens: a lifetime of uncut hair piled on top of her head, a pair of the largest breasts ever, and an air of *I'm not like you* that looked heavier than either.

She seated them in a booth with turquoise vinyl seats held together with duct tape. She turned and left. Zahnie said, "Thank you, Coralee," to her back.

Red whispered, "What's with the dress?"

A pretty blonde waitress came toward them bearing water, napkins, and silverware. She was a teenager and wore the older woman's face and an almost identical dress. "Behold the granddaughter," Zahnie said, after the young woman walked away.

Zahnie shot Red a quirky smile. "Splendora's a polygamous colony. You know about it?"

"No."

"Look at her ankles." As the young waitress walked away, her blue jeans were visible under the pioneer dress. Red and Zahnie grinned at each other.

"You're sitting smack in the middle of their business empire, such as it is, but where they live is eight miles to the southwest, up Dry Creek. Old-time Mormon polygamists. I don't know exactly how many, but in the low thousands. Leftovers. About a century ago, when the Church abandoned plural marriage, they went up there because it's a place no one would want and they could be undisturbed forever. It's right on the state line. They put their houses on skids. . . ."

Red gave her a look. "Okay, now you're pulling my leg."

"No way. When they saw the law coming, they used teams of horses to skid the houses over the state line, one way or the other, depending on which state was coming down on them."

"Man, I thought Californians thumbed their noses at the law."

"These people are passive. I started to say they do 'passive resistance,' but I won't. 'Passive' is it. You're lucky Coralee's husband isn't here gooing things up. They call him Whip. I don't know what it's short for, but it's a perfect description of his personality: whipped cream. Even his face and hair look like whipped cream. He has no definition."

The waitress came back with a pad.

Zahnie ordered *ha-nii-kai* for both of them. "Stew of lamb marrow and white corn with fry bread. Navajo. It's great."

He nodded at the waitress, who disappeared without a word. "Chatty little thing, isn't she?"

"They try not to have much to do with the outside world. This business is it—they only want to be left in peace with their religion."

"And they build their houses on skids."

"From time to time they used to get busted, but now Utah has an unofficial-official hands-off policy."

"Ah, free lust."

Zahnie looked sharply at him. *How much of your life has been free lust, stud?* She thought miserably of her skin, which was far from fair, her lips, usually chapped, her eyes, muddy brown. Her chest tightened. It'd been a long time since she'd been attracted to a man. *Lousy choice*, she told herself.

"It's not free anything," she said carefully, "I've known them all my life. For them it's a responsibility. The men are mild and the women are stern models of duty. You'd find more lust in a convent."

"You're defending them?"

She shrugged. "My great-grandfather Winsonfred, he had three wives."

"I had two. Disaster."

She threw him her *don't-mess-with-me* look. "You know I mean three at once. The government should damn well let all of us live the way we want to."

"I couldn't agree more."

The waitress set flowered cups of steaming coffee in front of them and left without a word or even eye contact.

"They serve coffee as a concession to the gentile world. *Gen-*

tile, that means you, me, black Baptists, Chinese Buddhists—
anyone who isn't Mormon."

Red lifted his brew and sipped. "Not bad."

"Sir Richard Burton," Zahnie said, "the guy who wrote *A
Thousand and One Nights*? He came here to check out Mormon polygamy and wrote about it. *The City of the Saints,* cool
book. Only thing he found wrong with plural marriage—that's
what they call it—is that it kills the romance. He wanted the
lust of a harem, and found out plural marriage was anything
but."

Red smiled at her impishly. "It's men who are romantic, and
women who're the practical ones. Too many practical people
living under the same roof."

"Somebody has to raise the kids."

"Zahnie, I'm picturing you as a second wife. You walk two
steps behind, and it's only the senior wife in front of you.
You—"

Zahnie threw a handful of Splenda packets at him.

"The man goes to the senior wife's bed every night. When
she's unwilling, he passes on to yours. He hasn't gotten through
the senior wife's door in eleven years. You have ten kids—"

She tipped his coffee in his lap.

"Whooee!" Red hollered. He flopped around on the seat
like a fish out of water. "Hot! A little bit hot!"

He grabbed his ice water and poured that on his crotch.
Then he let out his breath and smiled at her. "Did I deserve
that?" he asked with a tease in his voice.

She eyed him. "Maybe not, but I enjoyed it."

"Grandpa Angus, he used to say, 'We men, we deserve whatever women give us, and it's usually better than we've earned.'"

Zahnie softened. "I like your grandpa."

"I did, too. Excuse me, I'm taking a trip to the men's room."

Red came back with a wad of paper towels.

"So, how you doing down below?"

"Strong and manly as ever," he answered.

She flashed a wicked grin. "I could fix that." She lifted her glass of ice water as a weapon.

"Hey, careful. I might need it again sometime."

The Navajo stew rescued them, and they both launched in with enthusiasm. Though Red said nothing, she could tell he liked the fry bread more than the fatty stew.

At that moment Gianni barged through the door, followed by Eric of the Young Mormon Youth. "Let's get to it," said Gianni. It struck Zahnie that neither of them was in a good mood.

They hefted the boat onto the trailer and tied it down in no time flat. All clambered into the Bronco, Gianni cruised through the dusk, and Zahnie watched the passing red rocks and hoodoos. The glow of lavender twilight on the stone was a beauty that always affected her. No one said a word.

When they'd unloaded at Harmony House, Eric went inside to help Jolo clean up the kitchen. At the back door he turned and called, "Hey, dude, how's it *really* feel to be dead?" The closing door cut off his cackle.

Just then Yazzie came rolling in fast and skidded to a stop, his truck roiling up the dust.

He jumped out and said, "The shit has hit the fan."

16

ENTER THE FEDS

Don't walk along the track of rainwater. You'll cause a flood.
—Navajo saying

"Yazzie, this is my friend Red Stuart. Red, Yazzie Goldman."

Red grinned at the guy. The name was a good joke, but he wore Navajo jewelry everywhere he could find a spot for it, and though his face was elderly, his hair was pure black. He was also as tall as Red, about six feet five, and still fit, with long, ropy muscles.

"Born to the Deer Spring Clan, born for Jew," said Yazzie Goldman softly. He added with a return grin, "You don't need the whole routine."

Red stuck out his hand and said, "Pleasure."

Yazzie Goldman squeezed the hand with a white-man shake. "I know. Unusual name around these parts," he said, "but my grandfather Goldman was a Jewish trader here."

Crazy country, all right, Red thought.

"I'm sorry, Zahnie," Yazzie went on. "I wouldn't have called out in trashy language if I'd known you had company."

"Let's sit," said Zahnie, and led the way to a picnic table. "Whatever business you have, Red and I have big news right off."

As they sat, Zahnie said, "Red, Yazzie is my boss at the BLM."

"I do the desk work, she does the river work."

Red nodded.

"Go ahead," said Yazzie.

Red could feel a huge dam of will stopping the man's tongue and his story. Zahnie spun the whole tale of the Nielsens, their probable looting, the intrusion of Kravin, his armed attack on her, and Red's taking him down and out.

Yazzie spoke to Zahnie like a cop. "You did not see the Nielsens doing anything illegal? You believed your presence would keep them from digging in the midden? You're sure the location was on private land? Kravin cut off whatever you wanted to say and came after you physically? Kravin didn't actually point the gun at you? Everything that Mr. Stuart did was in your defense? Nothing you saw would constitute excessive force?"

Her answers sounded like courtroom stuff, and her descriptions were exact. She added at the end that Red's threats might have been excessive, but his actions were not.

"You believe that Mr. Stuart's actions saved you a beating?"

"Maybe my life."

Yazzie turned to Red. "Mr. Stuart, may I call you Red?"

Red was always uneasy around cops, but he said, "Sure."

"Your testimony would be that you judged Zahnie was physically threatened by Kravin, perhaps gravely threatened?"

"Absolutely."

Suddenly, remarkably, a big change came over Yazzie's face. He smiled, shrugged, and said something in Navajo.

Zahnie translated, "Now we're done with the white-man shit and everything's copacetic."

They all laughed. Yazzie Goldman slapped one thigh, and his face turned impish. "Sure wish I'd seen that. Red, you are the *man.*" Yazzie fished in a shirt pocket and tapped out a cigarette for himself.

Red took a chance. "Allow me," he said, and offered his pack of Balkan Sobranies. Yazzie took one, then accepted a light. He drew deep while Red lit up, and seemed to pay great attention to the tobacco taste. "That's the best smoke I've had since . . . Never mind."

"Since he was around those Hollywood people," said Zahnie.

Red kept from dropping his jaw. "*Hollywood* people?"

"That's a story for another time," said Yazzie. "Back to where we started. Even bigger shit has really hit an even bigger fan. Better take some notes."

He handed Zahnie a notebook and pen and got out his own assorted pieces of paper, alternately scribbled and typed on.

"Whenever you smell a stink," said Yazzie to Red, "it's federal." He took a big breath and launched. "This morning, on a weekend when all BLM officers were on the river or having a day off, like us, the U.S. Attorney General sends agents into town like paratroopers. They arrested twelve of our Moonlight Water citizens." He paused before adding, "All from the west side. Anyway, arrested twelve people for trafficking in protected Native American artifacts. Mind you, all charges are for dealing, not looting.

"The big deal here, at least to you and me and the sheriff and every law officer in the county, is that this was a huge federal operation all the way. They didn't cooperate with us small-time law enforcement, had no use for us. We live here, we know the people, but we're small-timers. Sons of bitches."

He smiled at himself. "Sorry again. Anyway, they found a guy in Gallup selling on the Net. Not a big dealer, it looks like. I got an inkling it was somebody who used to be a local—he only deals with people here.

"Seems they had this guy by the short hairs and offered him a deal. If he would give them all the dealers he got artifacts from—again, not looters, mind you, just traffickers—they would . . . Actually, I don't know exactly what they promised him.

"So, he gave them depositions and they invaded. Obviously, they didn't trust us to be in on it, thought we'd tip people off."

"They're right about the sheriff and deputies."

"Hell," said Yazzie, "the sheriff's brother got arrested. So, the sheriff is pissed off, and I am royally pissed off. This is my job in my territory. I've been fighting these looters for thirty years, you for a long time, too, so why don't they trust us? We get pushed to the side like kids."

"Jeez," said Zahnie, "twelve arrests. Everyone on the west side is related. That will touch every family."

"Just about," said Yazzie. "I wondered at first if your run-in with the Nielsens and Kravin would make trouble for us, make the feds think we were intruding, but I don't think so."

"So you came to tell me to back off and stay backed off."

Yazzie gave a smile that was angelic and demonic at once. "Not really," he said.

The front door opened, cutting off whatever Yazzie wanted to say. Winsonfred led the way. While he padded, Gianni, Tony, and Clarita clomped down the stairs.

"Yazzie Goldman," Clarita said in royal elocution, "we have some questions to ask you."

The four jammed themselves onto picnic benches.

"What on earth is going on?" said the empress.

"It's got nothing to do with us, Clarita," said Yazzie, "no trouble here." He sounded comfortable. Red wondered if Yazzie and Winsonfred were the only people Clarita couldn't intimidate.

She lit up a joint, maybe thinking Yazzie would see it as a bull sees a red cape.

"Anything that happens in Moonlight Water affects every-one. For heaven's sake, you know that."

"Clarita, slow down."

"*It's a federal issue,* you'll say, Yazzie. But you would have arrested those people, too."

"Yes, Grandmother," said Zahnie, "and I did something very much like it today."

"What?" Clarita sounded really alarmed.

"Wayne Kravin and the Nielsens. But the Nielsens won't be charged, and Kravin didn't loot. He assaulted a law officer with a deadly weapon."

Clarita studied her face, puzzling her out.

"The point is," said Tony, "a lot of local families are going to get hurt."

Clarita hammered out the facts. "Yes. If those men go to the federal penitentiary, children will be fatherless. Families may go bankrupt. Others will leave for other towns, other marriages."

"I can name three elderly people," said Tony, "who would end up right here with us within a year, and we don't have the room."

"Maybe they'll learn to obey the law," said Zahnie.

"Excuse us," said Clarita to the world at large, "for using our tongues sharp like white people."

"We're half-white," said Tony. "We're already excused."

Very casually, Yazzie said, "We don't know what the outcome will be. I expect a lot of plea bargains."

Now Gianni butted in, "Damn it, this trading has been going on for generations. It's practically a local tradition." He hesitated. "Maybe even honorable."

Clarita said, "It is. My husband was paid by the Smithsonian Institution to do just what these people are doing. He found artifacts, or bought them from locals who found them, and sold them to the museum."

"That's right. And the government thanked him for it," said Gianni.

"Two of my sons did the same," said Clarita.

"To hell with a government that acts this way," said Gianni. His eyes looked rougher than his voice sounded.

Yazzie held up a hand. "Times change, laws change, thank God." He took Zahnie's pad and pen, wrote, tore out the sheet, and handed it to Clarita. "Grandmother," he said, "I ask you to take your grievances to this man. He's the head of the federal operation here."

Yazzie rose to leave. "Call me in the morning," he said to Zahnie. "I'll have news about Kravin and the Nielsens."

Red and Zahnie found themselves alone in the warm night.

"I don't want to be around any of them right now," Zahnie said, nodding to the house. "Want to go down to the river?"

She took a thermal pad to sit on and led him to the water's edge, then along the bank. She was always more at home outside, and at home most of all where she could hear the river running. Running-sliding-whisking.

She sat on the pad on a bench-like chunk of sandstone, felt him sit next to her. River air felt different from the air of the bluffs, the canyons, the sand flats—gentler, moister, cooler. Feminine. She knew the mountains where this river came from in Colorado, where water fountained everywhere. She found water more a grace here in the desert. Rare and precious, a coral and turquoise gem.

She looked at the dark waters of the eddy below them. Though she couldn't see them, she pictured the depths. Water-borne food was drifting to the bottom there, and in the cool darkness catfish fed languidly. She liked to imagine those catfish finning around, shadows in aquamarine darkness.

"You saved my skin today. I owe you."

"No debt," he said. "It was exhilarating to fight for something, someone. It was real."

"Tell me who you are, Red Stuart. Tell me what you're running away from."

"I'm just a guy trying to find his way."

"Just a guy. The Navajo way is to say who you are by telling what two clans you come from. That helps *you* know who you are, what you'll do."

He stared into the flowing waters, and she wondered what his mind was on.

"Scots both sides. My dad was a tough union guy who drove a cable car in the city. He died when I was ten. My mom, she skipped out after that. Her allegiances, judging by her actions, were the Catholic Church and middle-class respectability. His was the union."

"Are you Catholic, then?"

"I ran far from it, and for years was an agnostic. Now I ponder occasionally about the Anonymous Source. That's what I call it, and it's as close as I can get."

Companionable silence.

Red broke it. "Know what my most vivid memory of Dad is? He used to take me on the cable car in the afternoon, after school. He had this glass eye, got it gouged out in a bar fight, what else? He loved the tavern life. Anyway, I liked those afternoons 'cause he told stories about the city. He knew everything that happened in San Francisco. He showed me right where the fires went after the earthquake, and how they rolled gondola cars into the burned areas and hauled the rubble away. How he watched the Golden Gate Bridge go up, later, the world's first successful suspension bridge. He was a big fan of Harry Bridges and the longshoremen, too. The first author I ever saw, my dad pointed him out, Eric Hoffer, wrote *The True Believer*. Mom's chorus was 'Blessed Virgin,' and Dad's was 'the workingman.'

"Well, this glass eye of his, one day on the cable car it popped out. I was standing just behind him, hanging on to a strap, and I heard this little clunk, and my dad says, 'Oh hell.' The eye poised there on the floor, for a moment, unmoving—we were sitting in the middle of a cross street, flat, blocking traffic. Dad had to ease the cable car forward.

"The eye started rolling. 'Grab it!' Dad hollered. He was

sensitive about it—I always figured he was afraid he'd get fired if the city officials knew he had only one eye.

"I started crawling between the passengers' legs, keeping my real eyes on a sharp lookout for the glass one. The eye would bop off one passenger's shoe, glance off a lady's high heel, pause against a man's briefcase, all like that. I hopped after it, dodging calves, to some considerable protests, but I never could catch up with it. Just as I grabbed, poof! The eye would carom off. I felt like I was playing a crazy game of pinball, and losing.

"Way at the back of the car, between a Chinaman and an elderly black woman, I dived like a shortstop and got it between my fingers. Desperately, I got my feet half under me. Just then Dad topped the hill and launched the car downward. The Chinaman looked at me like fate, almost smiling. I spilled over onto my shoulder, and the eye flew from my fingers.

"Back toward the front of the car it rolled, bouncing off shoes like pinball cushions, me right behind it like a frog—*Hop! Hop! Hop!*—never quite catching up.

"The cable car swung to the right, around a corner. I swung to the left, into an old gentleman's lap, or at least against his bony knee. He was wearing a straw boater and a carnation. He was so mad, I thought he was going to stuff that carnation up my nose.

"I hopped again, and the eye jammed under the arch of a woman's high heel, and an expensive-looking heel it was. I clamped my hand onto the vagrant eye, and then I looked up. A very elegantly dressed blonde and a looker—a generation earlier and she might have been one of William Randolph Hearst's mistresses headed for a rendezvous.

"Now, the painted part of the eye, the iris, had been rotating up and down, up and down. When it jammed, as fate would have it, the sightless iris was pointed straight up her skirt. The blonde looks first at me, like I was something she'd stepped in. I drew my hand back. Then she saw what direction the eye was pointed. She gave a high, little yip, like a terrier, and she crossed her legs real tight, like vines wrapping around each other. Then a 'Shoo!' as if I were a fly on her nose.

"Dad stops the cable car. He walks back, and he's just tall enough to face her chin to chin.

"I slip the eye out and hand it to him.

"She does that weird little yip again.

"He fixes her a glare, a most worthy one-eyed glare.

"She puts her hand to her face in false, blushing modesty.

"He musters his most baleful expression. Then, slowly, with an extravagant, grotesque style, like Vincent Price in a horror movie, he rolls the eye around inside his mouth to clean it, and he pops it back in.

"She breaks into a terrier titter of yip-yaps.

"'Milady,' says Dad, 'concern yourself not. The eye sees all, but it does not tell.'"

Zahnie laughed out loud, but she also watched him. "Is any of that true?" she finally said.

"We Scots tease the best out of a story, but we do not lie."

"Except when you're horny."

"There's that, too." To his credit, he grinned.

"What else do you want to know?"

What to ask? I even bewilder myself. So she asked the obvious. "Why did you come here, here of all places, Red Stuart?"

"I came to Moonlight Water because Gianni asked me to meet him here, and because he said it's the uttermost end of the earth. What's more important is why I went away from there."

"So tell me."

"I want to be more like my Grandpa Stuart, the one who told me the old stories of the Highlands and the west of Scotland, where our family came from. He spoke of magic and pookahs and monsters like a poet, and he seemed to walk a wiser way. He enjoyed his life more than I do. And that was from a wheelchair.

"You know the last thing he said to me? I poured him a

single-malt Scotch as I left for rehearsal that evening—he liked the really peaty ones. He raised the glass and said, *Slainte!*, meaning in Gaelic, *Health to you!*, with a sly grin. That was Grandpa, a poem, a toast, a sly grin. He died in his sleep that night, and I've always been sure he knew he was going."

Zahnie let his words fade into the evening. She looked into the sky and imagined multi-colored figures against the darkness, figures moving ever so slowly horizon to horizon, dancing ever so slowly, a reflection of our lives on the earth, one line of melody in the dance of the vast harmony of life on the planet. Maybe since these figures were spirits, they danced forever, never had to stop to sleep or wake or laugh or cry or make babies. Always dancing forth their energy, whirling the great fandango to the music of time.

Zahnie looked into his face, starlit, almost magical. Putting on a light Scots accent, she said, "And is that exactly why you've come to Moonlight Water, Red Stuart? To learn to enjoy it all? To be like your grandpa, with a poem, a nip of whiskey, and a sly grin?"

"Yes. I think so."

"I think you want more."

But Red didn't want to talk about his recurring dream and "T'ain't What You Do" and his setting forth, not yet. He turned slowly and searched for her eyes. "Turnabout," he said, "is fair play. Your time to answer questions."

Zahnie didn't like that. She bit her lip until she thought of an excuse. "I have a better idea."

He cocked an eyebrow at her.

"Let's make music together." She reached across and tapped his shirt pocket. "My voice and your harmonica. Don't deny it. I've seen it there all day."

He showed the good sense to say nothing, just plucked his mouth organ out of the pocket and put it to his lips. She saw him hesitate, and then he began to play. A slow, sad tune, one she didn't recognize for a moment. Then she knew— *You* are *telling me something.* When the four-bar intro closed, she sang the familiar words in her throaty alto. Though the loneliness was hers, too, and everyone's, the way he played it . . . She knew, at least at that moment, he had the notes written on his heart.

> "*I am a poor wayfaring stranger,*
> *A-travelin' through this world of woe.*
> *But there's no trouble, no toil or danger,*
> *In that bright land to which I go.*"

The harmonica felt rich, the minor chords sucked in and blown out like the soul's sweet air. She opened her throat and sang the words fuller, opened her heart and sang them truer.

> "*I'm going home to see my father.*
> *I'm going home no more to roam.*
> *I'm just a-goin' over Jordan.*
> *I'm just a-goin' over home.*"

She looked at him. The moon gleamed on the dark river now and threw a silvery light on his face. Regardless, she thought she saw a spark in his eyes. He said he didn't believe in anything. She believed in *Nizhoni.* She hoped she could walk in it every day, and she hoped he would find it.

She'd imagined an evening of playing music together, a much longer evening. But she reached over and put her hand on his cheek. She caressed it a little. Then she leaned across and kissed him, lightly, on the lips. Red returned the kiss. His lips felt full and good, and they were leading somewhere she was surprised to go. Didn't really want to go, when it came down to it.

Zahnie slammed on the brakes. She took his face in both hands, looked with feeling into his eyes, and said, "Sorry. It's not going to happen."

She could see Red was not surprised. Disappointed, but not surprised. "Maybe you can just enjoy my company."

17

TROUBLES TO THE LEFT OF US,
TROUBLES TO THE RIGHT

Don't hate anyone of the opposite sex, especially if he's ugly.
You might end up marrying him.

—Navajo saying

Wrapped around her pillow, Zahnie felt sensuous. Dreams
drifted sweetly by. She indulged herself.

What are you doing, Zahnie Rae?

She woke up hard and fast and gawked around her cabin.
Unmistakably, that was her grandmother's voice rattling around
the walls. *You crazy coyote,* the voice went on. Calling a Navajo
a coyote was rude—coyotes always got things wrong.

Thank God, her grandmother was long gone and couldn't
carp forever about Zahnie and Red Stuart or anything else.

She pictured Red at the main house sleeping in Winsonfred's
bed. Though Red was no prince on a white horse, he was attractive and fun and intelligent, a warrior with heart. She saw
world-weariness around the eyes, which felt to her like character.

She sat up and put her feet on the floor. *At least I didn't in-
vite him to my cabin.*

Don't walk into a dust devil! It will affect your heart.

Yes, Grandma, I did flirt with him.

You almost got carried away. And you were the one who started it!

Amazing how Grandma could make her voice real in the room.

Zahnie grumbled at herself silently. *At my age flirting with a two-time loser at marriage, a man dedicated to nothing, running from everything.*

Her grandmother chimed in, *Some way to act, Zahnie.*

Grandma, why do you wake me up with your griping?

Zahnie Rae, you act degees [*like a madwoman*] *around this* bilaganna [*white man*].

Zahnie didn't need Flora Kee's sharp tongue this morning. She was irritated with herself, irritated enough for both of them. She told her grandmother, "Shut up!"

Don't stare at the moon, came the voice again, another Navajo proverb. *It will follow you.*

Carefully and quietly, Zahnie stood up and slipped some clothes on. *The ceiling and walls feel too close.*

She stepped out onto her front stairs, pulled on her river sandals, and looked up to see Gianni sitting on the back steps of the main house, smoking. He gave her a big smile. She wasn't up to a smile. She walked past him without acknowledgment and went straight to clanking pots and pans in the kitchen. She wanted waffles, and she intended to have them.

In moments Red and Gianni were sitting at the table, trading talk she paid no attention to. Her mad was a hard-charging train, and nobody had better get in its way.

Winsonfred soft-padded to the table, sat down, and whispered something to Gianni. In a moment Gianni was standing next to her, mashing out sausage patties and throwing them into a hot skillet. She ignored him.

Breakfast passed in sweet, syrup-soaked silence. All three men looked a little tickled. If one of them said she was cute when she was mad, she'd clang him with her iron skillet.

The phone *brr*-rang across the room. Zahnie jumped to answer it.

"Oh, hi, Yazzie. Are the Nielsens and Kravin back okay?"

"Yes. Now get ready. Your name among the feds currently is, get this, *Heroine*."

"What?"

"You did really good yesterday. They're impressed."

"They don't say I was interfering?"

"Uh, Wayne Kravin and the Nielsens were the last warrants the feds had, but they couldn't find them. They appreciated you."

"Coincidence, you suppose? Any chance the Nielsens and Kravin got tipped off? To save them from the federal bust?"

"Hell, even we didn't know. Listen, I have something for you, something good, and we'll rub the feds' noses in it."

He paused and she heard paper crinkling. "I got a report last night from two hikers. They saw a flatbed truck loaded with heavy equipment on the trailer heading up Lukas Gulch. The women couldn't say what kind of equipment. They don't know a bulldozer from a backhoe from another."

"Heavy equipment," she murmured. Lukas Gulch was a roadless area. It would be hard to get anything wheeled in there. Besides, no one but Travis Kravin, as far as she knew, had been jackass enough to take yellow iron to get at a ruin.

"Yeah," said Yazzie. "Yesterday a big sting and today this."

"The timing is weird, Yazzie."

"Definitely. Look, as far we know, no way the fed bust has anything to do with Lukas Gulch. The government yo-yos are probably pulling out this morning anyway. You're a heroine, and this is our job. Go take a look."

She thought. "Are you sure the feds are leaving?"

"That's the way I'll remember it. No charges of obstruction."

She was silent, stalling.

"I know," said Yazzie, "it's boring. These tips rarely lead to anything. Humor me."

"Deal." She called to the room at large, "I gotta go hunt bad guys."

Red stepped out from the foyer where Winsonfred reclined. Red said, "And I'm going with you."

She studied him.

"I saved your skin," Red said.

It was irregular to take a civilian, but this would only be a long drive in the backcountry. Zahnie said, "Yeah, yeah, okay." To Gianni she called, "Do not tell me you want in, too."

Gianni shook his head. "Closing a mineral rights deal today." He smiled at Red. "Got to take care of me and my friend."

She was comfortable out here. True, not many people would call what they were driving on a road. A track, maybe, or a trace. Parallel bare spots through the sand and sometimes across the naked rock. You had to be a longtime local to navigate this part of the planet.

The country bumped by. There was strange stuff out there, the slickrock, sand blowing and rolling and somehow frozen in place. It was like the Anonymous Source (she had to admit she liked that term) poured it molten and it ran across the land like lava and stiffened into curvy sculptures. The Anonymous Source was definitely being playful when She made this place and when She carved the hoodoos. Playful and in a semi-spooky mood.

From time to time Zahnie slowed down and eased the four-runner diagonally through soft sand, or across the rocky bottom of a wash, or once through a piddly excuse for a creek.

She turned onto a dirt road. This was actually a bad road instead of a track.

"More big rock walls," said Red.

"And more," she said.

He rested his head on the seat back and closed his eyes. She knew that only a native could tell what direction they were headed, where north and south were, where the river was, anything.

Then she heard it.

"Damn it!" she said. The whirlybird machine-gun *whap-whap* was unmistakable.

"Who the hell?!" Zahnie again.

She slammed on the brakes, yanked some binoculars out of the pack. Then she realized she could already see it with the naked eye. Helicopter, one o'clock, low, way out, but moving fast.

Zahnie jammed the car into gear. "They're coming hard," she said. "They spotted us."

"Who? Why?"

"Who knows? Listen, you've got to hide."

"I'm not a criminal!"

She ground gravel as she stopped. "Gotta be feds. They'll say Yazzie and I are ignoring their orders by doing this on our own. I am violating regs by bringing you along and could lose my job. *Out! Go!* Into those rocks. *Now!*"

Red fumbled with the door handle and half-fell out of the car. "*Go!*"

He skedaddled.

Zahnie followed him, intending to create visual confusion. As the sound from the helicopter got louder, she considered. Red was already plunging in between two big slabs of rock shaped like pieces of bread leaning against each other. She needed a distraction so he could get hidden—good luck, with that bulk of his—and she needed a reason for being out of her truck.

What to do, what will work?

She put on her uniform hat, as if it would help her think.

The helicopter *whap-whap* was nerve-wracking.

Eureka! She grinned.

Hands shaking, she reached for her belt and started unfastening her shorts.

18

ZAHNIE AND THE COPS

Don't wear two hats at once. You'll get twins.

—Navajo saying

Red felt like a giraffe trying to hide in a petunia patch. He pushed his way forward. Hell, anyone could see right through the crack in these slabs of rock, sky at the top and musician in the middle. He had a sudden thought. About twenty feet up, a boulder the size of a VW was jammed like a chock stone, suspended in the air.

He damn well could turn into a rock climber.

It wasn't bad. He found footholds and handholds and reached and struggled and slid into a slice of shade between chock stone and slab. He raised his head and peered over. Beyond the hood of the Bronco he saw Zahnie's head or, rather, her flat-brimmed uniform hat. Why'd she put her hat back on? From the angle of her head she was staring forward along the road.

The *whap-whap* grew crushing overhead. For some reason they weren't landing yet. On the passenger door of the copter he could see the insignia of some federal agency, eagle wrapped in blue and white.

Eyes back to Zahnie and he got it. In the red sand of the road she squatted. Her drawers were dropped, hind end exposed.

Whap-whap-whap-whap!

Zahnie stared at the horizon out from under the brim of her hat with a peculiar concentration familiar to everyone.

The copter's shadow flicked over Red and then stopped in midair above Zahnie. He pictured the guys' faces

Leisurely, she took something white out of her shirt pocket, made a swiping motion in her nether region, pulled up her underwear, wriggling her bottom the way women do, stood up, raised and buttoned her shorts, and cocked her head up toward the copter. Casually, she tossed the white whatever onto the floor of the Bronco and looked up at the feds.

Red pulled his head back down. *Goddamn! What a woman!*

Red had a clear view of Zahnie and the copter. He figured there were two advantages to being this close. (Though he would have preferred farther away. Like Nebraska.) Advantage One: If the guys stood near Zahnie, he might hear what they said. Two: He could sure tell if she was in the kind of trouble that would require a quick assist from a hidden friend. Not that jumping in between over-amped cops felt healthy. Especially when you're carrying a concealed .45 auto without a permit.

Zahnie stood and squared her shoulders. *She's calming herself down,* he thought. He watched her like observing an actress from backstage. She pulled out her Attitude makeup, applied it to her face, and spoke her lines.

"You buncha dripnoses," she shouted. She shook her fist at the descending helicopter.

They probably couldn't hear her over the rotors, but she was letting them see she was going to be in their faces big-time. The copter sidled sideways and teetered gently to earth. They cut the engine. Two men wearing camos with sidearms jumped to the ground, a little white guy and a big Mexican.

When the rotors stopped, the Mexican grinned and started out, "*Chiquita*—"

"That's *Officer Kee* to you," she interrupted. Zahnie stuck her ID toward him.

He took it. His lips smiled faintly as he read.

"I'm Lieutenant Roberts." This was the little white guy, younger than her but with just a ring of hair, like a monk. He double-checked the name on the ID. "Zahnie Kee," he called to the copter pilot, spelling both names. "BLM. Check her out, McFay."

"*Chiquita*," began the Mexican

"Again, it's *Officer Kee*. And I'm Navajo, not Mexican."

"Okay. I am Agent Hernandez," the Mexican went on, "Officer Kee." His tongue nearly licked the words. "Don't worry, we ain't after you for a public indecency rap. We wanna know what the hell you're doing out here."

"My job. And you're interfering with it." Zahnie kicked a little sand on the ground between her legs to cover the fluid that wasn't there.

Attitude. Go, Zahnie.

"And just what would your job be," said Roberts, "forty miles from freaking nowhere?"

"When did you get into my chain of command?"

Hernandez twisted a corner of his smile. "You'll have to do better than that."

Red's mind spun like a clothes dryer, thoughts tumbling. He wondered what story she would come up with.

"We got a report of possible looting in Lukas Gulch, I'm checking it out," she said.

Whoops, she told the truth.

"We got the same report, Officer, this is our sting, and you locals are getting in the way." This was Roberts. "Albuquerque office told your boss and the sheriff, all local law, to stay out of this, all the way out."

"We thought you'd gone back to your air-conditioned offices. Besides, we get reports like this all the time." Red figured she was whistling "Dixie" now. Her mind was probably more on whether the feds would spot him.

McFay called from the copter, "The head guy at Moonlight BLM, Yazzie Goldman, says she's out of his headquarters and following his orders." He jumped to the ground, which was surprising. He must have weighed three hundred pounds. He had a pasty face that read *smiley-but-dumb*.

"He lying to cover for you?" said Roberts.

"What's going on, Officer?" said Hernandez. "You trying to get in on the action? Or are you trying to protect some friend or relative from what's coming down?"

"You don't know up from down in this country. Go home," Zahnie snapped.

Jeez, Zahnie.

Roberts pulled out a handheld GPS and said, "Latitude thirty-seven degrees, fifteen minutes north, longitude one hundred nine degrees, thirty-eight point zero four minutes west."

"That's what I mean. This country is not a map, and this place is not a GPS number. It's a real spot in a hostile desert, where mean critters live, and city boys die."

Red's skin crawled. *Easy!*

"We think you need to learn to be a team player," said Roberts.

"We could overlook it, maybe, for a little better look at—"

That was it. Red started to launch himself out of the rocks and realized his foot was caught in the crevice below the chock stone.

"Shut up, Hernandez," said Roberts. Then Roberts's eyes turned to Zahnie and bored in on her. "Get in the copter."

Red heard Roberts's tone, saw the effect it had on Hernandez. Some kind of power struggle was going on between those two.

Roberts's barked order had the effect of a slap—Hernandez seemed to shrink several sizes.

"What about my vehicle?" said Zahnie.

"Not my problem."

"What about—?"

"Get in the copter."

Zahnie hesitated. "No."

"Cuff her, Hernandez."

The big Mexican strode two steps and grabbed her elbow.

She jerked away. "Never mind," she said. "I'll go easy." She turned her head sideways to glance toward Red. Her eyes said, *I'm sorry!*

Roberts smirked, mistaking her expression. "Smart choice."

Hernandez added, *"Chiquita."*

Zahnie looked at Hernandez like she was queen of the desert, her chin in the air. "Now I understand why generations of Navajos have disliked Mexicans."

She walked to the helicopter like it was her idea. Clarita in training. With Zahnie's lip and her attitude, she could probably stand the assholes off. Or was that himself, whistling in the dark?

People climbed up, the rotors whirled, and the bird carried Zahnie away.

19

STRANDED

Don't pretend to pray or cry. It's asking for someone in your family to die.

—Navajo saying

And now what about Red Stuart, previously Robbie Macgregor and Rob Roy—what would he do out in this desert?

He smiled at himself. *I set out to get lost, and this is about as far as lost goes.*

He looked at the sky, a perfect azure, innocent of a tuft of cloud or even a speck of dust. "Grandpa," he whispered, "I don't see any messages written up there."

As the last hint of sound of the copter faded, Red mulled over the spot he was in. He wouldn't worry about Zahnie, he told himself. She was a cop in the custody of cops, headed to face the questions of more cops—probably just bureaucratic bullshit. Might be smart to keep his mind on his own circumstances. His hands had just stopped shaking. What could he do to send the last of his over-pumped adrenaline out and away?

He said aloud in a mock-musical voice, "Let's find out if the keys to that Bronco are in the ignition." He pictured driving into town, finding that guy Hernandez, and—

Red clambered down the crack and out into the sunlight. He swallowed hard. *What if?*

He tiptoed to the passenger side and stuck his head in the window. No keys in the ignition. Check the floor—no keys. Check under the front seats—no keys. No spare keys in the glove box or above the visor, either. None in any of the four wheel wells in a magnetic box. None under or in back of the bumpers. None on the frame. None, none, *nada*.

He got the gallon plastic bottle off the back floor and swigged some water down. He thought word by word, *I will act cool. Be cool. Sit and eat lunch and enjoy and not worry about being stranded in the middle of the freaking desert with no idea which way is home and no way to get there anyway.*

The word *home* stumped him for a minute. *I don't have a home.* He cackled. Then he yelled, "This is my destination, this Epicenter of Nothing at All. This is my heart, the holy chamber of Nothingness. This is my home, vista upon vista of emptiness!"

He heard Zahnie's voice. She was right. He needed to get over himself. He should start with dumping the theatrics so that he could think straight. If he didn't pull it together, he wouldn't be *on* the planet long enough to get over himself.

He took his pack and two sack lunches out of the backseat. A banana in each and a sandwich of braunschweiger, overheated and slimy. The water bottle.

He didn't feel safe in the Bronco. If the assholes came back, he wanted to have a choice about meeting them.

He decided to go for a new hiding place. He filled a pack, tromped some scrub desert, scrambled up a shaley slope, and sat against a boulder that offered shade and a good angle for his back. He splayed his legs and ate all of what he had.

Then he lifted the gallon bottle and drank deep of the water.

Better mete out the water wisely, he lectured himself. *You can die in the desert without water.* He thought of the headline:

ROB ROY DIES OF THIRST IN DESERT
Contrast with First Death by Drowning

He splashed water over his head, wiped his eyes, and ran his fingers through his sopping hair. Then he capped the bottle, stepped into the sunlight, and eyeballed the ultra-blue emptiness of sky. He scanned the red emptiness of desert. Well, the thing about emptiness, there ain't nothin' to see, nothing at all.

Vigorously, he launched into his own version of an old song:

> *"Oh, I got plenty of nada,*
> *And nada's plenty for me."*

"Bleak," he whispered.

On that note he turned onto his side and propped his head on the pack. He let his mind drift back to last night, a wild night of dreams and fantasies about Zahnie Kee, all unmentionable. Maybe sometime he'd be allowed to touch the real woman again. He then exercised one choice that hadn't abandoned him. He went to sleep.

Through the late afternoon Red dreamt of shadows flitting across his sky, boiling into black clouds. Or were the shadows giant black buzzards that had gobbled up all brightness?

"Ed?" he called in his sleep. "Ed?" But the bird, the one enormous bird, it wasn't Ed. Red could tell.

Lightning flashed and turned into thunder.

Red shuddered and started and sat up, half-awake. He was shivering, in a drizzle. *Holy shit, San Francisco weather in the June desert.*

He looked up higher and saw an overhang that sheltered a small ruin. "Hey," he said out loud to cheer himself up, "Heartbreak Hotel."

The slope felt a little slick, but a fraction of an inch below the gooey surface the earth was parched. He muscled himself up twenty steps and into the alcove. It took a moment for his eyes to adjust to the darkness of the overhang. Then he took in the white walls and ancient mud mortar and—*incredible!*—on the wall above there were dozens of figures drawn on the red rock. They danced around the stone corner and into the twilight.

He lay down and dozed off again. The last twenty years had been pretty exhausting.

Later Red woke up restless and wondered, *Where the hell am I?*

Oh yeah, the rock figures. They'd been pecked or chipped into the walls. There were animals—goats or mountain sheep, from their horns. Also antelope and one gigantic bird. Oddly, the sheep and antelope looked real, but the bird looked mythic, a creature risen from the eye of the imagination, not the eyes of the head.

Red wondered what he'd been doing in his dream. *Well, goofus, maybe you've been dancing with these old guys*. He missed dancing. His body missed dancing.

Red creaked to his feet and meandered in and out of the four rooms of the little ruin. He snuffled the air and tasted it on his tongue. He watched out of the corners of his eyes, on the chance he might see something. He chuckled at himself.

There was figure after figure here—what seemed to be a waving rope but might have been a snake. Zigzags of mysterious purpose. A sun, with beams radiating out. Two spirals of different sizes. Then there were lots of handprints and a score of human figures. In one group three human stick figures lined up, each with one knee raised, dancing.

Wait, around one corner was the humpbacked trader who played a flute. Miss Clarita's personal angel. Name . . . ? Kokopelli.

Red shook his body like a dancer. *Do they still step to your tune, Old Koko?*

The main thing to Red was that Kokopelli was a musician. *When you play it, will I get to hear it? If I stay long enough, if I listen hard enough? If I catch your rhythm, can I sing along with you? Are you playing the music of the spheres?*

He looked at the big stone flutist. For now he couldn't hear what Old Koko was playing. Red went close and put his ear on the stone just below the end of the flute.

Oh, spirit trapped in stone—do you want to dance?

That tickled Red. *You do. You want to bust out of the rock and step lively.*

Here's an idea. You pipe your tune, I'll back you on the guitar, and you'll be set free for the first time in a thousand years. You'll boogie.

In the last of the light Red pulled the sweater on and he rolled up in the poncho. Though he thought of using one of the rooms in the ruin, he made his bed outside. Wide awake, he propped his head on his pack and looked around at the desert. A tough environment it was, even hostile, but it was intriguing. Both the desert and Zahnie Kee were intriguing. And forbidding.

Red had no idea where civilization was, no idea where water might be, no idea how to find food. He was on a short leash out here, and suspected there would be no manna dropping from heaven. For whatever reason, he wasn't scared.

Then he heard the growl. He sorted out the textures of sounds, so he knew what it was before he saw it. In a few seconds a purple and white ATV came into shadowy view, cruising up the road in the half dark.

Was the ATV really purple and white? Twilight could play

tricks with colors. Red wondered if it was really Kravin. *And where are you sneaking off to, you stinking bastard?* Red grinned. *I've got your weapon.*

The ATV driver stopped at the Bronco, walked around the car, and seemed to check the license plate. Then he opened the front door and rummaged around, then the back door, then the rear hatch. Thief? Or just nosey? Kravin? If Kravin was looting ruins, he'd damn well want to know who else was around. Red would tell Zahnie all about it.

Red looked up into the violet sky and saw it—a buzzard circling right over the Bronco and ATV. *Hi, Ed!*

Red chuckled at himself.

Kravin mounted the ATV, started the engine, and buzzed off.

The vulture left its circle and wing-flapped off to the left of the setting sun, the south, probably toward the river.

The ATV turned north off the road into a side canyon where Red could see no road.

Curiouser and curiouser.

20

THE RANGER RESCUES TONTO

Don't laugh at old people, or make jokes about them. One day
you'll be worse off than they are.

—Navajo saying

Honk-Honk!

Red blinked. Light all around him, full sunlight.

Honk-Honk-Honk!

He sat up. The sun was shining directly into this overhang
early in the morning.

Honk-Honk-Honk!

He shook his head but didn't get all the cobwebs out.

Honk-Honk!

He looked out toward the road. A white van with the Harmony House logo stood bumper to bumper with the Bronco. A
head craned out the window. Zahnie, the lonely ranger rescuing
the lonely Tonto.

Red wondered what her mood would be this morning.

Honk!

He tiptoed out into the sunlight and waved at her. She was
out of the van now, next to the driver's window, peering around.

Honk-Honk-Honk! She didn't see him. She was going to wake up the whole country. Good joke.

He yelled and waved.

She turned around and around.

He yelled again.

She kept turning. At least she'd stopped honking. When she spotted him, he grabbed his gear and slipped his way down the damp slope.

"They held me for hours asking questions," she said. "Let's get moving."

"You may want to hear something first. Wayne Kravin stopped here last night. Riding his ATV. Got out and checked the Bronco inside and out, like a sniffing dog."

Instantly, she was in the driver's seat of the Bronco and talking into the radio.

Yazzie was so loud he hurt Red's ears, and Zahnie was whispering into a cupped hand.

"No, *hell,* no," her boss said.

She whispered.

"You will *not* follow up."

Whisper.

"You *were* a heroine. Now they're thinking of filing obstruction charges against you for yesterday's bullshit."

So few Navajos cussed that it was a pleasure to hear.

"Yes, I said I would lie for you, and I will. You're covered."

Zahnie's lips moved.

"If I don't see you in two hours," her boss barked, "I will charge you formally with being insubordinate to *me*. Get your ass back here."

Red thought she must have the best boss in the universe.

Red was glad to climb into the Harmony House van and not ride with Zahnie. Not good company right now.

Finally, his bumper followed hers into the dirt parking area at the rear of Harmony House. It had been a long, hot, and miserable ride but better than being stuck in the outback. No question.

When they rolled to a stop, she jumped out, slammed her door, and said four of the worst words a man can hear from a woman: "We need to talk."

"Can we eat first?"

She opened her mouth to say no, and grace soared from the windows. Zahnie stopped to listen, and the challenge on her face metamorphosed into pleasure. "It's Clarita," she said.

Red nearly laughed. Incredibly, Franz Liszt's "Liebestraum" sailed out the windows and through cottonwood leaves gently stirred by a breeze. The granddame was playing a song that Red had loved to play as a kid. Even on an out-of-tune piano it blessed the desert afternoon.

"'Dream of love,' it means," he said.

Zahnie looked at him, puzzled.

"The German—" He stopped himself. Bad time.

Tony saved them by opening the kitchen door as wide as his smile. "Want some lunch?"

"No mobs in my kitchen," said Jolo, pointing all of them through the wide door to the dining room.

"Please, go on," Red said to Clarita at the piano. "It's lovely." "Liebestraum" was one of the few classical pieces his grandmother had taught to him. Looking pleased to have the attention, Clarita turned her fingers and her imagination back to the music. It seemed like a message from a more genteel world. *Fairly amazing,* he told himself, *considering where we are.*

"I have stuff for egg salad sandwiches left from lunch," said Jolo, putting plates on the table.

Tony told Red with a smile, "Applesauce on the side with the sandwiches. Egg salad and applesauce every day for lunch, sometimes peanut butter and jelly, oatmeal every day for breakfast, mashed potatoes for dinner, and tapioca pudding or chocolate pudding for dessert. Our folks aren't going to die of old age. The food they've got to eat because of their bad teeth, if they have any teeth left, is gonna bore them to death."

Clarita sat down at the table. Jolo put a platter of sandwiches and sweet pickles in front of everyone.

Tony said, "Living with old people, it changes your life. I read a really good story the other day."

Zahnie said aside to Red, "That usually means in *The National Enquirer*."

"Of course *The Enquirer*," Tony exclaimed. "My favorite. Anyway, the Queen Mum went to visit an old folks' home. She was nearly a hundred then, but she did those things, royals among the ragamuffins. She's walking through the ward and stops to talk to a sweet little old lady. 'How are you? You're certainly looking well,' that sort of thing.

"Well, the old lady gets a blank look on her face. The Queen Mum considers. 'My dear, do you know who I am?' she asks nicely.

"'If you've forgotten that,' says the old woman, 'you can go to the nurses' station and they'll tell you your name.'"

Tony gobbled up one of the sweet pickles while everyone hooted.

"Any news?" Red asked the table at large.

"The local paper put out a special edition with full info on the warrants, and gave Zahnie credit for Kravin and the Nielsens, the biggest fish. But it wasn't exactly welcome news. The paper is nine-tenths letters from angry citizens wailing and bellowing. 'Don't the police have anything better to do than bother good citizens? With the streets of Salt Lake City full of rioting gangs? With the Mexicans motoring marijuana through our county in the dark of every night?' Et cetera, et cetera. No citizen opposed to looting has dared open his mouth, not yet, not in print. And that's the news from Lake Wobegon, where the women are queens, the men are good-looking marshmallows, and only the little kids act all the way alive."

"Where's Gianni?" asked Red, noticing the empty chair.

"He said to tell you he's gone to reap the first rewards of your investment." Tony raised an inquiring eyebrow. Red thought, *It sure would be okay for my ship to come in.*

"You look like a young man who would play the piano." That was Clarita. She had the lid of the piano bench up and was rummaging inside. "I have lovely four-hand arrangements here."

"I have a better use for him," said Jolo from the kitchen. In an instant "The Blue Danube" lilted forth and Jolo was in Red's arms, waltzing. "Clarita's divine," Jolo said.

At the end of the waltz Clarita said, "Do you like Cole Porter?"

She launched into a sprightly version of "I've Got You Under My Skin."

Tony clinked out a beat with his fork on his drinking glass.

Red felt his hips loosening, and his feet got into the groove. Mmm, it felt so good to move.

The back door opened and a young man came in carrying an infant. Just as Red recognized him, Eric grinned and slipped into the dance embrace, complete with baby. The four of them boogied, and the baby looked delighted. When the song changed, Eric danced away with the baby and Jolo.

Red had a yen to be alone. Too many complications in this room. "Tony, is it okay if I lay down upstairs for a while?"

"That bed's yours as long as you want."

After supper Red sat outside in the evening light. He had a bench, some pleasant evening air, and a half-moon to indicate that his life could be waxing or waning. He decided to risk playing the harmonica and not fret about Eric.

Red played old American music, first a Stephen Foster tune called "Hard Times," then a couple of spirituals. He fooled around with the spirituals. He found a little suck-quick-in-and-out trick at the end of one spiritual that he liked.

He didn't care whether they heard him inside. The music could be a gift of the evening breeze, which blew it to them or blew it away. He played "Tain't What You Do" and thought of getting up and dancing, but he wasn't good at the steps of the soft-shoe that went with it originally.

Abruptly an audience of one opened the door. "Right back," said Zahnie. She disappeared toward the back of the property. When she returned and sat down on a nearby boulder, she had a cheap guitar. "A G and a D, please." She tuned all six strings. At last she said, "Anything. I'll follow."

Red thought and then dived into one of his favorite oldies, Hank Williams's "I'm So Lonesome I Could Cry."

She joined nicely, no big deal in her playing, but she was in the swing of things. Making music together felt good.

The second time through he sang the words, sweet and piquant and full of longing—the blue whippoorwill, the midnight train, the star falling across a purple sky.

When they finished, he tried to hear the last chord zephyring out across the red sand all the way to the highway and the town and beyond to the river. Maybe Ed could hear it.

I need to make music.

Their eyes met and held. Zahnie said nothing. Red nodded toward the nearby building and said, "Show me your house."

She smiled. "That cottage isn't mine. That's the Annex. Tony's fixing it up to move into. He needs his office, and his own space, and eventually he'll still need the upstairs bedroom he's using."

Red shrugged.

"But if your clock ticks that tock, Tony's usually up for it."

"Pass."

She grinned. "C'mon." She jumped up and led the way.

Behind Tony's cottage was the Granary, a funny little structure two stories high and taller than it was wide, like an over-grown outhouse. It had an enclosed porch full of outdoor gear, one big room with a gas stove, refrigerator, table with two chairs, and woodstove, plus a loft that must hold the bed. Cramped and improvised, a camp as much as a home.

She didn't speak but waited while Red looked.

He reached out and took her by the shoulders. She held back.

"Red, I said it's not going to happen. I'm not . . ."

He took his hands away, felt a little pang in his heart, and made an effort at a smile. He looked into her eyes. No crack in her shell tonight.

Bright headlights and a siren invaded the room.

Zahnie looked out the window and then moved fast. Over her shoulder as she went out, she said, "It's Charlie Lyman. Give me that gun you're carrying."

Red flinched, but he did it. She opened her freezer and stuck it behind her ice-cube trays.

"Don't say one goddamn word."

21

BUSTED

When you cannot catch your enemies, it's because you don't
have Coyote's help. He can jump over four bushes with one
jump. Ask for Coyote. He's a trickster, but he likes to help.

—Navajo saying

Zahnie and Red shielded their eyes as they walked toward the
cop car. She yelled, "Kill the lights and siren, Charlie!"

He slammed the door and stuck out a piece of paper. "I have
a warrant to search this property!" he shouted over the whine.
Charlie could get about any warrant he wanted. The judge
was both his bishop and his uncle.

"Kill the damn lights and siren!" Charlie did. She took the
proffered warrant and read it. *Oh, shit.*

At that moment Deputy Hicks got out of the county car. At
least he had the decency to look sheepish. "Let's the four of us
go inside," Charlie said, "and have a good visit. You wanna be
a cooperating officer and show us where it is?"

Zahnie's heart sank, and she didn't budge.

Charlie Lyman banged open the door of Harmony House and
filled the frame. "Calling all lamebrains," he yelled, "front and
center! Your asses are busted!" He stomped in, and she followed.

Virgil wiggled in his seat like he might rise from the couch.

Jolo came to the kitchen door and gave the intruder The Eye. Tony looked up from the small desk where he was paying bills and rose slowly.

Zahnie wondered how many people in the room felt little water snakes swimming up and down their spines. Herself, for sure. Tony because he ogled men and once touched Charlie Lyman. Probably even Virgil Rats half-remembered an imaginary crime fifty years ago and was on the edge of wetting his pants. Luckily, Eric was gone, and Miss Clarita had finished her evening joint.

Everybody thinks they're guilty of something and that one day they'll be found out.

Charlie swept his malicious gaze around the room and then fixed it on Tony. "To stay clean with the judge, I have to say this stuff. I have a warrant permitting me to search this property thoroughly for marijuana, which I have probable cause to believe is grown, distributed, and used on these premises. Deputy Hicks, get started while I ask Anthony Begay some questions he won't want to answer."

Zahnie said, "Charlie, this is bullshit. I'll take you to the pot plants." Everyone in town knew about it.

"Take me to whatever you're willing to show."

"The attic," she said.

"Deputy Hicks, start searching this floor. Don't miss an inch."

Zahnie could hear the clomp of Charlie's boots behind her as she climbed a set of steep stairs with a landing and a turn. At the top she opened the door with a skeleton key. "The old polygamist intended to fix up this attic for a third family," she said, "but he didn't live long enough to have one."

She flipped a light switch. It was one huge room, the floor finished but not the walls. In the gable at the southern end hung a telltale pair of fluorescent lights, right next to a captain's window that let in the winter sun.

"There's your evidence," she said, extending her arm like a headwaiter saying, "Right this way."

Beneath the lights sat two white five-gallon buckets, each with one flourishing marijuana plant.

Charlie hefted one and said, "Get the other for me."

"Go to hell," said Zahnie.

The cop lifted them both, labored back to the door and down the stairs. Then he and Hicks spent over an hour turning the house inside out. The Harmony folk huddled in the living room in front of the TV that only old Virgil watched. No one spoke—it felt like a funeral. The cops found not a speck of marijuana elsewhere. They missed Clarita's spice jar full of weed labeled "Oregano."

At last Charlie marched into the living room, trailed by Hicks like a whipped dog. "Anthony Begay," Charlie barked, "stand up!"

At Charlie's motion Hicks went to Tony with cuffs out and open like lobster pincers.

Tony stood.

"Hands!"

Tony hesitated.

Zahnie said, "Tony." She gave him the most significant look she could and sent him a mental message: *Use your get out of jail free card. Let him know you'll tell all if he busts you.*

Tony stuck out his hands.

She said sharply, "Tony!"

He looked at her with hound-sad eyes and gave his head a minuscule shake—*no.*

At that moment Zahnie noticed how Tony looked at Charlie, and got a glimpse of his heart. *My God, Tony still has a thing for him. After all these years.*

Hicks snapped the jaws of the cuffs shut, and Charlie gave a rooster-crow smile.

"Young man, what are you charging us with?" This was Clarita at her most imperial.

Charlie grinned savagely. "Possession and cultivation of illegal substances for purposes of use and distribution."

"I remember you perfectly. Aren't you Roddy Lyman's youngest? Charles, it would be. Why are you doing this, Charles? Everyone in town knows what we grow here, and why."

"Miss Clarita, I haven't had to answer your questions since fifth grade." He turned to Tony and started to read him his rights.

"Charles," Clarita interrupted, "I have cancer of the colon."

Charlie started in on the rights again.

"The pain is sometimes intolerable. Tony grows it for me. I smoke a marijuana cigarette every day, sometimes two. I'm sure you don't want my days to be pure pain."

"Oh, don't I?" Charlie snapped. "Why not? Tit for tat."

She opened her mouth once more, but Tony said, "Grandmother, enough."

She made herself half-visible.

Charlie finished reading Tony his full list of rights. "Anthony," he went on sarcastically, "is this property yours?"

"It belongs to Harmony House. I am the executive director of Harmony House and fully responsible for everything that goes on here."

"You have full cognizance of what's being cultivated in those buckets?"

Tony let out a big breath. "I want a lawyer."

Charlie looked around at everybody and called out, "Perps and jerks, we're taking those buckets as evidence." Hicks picked them up. "And we're clapping Anthony Begay in jail."

With a shit-eating grin, Charlie marched Tony to the car and pushed him into the backseat. Charlie and Hicks spun out for the county jail with lights and siren going full blast.

Clarita wept quietly.

They ate supper in silence. When the last pudding was eaten and the last coffee cup drained, Clarita said, "Tony did it for me." Her voice trembled. Her cheeks glistened with tears. Red thought her face looked like water-stained silk.

"This train has been coming down the track for twenty years, and it just ran over us," said Zahnie.

"What do you mean?" Red didn't get it.

"Tony and Charlie's week in San Francisco." Zahnie added, "God save us from other people's guilty consciences."

"You figure Charlie doesn't care if Tony exposes him?" Jolo asked Zahnie.

"Tony won't. Ever."

"Why in heaven's name not?"

"He still loves Charlie," said Zahnie. "But I might blow the son of a bitch out of the water. That would fix him with the sheriff and most of the county."

"My fear is," said Clarita, "even if the people around here turn their backs on Charlie, the state board will still shut us down because of the marijuana." She stared at space, thinking. "Zahnie, you tell Tony he can use my money to fight this," she said. "Whatever it takes."

A sweet, reedy voice came. Winsonfred. "I have an idea."

They waited. They hoped.

"Let's all go to Navajo Fair over at Mythic Valley."

Red looked at Zahnie, but her face was freeze-framed. "Have you totally lost your marbles?"

"I'm no crazy person, and I say it's as good a time as any to back out of this . . . mess," said Winsonfred in his soft voice. "Hey, the fair is a lot of fun. Mostly it's races, horse races and footraces, little kids, old ladies, everyone, the way old-time Navajo fairs were."

"Zahnie and I talked about going tomorrow," said Clarita, looking mystified.

"Well then," Winsonfred said, "let's Red and me just go ahead now and meet you there."

"Okay," Red said, carefully not looking at Zahnie.

"Good," said Winsonfred. He leaned forward. In a stage whisper, he said, "I'm going to be in a race myself."

22

THE HOSTEEN HOP

Don't weave if you don't know a weaving song. It won't be any good.

—Navajo saying

"Across is better," said Winsonfred. "People there know how to live." This was the "across" that meant over the Old Age River and on the reservation, the most remote old-time part of the rez. "Funny, you white people, you're so smart, you can make all sorts of clever things like television, but you don't know how to live."

Red drove through the dark, next to an old-timer whose confidant was a buzzard, headed for a town of throwback polygamists and, after that, across into a world that would be . . . What? Even more than when he started east across the Bay Bridge, Red didn't know where the hell he was going. And now Winsonfred seemed to have gone to asleep.

"Let's stop at Splendora for coffee," he said with his eyes closed. "I like Splendora."

"You like the polygamists?"

"I had three wives." Then he read Red's mind again. "No, not like you white people, I had three all at once. My first marriage, that was pretty funny. We were teenagers, me and this girl, and our parents arranged for us to get married. Them days, that's how it was done, the families talked, the man's family gave the woman's family some horses, or something else her family wanted, and it was set. I didn't know her, of course. We didn't marry girls we knew. If you'd hung out with her, got to know her, that was like marrying your sister or your cousin. Also, if you called a girl 'friend,' then you could never marry her—the two don't mix.

"Anyhow, at the ceremony her and me, we looked at each other and no way liked what we saw. All our thorns got sharp. Even after the ceremony she said no. I wasn't gonna take a backseat, so I said hell no, or as close as one of the Dineh can say something like that to his parents. Them days that wasn't done, saying no to your parents.

"So our families, they took us into the hogan where we was supposed to live and boarded up the door. Three-four days we was shut up in there together. When we came out, we liked each other good. Real good." His smile gleamed of sexy memories.

"What about your other wives?"

Winsonfred opened his eyes. "They came along later, when we were doing better. It's a responsibility, a big family. And they were her sisters. We all got along real good." Red glanced sideways at him. "Hey, somebody's got to balance you out. You divorce them. I marry them."

"How did you get along with all three wives?"

Winsonfred's voice was merry. "What you mean is, how did it work with three?"

The silence twisted Red.

"You know better than to ask that," said Winsonfred easily. "So. You know what makes up a typical Navajo family?"

"No." Red had never felt more ignorant about more things in his life.

"Two parents, four children, one grandparent, and an anthropologist."

Red grinned big.

Winsonfred closed his eyes again. "Wake me up at Splendora. I like to look at that young woman works there, has big breasts."

Red drew a careful mental picture of the waitress. Then he said, "*Hosteen,* she can barely fill out her dress."

Winsonfred flicked his eyes open in surprise, then suddenly smiled. "No, that's the baby. I mean the young woman, her grandmother."

After Winsonfred spent half an hour paying due attention to Coralee's well-encased bosom, and they were back in the van, Winsonfred screwed himself around and studied the Big Dipper. "We'll go the short way."

That worried Red.

They wound uphill, apparently onto the top of a mesa. As they cruised at sixty-five, Red could see the dark shapes of mesas and monuments on both sides but no vegetation at all. He pondered his bleak future as a homeless person, ignoramus, and rejected suitor of the thorny Zahnie Kee. *This is adventure?*

Every once in a while he also made time for a thought of the bleak future of his new friend Tony, now in jail.

Suddenly Winsonfred said, "Turn here. To the right."

Red throttled down to dead slow. There it was, a double dirt track in the sand. Red turned. He stopped. He said a quiet thank-you for all-wheel drive.

He drove for five minutes, ten, fifteen.

"I'll tell you when," said Winsonfred.

Red pushed the van through desert scrub. From time to time in the darkness he thought he saw shadows off to the left or right, maybe long shapes like trailers or round shapes like hogans. On and on they pushed, endlessly. Other two-tracks

MOONLIGHT WATER • 165

dived off to the left and right. Winsonfred didn't speak, or he just said, "Straight." Red wheeled down the widest swath of sand he could see. *Well, I asked for somewhere new to do my dancing.*

Suddenly Winsonfred said, "To the right."

Red steered down an even narrower track. After a couple of minutes shapes took form in his headlights. A stock pen, maybe another stock pen, a trailer, a hogan. Then a ragged line of vehicles appeared, mostly pickup trucks. "Find a parking place. That's the track in front there. Most people will come in the morning. It's late, let's sleep." He put his head back. "The young men will prowl up and down in their chiddies all night. Hope it don't keep you awake."

"Chiddies?"

"Pickup trucks. Chevvies."

The old man seemed to drift away. Within seconds he was switching back and forth between a light snore and a light whistle. A chiddy rumbled slowly down what must be the track in front of them, growling. The flesh it was hunting was surely young and female.

Red gazed out the windshield at the stars. *It's true. Out here where there are no lights, you can see ten times as many stars.*

He started checking them out, looking for the Big Dipper, though he didn't know how to tell time by it. He checked out a dozen stars, then a hundred, then gazillions, and he was still awake. He had fantasies about some of the people who lived on them, how they had ears like conch shells or their noses were broom brushes. He imagined the orgies they conducted with their impossible equipment. He got some chuckles but couldn't get to sleep.

And the chiddies growled all night. At some point the growl turned into Red complaining loudly. He was in a big, old four-poster bed with three women and a passel of kids. The kids were running around the bedroom, hopping onto the bed, bouncing off, and running around the room. The women were each trying to screw Red, all at once. The problem was that no one's equipment fit. Red's equipment was five gold hoops, like the Olympic rings. They dangled and clinked, but were useless. One by one, fast as a monkey chasing around a tree, the naked women tried to find some sexual use for the rings, but their equipment was bizarre, too—one had a mussel shell, another had a long fork like you barbecue with, and the third had a flopping fish. No matter what they did, nothing worked, and they got more and more frustrated and started yelling at each other and at Red. One of them tried something that went *squeak, rattle, clank, sque-e-e-eal!,* and that woke him up.

Red blinked out of the stupid dream, hoisted himself by the steering wheel, and peered out blearily. A chiddy rocked on its springs noisily in front of the van. Another slid in beside him and stopped. Wake-up colors paraded in front of the van, a flamboyance of velveteen—rose or purple skirts, turquoise necklaces, silver belts, jet hair, shell-white teeth, brown-red faces. It felt like the moment where Dorothy gets to Oz and the movie bursts from black and white into Technicolor.

He snapped the seat upright.

From the pickup by his window climbed one old Navajo man, one young man, four women of various ages, and a pack of kids.

"What's going on?" Red asked. He turned his head toward his companion.

Winsonfred was gone. He was perched on the chiddy's hood.

Then Red's eyes went beyond his friend.

Mythic Valley.

Words couldn't touch it.

His eyes feasted while his spirit held still.

Red knew this place, sort of. His mind struggled to bring into focus old John Wayne movies. Monuments stood mute and eloquent as gods. Stony slopes angled up to the base of each one, and from there the towers rose straight against the sky in simple, pure majesty. Spaced across the landscape, stone giants made their statements against an impeccably blue galaxy. Somehow, Red understood that life was simpler than he had ever known and more original. Better.

He got out of the van and looked up at Winsonfred.

"It's heady up here," said the old man, grinning. He reached for a hand down.

As Winsonfred slid to the ground, the light changed his face. Red turned. In the east, the sun butterscotched low ridges. For a moment the sky turned a color he'd never seen before, and above the darkened earth was a blush of mint green. Then the sun rose, and abruptly the red rock of monuments glowed gold.

The morning air was cool. The desert sun, gathering itself on the horizon, seemed to freshen and sweeten the air.

This felt anything but lost.

"You know," said Winsonfred, "the white people, the scientists, they tell us a lot about these monuments. About the big rock walls in the canyons, too. They're full of fancy words, and I like them okay, but I don't understand."

Red reflected that he didn't understand them, either, and didn't much like them. Analytical words.

"It's good to know about the rocks, the old, old story of our mother the Earth." Winsonfred was measuring and polishing his words. "This one brother-in-law, he was a Lakota guy. I met him in the army, World War One, you know, France. Afterwards he visited me at home and married two of my sisters. He said, 'The Stone People are the oldest people. They were here before any other people, two-legged, four-legged, rooted, or winged. They were here before the rivers and the sky and even the sun. Their stories are the first stories.'

"I like that. I'd like to know those stories, along with those scientific men's stories. Also, I think it's good to know the stories of what people did here. The white people tell you how a big rock was formed—wind, rain, snow, ice—but they don't know the stories of the people who lived below the rocks. Funny idea they got, of what's important.

"For instance, you look out to the east, all the way to what we call Male Sleeper, that's the Lukachukai Mountains and the Carrizos, with Gray Mesa as the pillow. Then you look west to Sleeping Mountain, the Female Sleeper with Navajo Mountain as the pillow. Across this country a hundred years ago some Mormons came, moving, going to a place their Prophet told them to go. In the end they made the dwellings in Moonlight Water, you know, that's what they did. When first they crossed this country, it was not so dry. Where Laguna Wash is now, below the Tsegi, the canyon, it was low green meadows, with water coming out of the hill like fingers.

"One day an old Navajo, they whispered that he was a witch, he said in a bitter way, 'There's not enough water here. In Floating Reed Canyon there are lakes. That water should be here, where we can use it.'

"So he went up, all the way to Floating Reed Canyon. There the water god lived, and twice every day he made the water spout up.

"The day the old Navajo got there and did whatever he did, black clouds formed over the canyon, and the rain slashed down in torrents. The lakes broke loose. Down came the water into the pass. It gushed along the lowland by the rock ridge. The flood bore old logs glowing with phosphorescence, and one log bore the water god. The people saw him pass by on the stream during the night, breathing fire.

"The old man, the people made him pay the price of death, as witches deserve.

"The meadows, though, they became sandy flats. Every year the wash got deeper. The country was drier, more deserty, and there were fewer places of living, green earth. From here, way to the east, to where the water used to come out of the hill like fingers, it's drier now.

"When the white people come out here, it's funny how they get the scientists' stories but not the stories of the people or the gods."

About that time two more chiddies stopped in front of them with dozens of Navajos, it seemed like. Winsonfred walked over to greet them. The air was sassy with the word *shicheii,* which Red later discovered means "Grandpa." He didn't know if Navajos had words that meant "great-grandpa," "great-great," and so on, but if so he figured Winsonfred probably got all of them. Red figured Winsonfred might even have a hundred-dred progeny altogether.

Clarita walked up and took Red's arm. She introduced him all around. Everyone greeted him with their eyes down and no show of interest in the white guy. One couple asked where Tony was. "I got Gianni on the radio. He'll bail Tony out this afternoon," Clarita said. The kids were ready to run off and find their friends.

"Winsonfred," Red said softly, "is it okay if I sleep? Didn't get much last night."

Winsonfred patted him on the back, motioned to the van in approval.

Red slipped into the van, and that was the last he knew until the passenger door opened, then closed softly, and he peeped between his eyelids to behold Miss Clarita in the next seat. "I hope you don't mind, Red," she said. "This walking around, I'm hurting." She plucked a plump joint from her purse, lit it, and dragged deep.

"Have a toke?" She held it out to him.

"I quit," he said, "many years ago. But thanks."

"My dear young man, you have no idea what an expanse of

many years is." She looked at Red with all those smarts in her eyes again. "You always seem to have something on the tip of your tongue around me. Why don't you come out with it?"

Okay, Red thought. "I still don't get it. How can you be a Mormon and a Navajo at once? They're so different, and you're so . . . you. Centered."

"Mmmm. At least with you the question comes from thinking Navajos are noble savages and Mormons wretches. From most white people around here, it's the opposite.

"Here is your answer. I have no sense of conflict. I was born a Navajo and raised in the traditional way until I was eleven, when I was adopted by the Allred family. But it wasn't the placement that opened the new door in my life. It was reading. You heard of Mose Goldman at the trading post, Yazzie's grandfather, the old Jew. Larger-than-life character, good man, taught me English, taught me to read, and loaned me books. Then at the Allreds', I again had access to books. My first great enthusiasms were the Bobbsey Twins and Laura Ingalls Wilder. I love literature. I could no more turn my back on reading than stop breathing."

She took another deep drag.

"For me, becoming a Mormon was embracing a culture that was literate.

"Oh, I felt torn sometimes. I insisted on a traditional Navajo wedding ceremony. When I looked into the eyes of my first-born, I knew I wanted her to walk the earth with two strong bloodlines flowing, not just one. So I asked a medicine man to do a Baby's First Laugh ceremony to welcome her to the world. The children and I always went to squaw dances, and to fairs like this one, and visited our relatives and slept in hogans.

"I raised them in town, though, and sent them to school. At the same time, I became a teacher myself. My life has been reading, family, and ceremonies."

She set the half-smoked joint in the ashtray and cocked her head at me for further inquiries.

"But the polygamy," Red stammered.

She chuckled. "A few plural marriages among the more prosperous Mormons when most of my poor Navajo uncles and grandfathers had more than one wife? Really."

She looked at Red and waited. At last her expression changed. "All right, what else? Out with it."

"The silly stories, the dumb theology."

"Oh, you." She shook her head. "At my age I should cease to be surprised. If you look at those stories literally, they're silly. If you seek the deeper truth in them, they will comfort your heart. The same is true of Bible stories, and the old stories of the Navajos, and the stories of the Greek, Norse, and Hindu gods. In the years I taught school, I taught all the stories this way. One bishop tried to correct my thinking. I told him to go home and grow up.

"The Navajo way is beautiful. It teaches harmony with the self, the family, the community, the earth. The Christian ways are beautiful, all of them, including Mormon. They teach people to love each other. If I were pushed, I might admit to preferring the Navajo, if only because they were woven into the fabric of my soul at an early age. However, Winsonfred and the local bishop walk separate paths up a single mountain, and they go toward the one summit."

Red felt properly chastised, and enlightened. Clarita pinched the dead-out end of the joint, put it in a Baggie, and dropped it in her purse.

A knock on the driver's-side window made Red jump. It was Winsonfred, and Zahnie stood next to him sporting the world's biggest grin.

"Time to play," she said.

She was spectacular. A scoop-necked velveteen blouse of pale, shimmery green topped a full purple skirt. Her glossy black hair was held back on the side by twin barrettes, each with fire opals. Her wrists flashed silver bracelets with gleaming topaz and onyx stones. Her feet were shod in Navajo moccasins, tops the color of the red rock of the canyons and soles bright white. Her neck was ornamented with a heavy silver necklace that showed off a huge and handsome oval of turquoise, with lovely meanderings of ochre through the blue.

When she saw him looking at it, she caressed it with a finger and said, "It's a Carico Lake stone."

"You're a vision," he blurted.

"You ready?" Her smile was luminous.

"Absolutely."

The fair was in full swing. The four of them sauntered slowly around the grounds. Booths were set up everywhere, jury-rigged affairs of plywood. Fortunately for Red's belly, they sold food. Fry bread here, mutton stew there, cans of soda pop.

"Over at Shiprock Fair," Zahnie said, "things are different."

"There's more *bilaganna* things at Shiprock," Winsonfred said, "like cotton candy, hot dogs, hamburgers, stuff like that."

"*Bilaganna* just means 'white man,'" explained Zahnie. "There's no offense in it."

Clarita stooped to pat a kid on the head and spoke to him in Navajo. The kid looked puzzled. She didn't resort to English but just strolled on.

"There's a story about that word, *bilaganna,*" Clarita said with a wide smile, a queen getting risqué. Originally, it meant 'those who fight with their penises.'"

"It was the first white men in here," Zahnie put in. "They took Navajo women."

"Of course," said Winsonfred. He looked Zahnie up and down. "Who can blame them?"

Clarita's eyes sparkled. Red couldn't keep his eyes off Zahnie.

They zigzagged on. Winsonfred acted a little tired, clutching one of Red's forearms. The Ancient One waved vaguely toward the center area with his free hand. "The main thing here," he said, "it's horse races. We already had three or four, but I didn't wake you. You'd just lose your money."

Zahnie said, "He's bragging. Winsonfred always wins. Show us your wad, old man."

Winsonfred rummaged in a pocket of his shapeless pants and after a long while pulled out a roll as thick as a baseball. He flicked the edges—no ones in it, just fives, tens, and twenties. He touched the roll to his head. "It's experience. Horseflesh is experience. But you'll like the next two races, coming right up." When he looked into Red's eyes now, his expression was almost flirtatious. "And I intend to compete myself!"

Zahnie and Clarita tittered.

Clinging to Red's arm, Winsonfred almost pushed them toward the starting line. When he let go and lined up with the other old men, though, he looked independent. There were maybe twenty men, and most looked a lot less fit than Winsonfred.

Red hustled back to Zahnie and the others.

The finish line was a pile, looked like clothing. The starting gun sounded. The geezers did their paddety-pad to the pile.

Winsonfred seized what looked like a 44 E-cup bra and modeled it. The cups perched in his armpits. He dipped into the pile and held up some pink panties, dangling from one finger and big enough to fit a water barrel. He stepped into them and pulled them up. They formed a moat around his waist and puddled between his knees. He preened for the audience, and everyone roared and whistled.

Red saw now that some old men were ahead of Winsonfred. Several were pulling up full skirts, and one had his head buried in a pullover blouse.

One geezer shoved the buried head, and the body toppled.

Winsonfred grabbed the hem of a skirt and pulled it down.

Two of the old men pulled a guy's skirt up over his head and started knotting it there.

Things degenerated fast. Instead of trying to win, Winsonfred had a good time hog-tying a man with a giant pair of panty hose.

Eventually a man got fully cross-dressed and hobbled back across the starting line, winning the prize. Red laughed like an idiot, but he decided never to tell anyone all the details, bearing yet some sense of the dignity of his sex.

And all this *hosteen* hop for the grand prize of a sack of groceries! Red thought for that performance the old guy should have won a trip around the world.

Just then Clarita touched Zahnie's arm gently and pointed with her lips. Zahnie said, practically in Red's ear, "Oh, shit!"

Red could get tired of "oh, shit" really quick.

Red followed Zahnie's eyes, and there loomed Charlie Lyman. Out of place and out of uniform, he was extravagantly western, from black ten-gallon hat to snap-down mother-of-pearl buttons.

"He here to roust us?"

"The reservation is not within his jurisdiction," enunciated Clarita.

"He's cruising for drunk women," said Zahnie. "That's what predators do, hunt."

What Charlie Lyman searchlighted at that moment was them. He cruised over like an eighteen-wheeler, clumsy and magisterial and arrogant all at once. He gave Red the cop look, and Red gave him a *screw-you* look back. It was Zahnie Charlie spoke to.

"We're treating Tony like any other jailbird," he said. "Who's next?"

"You," said Zahnie.

That earned her a good, solid cop glare.

Red offered, "You got a vein in your temple turns the color of eggplant when you get mad. Cute."

Zahnie laughed.

"Where are you staying in Moonlight Water, her bed?"

"Who could resist her?"

Zahnie arced her hands over her head and did a show-off spin.

Charlie flashed a look at Zahnie that was truly ugly. "You deserve to get your ass kicked," he said with a snarl.

Suddenly Clarita spoke. "Charles Lyman, you're a bad man. Even in the fifth grade you were rotten."

Charlie's smile turned rictus. "You're a wonder, Miz Shumway."

"Begay-Shumway," Clarita said softly.

Charlie fixed his eyes back on Red. "Keep an eye out. The Redrock County jail ain't got the amenities of the Granary." He winked and strode off.

"Asshole," said Zahnie.

Winsonfred creaked up to them just then. Just like he'd heard everything, he said, "Phoo. That Lyman boy is not a problem. Let's eat!"

This from the guy who never ate.

23

THE PAST LEAPS UP
TO BITE YOU

Don't use your own name. Your ears will fall off.

—Navajo saying

"Leeja's not here," said Zahnie.

Red took a moment to register the name—Zahnie's sister, the one with the hanky-panky daughters.

"A big bird told me where she is," said Winsonfred with a wink. He took Red's arm and, with his distinctive way of leaning and leading at once, guided everyone across the racetrack, between some chiddies, toward where a canvas shade was stretched over the back end of a pickup. There was a big pot simmering on a camp stove on the tailgate. Off to the side a couple of teenage girls acted out adolescent gloom, and two younger boys played with Hot Wheels. Under the tailgate a man was passed out. At a Dutch oven full of oil a woman was making fry bread. She was thirty pounds heavier than Zahnie but with almost the same face.

She turned toward them and shrieked with joy. "Hey, Grandpa, Zahnie, Clarita. Where's Tony?"

The news sobered her. Then her eyes fixed on Red and she

gave a big grin. She looked from Zahnie to Red to Zahnie to Red, her eyes getting merrier with every glance. "What kinda joke is this?" Eyes back and forth. "You've come off your everlasting mad, right, Sis?" Eyes back and forth. Her wide mouth wiggled, her lips like cartoon worms. "No, it's your revenge. Finally."

Zahnie simply looked puzzled.

"Come on—tell me, Zahnie!"

"What are you talking about?" Zahnie said stiffly.

Even the teenage girls were paying attention now. Leeja threw her arms up in the air, bent from the waist, and slapped her thighs. "I'll be damned," she said, "this is . . ." She hooted, and then hooted some more.

Clarita truly looked at Red with deep interest, a vessel that had hoisted sail in a very personal part of her universe.

Zahnie's color was rising. "What the hell are you going on about?" The straight sister calling the loose-goose sister on the carpet.

"Oh, come on. If you're gonna pull this, don't play the innocent."

"Pull what?"

Red couldn't guess either, but he was nervous.

Leeja waggled her generous upper body, like the fun of it was busting out of her. She flabbered her lips. The teenagers were grinning at Mom's antics now.

"The first man you ever bring home, Roqui, I steal, or that's the way you see it." Leeja waved an arm theatrically in the direction of the man under the tailgate. "This prize, this charmer, who wouldn't want him?"

She kicked Roqui in the sole of his cowboy boot, but he didn't stir. "When you shoulda thanked me for taking this loser off your hands."

She stared at the two of them, grinning, practically quivering with hilarity. "And the second you bring home is my old heartthrob Rob Roy."

Busted!

Leeja danced over to Red–Robbie–Rob Roy, put an arm around his waist, and leaned her head and torso way back, like the two were auditioning for the cover of a paperback romance. "Oh, heartthrob, I beg you, take me away from all this!" She stood up and waved a circle around the whole scene, kids, Roqui, the rest of her family.

"Rob Roy?" Zahnie said in Red's face. "I knew, goddamn you! Goddamn you!" Her face was a dust devil of fury.

Clarita turned and smiled at Zahnie, then at Leeja, then at Red as only a great lady can smile, and pronounced, "We will have stew and fry bread and several of you will explain all this. I'm having a very fine time."

They sat around two folding tables and ate off paper plates. The teenagers, who'd been introduced as the wayward boaters Sallyfene and Wandafene, were interested now, like they were unfolding a *National Enquirer* story. Red was introduced to the boys, who were named Devin and Dino. The mutton stew was fatty, but the conversation was delectable.

"Tell us who you truly are, Mr. Red–Rob Roy," said Clarita.

Truly? Okay.

"All of the above."

"Insufficient," said Clarita.

"I am a middle-aged man lost at sea after jumping off the ship of his life. That ship was a band, the Elegant Demons, and I was the lead guitarist, keyboard player, and dancing maniac, stage name Rob Roy."

Clarita asked a question of Zahnie and Leeja with her eyebrow.

"The best cosmic band ever to come out of the Bay Area, next to the Grateful Dead," said Leeja.

Sallyfene and Wandafene squealed.

"But *way* after the Dead," said Zahnie.

"They had cuter guys, though," added Leeja. "I had a big crush on Kell Stone."

"Our lead singer," Red said to Clarita, hoping to imply that it's a big step down from lead singer to keyboard player.

"My room," Leeja said, "was papered with posters of you guys."

"Our room," said Zahnie.

With the other eyebrow Clarita Ping-Ponged the inquiry to Leeja.

"The band did this big tour, came to Albuquerque."

"The Lick-Free tour." Red remembered it well. The band went to a lot of towns he'd never seen, like Albuquerque, and at that time hoped never to see again.

"I scammed tickets," Leeja plunged onward. "It was a g-r-e-a-t concert"—her eyes flashed just how great—"and like every other teenage girl in New Mexico, I wanted to meet Kell. Somebody knew what hotel they were staying at, I forget the name. Zahnie and I went down there—"

"Leeja dragged me—"

"Oh, poor, helpless older sister. I gave a bell guy twenty bucks to tell us what room Kell was in. Twenty dollars, you have no idea how much money that was to a fifteen-year-old Navajo, and how wide I had to waggle my ass to persuade that guy. So." She looked at Zahnie with a grand conspirator's smile but got no smile back. "We went upstairs. To the floor, I mean. We had to hang out by the elevators for a while, thanks to Little Miss Chickenshit—"

Zahnie stuck out her tongue at Leeja.

"Finally, I got up the nerve, walked down the hall alone, and knocked."

She looked straight at Red with both a twinkle and an accusation.

"You came to the door. Wrong guy, not Kell, but it wasn't the face I noticed first. You were naked, and what, well, caught my eye was your erection. It looked like a baseball bat, cocked and ready to swing. To a fifteen-year-old who'd never seen one before, not in the flesh, it was . . ." She grimaced and waved her arms defensively.

Clarita gave the universe a delighted whoop.

Yeah, Red remembered doing things like that in those days, when he was tripping, tired, drunk, and toured-out.

He looked shamefaced at Zahnie. She cast her eyes down, and then flushed when she realized she was looking at his lap. Red managed an inward smile at seeing her red skin blush.

"Without even trying to cover up, you mumbled something about expecting someone else. I shrieked and ran. Ran all the way down the hotel stairs, didn't even wait for the elevator. After that, I spent a lot of time looking at your face on those posters, not just Kell's."

"God, Leeja," mumbled Zahnie. Humiliation squirmed in her.

"However, as you see, I'm happily married—behold the white knight, father of my children and Zahnie's son, sleeping it off under the truck. My sister, though, is eminently available."

Leeja giggled maliciously, and Zahnie turned a deeper red.

"That lovely act of your forever mad? Don't you think it's time to let go of it?"

Zahnie looked at her sister coldly. "What act? I was pregnant. I brought Roqui home. The next thing I knew *you* were knocked up. And the next thing was, you hauled Roqui off to the altar, or rather the county clerk. How was I supposed to feel?"

"Like it was a lifetime ago. And not really my choice. And the best break you ever got. Anyway"—Leeja cocked her head rakishly at Red and slapped his behind—"here's your big chance to waltz off with my heartthrob."

24

TELL THE TRUTH

Don't look at a falling star unless you blow at it. You'll have bad luck.

—Navajo saying

Zahnie and Red walked out past everybody and everything to nowhere in particular. In a few minutes they climbed a red-rock outcropping and sat in the shade of a cedar tree. The sun was setting, but he wasn't paying attention to how splendid the scene was or wasn't. He felt his face was burning red. He tried starting things. "You first."

"Okay." She looked him straight and hard in the eyes. "I brought Roqui home from college, he seduced Leeja, I got mad and ran back to Albuquerque, and they stayed at Mythic Valley. Their first, Sallyfene, was born three months after my son, Damon. That's why I keep a little distance from them." More challenging eyes. "Now you tell me everything." She paused. "On the other hand, why should you?"

Red thought before he spoke. "You're becoming a real friend, maybe more. I'm getting attached to you. So I tell you, or I lose you."

————————

Red let his mind slide back to the dream. He saw himself plunge into the bay as one man and come out another. When he felt it to his toes, he told her about it.

"A couple of months ago, I was half-famous and half-rich, and dead, dead inside."

He couldn't go on. He let his eyes roam across Mythic Valley, to a horizon far from Zahnie. His story turned paranormal now. He told her of the many nights of the same dream. He spoke of the baptism of his old self and the emergence of the new. "Weird. I climbed out naked and invisible. And wondered, *Am I alive or dead?*

"When they hauled the car up, the driver's seat was empty. The new man was sitting right on the bank, exposed and unseen.

"So. I saw a way out. An invisible man could walk away and start over. But, and this was real strong, if I walked away, I'd have to go naked. No band, no money, no nothing."

He started to reach for her hand and pulled back.

He thought maybe she'd say it, but she just looked into him.

He stumbled onward. "I guess it's every man's fantasy, in a way. Death and resurrection. Burn the old life on a pyre, catch the energy as it rises up, become a new man."

He looked at her, wondering. She was unreadable.

"Anyway, I knew when I was ready. Cut my hair short and grew this beard, so that my hair is in the wrong place." He pulled at his whiskers. Then I blew up my beautiful sailboat, which I called the *Elegant Demon,* got a new ID, new everything, headed into the nowhere-everywhere. I was happy and scared, more scared than I've ever been." He spread his arms. "The Demon is dead, full fathom five. Here's the new guy, Red Stuart."

He looked at her and waited.

"I'm glad you told me."

Red sat back and put his knees up to his chest. "For me, in this moment, in this incredible place, you are part of the magic."

Her arm slipped around his shoulders. It felt like the way you comfort a friend, or even a stranger, when comforting is called for. He thought, *I've blown it with her.*

"Red," Zahnie said, "I forgive you for being Rob Roy, and for fooling me. I know why Leeja recognized you. More than your face was engraved on her brain."

They laughed together.

"Can I say I'm sorry for being an asshole and have you believe it?"

"You can give it a try."

"I'm sorry for acting like an asshole."

A nod, no words.

"What are you looking at?"

"You." She hunted within herself. "I expected a *poor-me* rich-guy wail, and found a real person."

"That's who you're looking at?"

"Yeah, I guess so."

"Zahnie Kee, you are indeed a magical creature."

"That's one of the nicest things a man has ever said to me."

"And I thank you. As I entered Moonlight Water, Charlie Lyman tried to take me to the dungeons, and you saved my soul."

She smiled at him. "More like your ass."

She watched him search her eyes. If he was looking for love, she let him see something else. She squeezed his hand and turned to look around at the desertscape. The last of a melting twilight in a country beautiful and forbidding, vibrant with life and an invitation to death.

"What do you want to do?"

"Go see the dances," she answered.

"Okay. I'm with you."

They walked halfway to the crowd with fingers locked, and then she slipped her hand away. After the spell of the world Red drew her into, the Navajo Fair felt to Zahnie like an assault, bright costumes, laughs, shouting, and lots of music. Over a couple of hours they watched a jingle dance, a women's traditional dance, a dazzlingly athletic men's fancy dance, and a torch run.

Tonight, for the first time in years, she compared her dress-up outfit with other young women's and thought she looked good. *Not that anybody looks as good as Navajo women when they are decked out.* Glossy black hair, beautiful skin tones, vivid colors, everything bold, nothing pallid. And even if she wasn't a flashy, silvery, jingle-jangle person, she thought, *I look good here.*

From time to time Red touched her hand, but she pulled it away—not a Navajo way, public displays of affection. She never looked at him, but she wanted to.

They saw Charlie Lyman in the audience twice, once caught him looking hard at the two of them. Red looked back just as hard, and deliberately put his hand on Zahnie's shoulder. For effect, Zahnie let him.

After midnight, when they were walking back to camp, she asked, "What did you like best?"

He gave her a quirky, funny look, made a motion like beating a drum with both hands, and sang, "Twinkle, Twinkle, Little Star" while making drumbeats out the side of his mouth.

She giggled. The band had done a powwow version of the nursery song, wonderfully silly.

Zahnie faced him, held up their hands, and looked at him. "I'm getting too comfortable with this."

"That sounds like a good thing to me."

"The comfort—it freezes me solid." She stopped walking. She faced Red and let go of his hand. "You're still a problem."

"My switch of lives?"

"Partly, yeah."

"What are we going to do with me?"

"Maybe lose you in Lukas Gulch?"

"Whatever."

"Red, I know what you want. I'd like to give it, but I can't."

He looked at her, opened his mouth like he wanted to say something, but closed it again.

"We're very different," she said. "Not white-Navajo stuff, or at least not just that. You have your dream, the zing of song, the uplift. I don't. It's not me. And I wish it was."

Into the night she walked.

Pretty soon the passenger door opened and Winsonfred climbed in. "Want company?"

"Sure."

"Don't worry about Tony. He's gonna be okay."

Red doubted that, and felt ashamed for being so absorbed in himself he almost forgot about his friend.

"Wanna talk?"

"Please," Red said.

In the eerie glow of headlights Winsonfred gave Red a look. "I watched you and Zahnie tonight. I know what troubles her heart."

This old man doesn't waste time, Red thought. *He reads your mind, sorts out the important questions, and answers them.*

"White people would say she has a hole in her heart. Navajos, we say she's out of balance, not in harmony with herself, the community, and the world. Maybe it comes to the same thing. No matter, she's my favorite grandchild. You want to know a little about her?"

"Yes."

"Zahnie would probably give you a lot of things, especially mulishness, before she told you her story. I call her Little Turtle

Without a Shell. She was nine, maybe—this was before her family left living with us around Mythic Valley. We had several hogans where we grazed the sheep, and we were at this one. She was the oldest child, Zahnie. She's had the least trouble to see from the outside, but plenty on the inside.

"Their mom and dad, Mirv and Lina, they converted to the Assembly of God and were thinking of moving to Grand Junction, near their church. No problem there. You're Navajo, you can keep your feet on the road of harmony, go to any church at all, makes no difference. You don't have to give up the Navajo way for any religion. The path of the Dineh, it's a way to walk. Religion, that's just a belief. A way of walking is something more. Mirv and Lina, they needed to quit drinking, and the Jesus of that church, he helped them quit, for a while.

"What bothered me was them going away from the family and the land. Good job, strong church, good schools, shopping, movies, learning the white way—all that is tempting. But Navajos belong between the Four Sacred Mountains. Maybe you go to a new place, find a new house, think you can live good in it. But a Navajo needs to be part of the big harmony of all the Navajo family and the land we were given to live on. You know, when we went on the Long Walk and lived in that place way south, outside our own country, we died. Outside the Four Sacred Mountains, we can't live right."

Winsonfred was silent for a long moment, his eyes on a long-ago time. "Anyway, that summer, after a gully washer, Zahnie found a funny little turtle crawling around the gully, or trying to. It didn't have a proper shell, that turtle, just a thin, soft, half-formed thing, no protection. You could see right through the shell. Poor thing wasn't born proper, misbegotten. I knew it wouldn't live long. The sun could shine through on its innards, and every stickery thing in the desert would scratch and hurt it. I told Zahnie to leave it be.

"She was entranced, though, brought it home. She kept it

under the trailer, in the shade, brought it grass and leaves, all like that. After a few days it died.

"After that I called her Little Turtle Without a Shell. She seemed like that turtle, too vulnerable. She was the oldest, but her brothers and sister, they seemed harder, tougher, not so easy to hurt.

"Mind you, I'm not sure hers is not the better path to walk. Living in your truth, you're vulnerable.

"After the parents took the family to Grand Junction, Zahnie went away to boarding school, then found a way to go to the university in Albuquerque, got a good education, lots of good things. She showed up back here one day, kinda lost. She was twentysomething, didn't know where her parents were anymore, probably in some gutter outside an Indian bar in Gallup, or dead. Barely had any contact with her brothers, them gone chasing a living, one of them even working an oil patch in Arabia. Her sister, Leeja, that's another story. She was back here, her and Roqui and their kids living with me. Zahnie had a little boy, no husband, didn't own any sheep, had no way to support the child. Hard path.

"She stayed with me and Leeja here in Mythic Valley for a couple of weeks, but her and Leeja couldn't get along. Anyhow, there was nothing for her here. She had a college education, studied environmental something, didn't want to spend her life on sheep, and didn't want the boy to learn just watching tails twitch, she called it.

"So she left little Damon with us and went job hunting. Two years she waitressed, cashiered, did everything. We all thought maybe being around his dad would be good for Damon, but Roqui, he's a no-good, then and now. Finally she got the BLM job and took Damon across the river to Moonlight Water. Boy went to school with other Navajos, had a decent place to live.

"Zahnie, though." He shook his head. "She never did fit. Acted like she wasn't Navajo, turned away from the Navajo path—explained to me once she's an agnostic. Best I understand that, it means a path of doubt, and I don't know how you get any footing on doubt. She didn't act superior or anything, but she thought the Navajos were a superstitious bunch of old fogeys. She didn't go to dances or nothing like that.

"How it come out, she wasn't Navajo, and she wasn't white. The white people let you know that pretty quick. Indian face—back of the line. Eventually, she came halfway back to being Navajo, and moved in with all of us at Harmony House.

"I kept calling her Little Turtle Without a Shell. She knows why, but we don't talk about it. Turtle always has a home, wherever it goes, because of its shell. Zahnie, she don't have no home, no matter where she goes."

Winsonfred stopped, and Red didn't say anything, didn't need to, a story like that.

The old man added, "She's got a good act, though, just like she's built a strong shell to keep you out."

They sat for a while. Winsonfred closed his eyes and Red thought he was asleep, but the old man's lips moved and he said pertly, "Ed says you oughta search out Lukas Gulch for some pot hunters. See them or not, they're around there."

Winsonfred was quiet for a long moment. "You wanna hear something else from Ed?"

Red said, "Sure," though he wasn't.

"That ruin where you slept when Zahnie got taken away on the whirlybird, Ed liked the way you took care of yourself, liked the way you used your eyes and ears and your true mind. You have possibilities, he says."

Red thought, *One reads my mind, the other spies on me.*

"Don't be scared on account of I know what you're thinking. I've learned a few things on this planet. And don't get rattled by Ed watching you—he's a good fellow."

"How come you call him Ed?"

"Why, that's his name. I knew him when he was a slouchy,

gray-bearded white man. That book you got in your glove box, the one Gianni gave you, he wrote that."

"Edward Abbey?"

"Yes, that was his name."

"Should I read it?"

"I never read any book, but that one seems to help white people. Ed paid attention and wrote down what his spirit eye saw.

"Course, he's got a better spirit now. He used to be kinda grouchy, which disturbs the digestion. Now he sails high, and he sees, and don't have to figure things out—he just knows."

Red let that sit. In a moment he heard the slow, deep breathing of sleep. He followed the Ancient One's lead.

Winsonfred and Red got home first. The next afternoon they were sitting outside in the shade when Zahnie and Clarita pulled in. For the first time Red got a good look at Zahnie's personal car, which looked like a Raggedy Ann doll stitched together from junkyard lots. It bore, in contrast, a clear message, black print on white bumper sticker: WELL-BEHAVED WOMEN SELDOM MAKE HISTORY.

Tony squirmed out of the backseat.

"Thank God, you're all here," said Tony. "I didn't meet anyone in jail I want to breathe the same air with."

He waltzed up the front stairs. He turned, faced everyone, and spread his arms wide. "Here's the story. I'm going to jail, and Harmony House is being destroyed. So I say, we are a family. Let's eat, drink, and be merry while we may."

He led the way in. "Jolo, lemonade!"

They sat around the dining table, and Jolo brought pitcher and glasses.

Clarita was practical. "How'd you make bail?"

"Gianni put it up."

"And the prognosis?"

"Simple. We're going to lose our license. We won't lose the house. You can stay, Clarita, and probably Winsonfred, since he's your uncle, and Zahnie, but we'll have to do something else with our residents."

"No chance of catching a break?" asked Red.

"None. People in this county are retro as rocks, and marijuana is one of their big bogeymen. The Mormons say we're dirty hippies who spend every night having orgies or tripping on weed. Never mind that their high school kids are snorting cocaine. The county is slavering to prosecute me."

His eyes red with unshed tears, he looked up into Red's face. Red wanted to reach out and cover Tony's hand with his, just for a moment. He made himself do it. Tony gave the hand a firm clasp and let go.

"The real problem is the state board. They will jerk our license. We may not even get a hearing. I don't know."

A tear leaked. "Virgil, Edie, Agnes, Bernice, Agatha." He raised a finger and circled it to indicate the bed-bound residents upstairs. "What are we going to do, send them to roost with the buzzards in the big cottonwoods on the river?

"Or the ones who would come after and don't want to be a punch card in this county's old folks' institution." Tony wiped his eyes, fished for a Kleenex, and wiped his cheeks. He sat back down in front of what looked like a stack of bills. "I've failed them, failed them all."

"What could you do different?" asked Red.

"Nothing. Sometimes it's against the law to take care of human beings."

With the tips of his fingers Red brushed away a sneaky rivulet, a tear of his own.

25

LUKAS GULCH

Don't walk along the track of rainwater. You'll cause a flood.
—Navajo saying

Red woke up when Zahnie sat down on the edge of the bed that Winsonfred never used. He looked into her face and felt a pang. *Close as I've gotten to you, or probably will, Little Turtle Without a Shell.*

"It's been long enough, and it's time to get mad and get going. Let's head for Lukas Gulch."

So, looking for looters. And she was treating him like the buddy she wanted along.

She already had the Bronco loaded with camping gear.

On the map, and to the untrained eye, the gulch looked like a Chinese painting of a dragon doubling back on itself in huge loops and with curlicues going out in every direction. Red figured it was almost as complicated as the human psyche.

"This may turn out just to be a camping trip," she said. "The canyon's huge and, with all these side canyons, nearly impossible to find anyone in. Our best hope is to see a track or hear an engine noise. A long, long shot."

Red wondered how many days for the camping trip. He hoped they wouldn't find any looters—maybe the trip could become a honeymoon of sorts. Unlikely.

Zahnie squeezed his hand a couple of times, but she was back in her cop mode. Also, it was hot, damned hot. Heat didn't bother Red. He much preferred Marin County's weather, which got into the nineties in August, to San Francisco's, where you were always chilly. But this desert heat burned away social graces, and most soft feelings.

She stopped where her SUV had been parked the evening Wayne Kravin had searched it. "We might be able to get a partial track here," she said, "but the ground is hard packed."

"Give me a minute, will you?" Red asked.

They were almost in front of the ruin where he'd spent the night, and he wanted a moment to remember. He'd made a promise to Kokopelli to come back with a guitar and animate the flutist's legs.

After a couple of moments, Zahnie said, "Forward, march."

When she cranked the starter, it struck Red that it would be very inconvenient, and perhaps fatal, to be without a vehicle this far from nowhere. *Keep the keys in your pocket.*

She reversed and took a track that presumably angled into the main gulch. In one muddy spot tracks were embedded. "ATV," Zahnie said. "Gotta be Wayne." Which did not thrill Red.

They rolled along at half speed. "I hope Wayne Kravin is as nasty as looters get."

"He's not. Used to be that pot hunting was mostly old-time Mormon families doing what they've always done, hustling up a few extra bucks on public land. The business has changed in the last few years. The crackheads are at it now. Half-crazed guys dig up dead people's belongings, sell them for a few grand, grab enough crack with the money to get really crazy, and do it all over again. They say some big-time money's moving in, too, for bigger rip-offs."

She cranked a hard left. "Road's gonna get rough now."

Unintentional joke. No road at all, just a hint of wear across rocks. It was bumpy and slow, like driving on the backs of giant tortoises. Two minutes later they were negotiating through soft sand, and Red was sure they'd get stuck. "We might have to let some air out of the tires," said Zahnie. But she kept going. Soon they were driving across slickrock, following slight scarring on the surface.

Red quelled his fear by looking at the canyon walls. It was like the Grand Canyon but more intimate—red rock, purple and ochre earth, green cedars, the walls shelving down in lacy terraces gracefully chiseled over millions of years by the wildest of sculptors, the deities Water and Wind. Though ruins must have been tucked into many niches, he didn't see any. He wondered at the human beings who lived here one or two millennia ago. He wondered at the human beings who ventured now into this remote, fantastical, beautiful place. *Mad seekers of life, perhaps. Like us?*

She said, "People have been trying to tear up this land for money for quite some time. In the nineteen-fifties we had uranium on the cranium, prospectors looking to get rich and helping the world blow itself up."

Grabbing for gold, Red thought, *instead of feeding their spirits.*

Though the tracks had been obvious at the turnoff, they'd mostly disappeared. Once in a while you could see a fragment in some sand.

"We're driving into a huge maze with no idea where we're going, right?"

"Worse. Recently the pot hunters have gotten desperate. They work with headlamps at night, in very, very remote locations. Our policy is to assume they're armed and dangerous. Word is, whether you're a civilian or you're government, if you come on what looks like a pot hunter in the outback, mind your health and keep going. They have guns, and they're nuts."

"So who did the feds arrest back in Moonlight Water?"

"The little fish, as usual."

A few miles up, Zahnie stopped at the mouth of a canyon, entering from the left. It ran back about a quarter mile and crooked out of sight to the right. Like all the deep-walled canyons in this country, it was a step into an alternate world. Perhaps a world of infinite curves of stonescapes, like mirrors receding forever within mirrors, seducing the unwary. Perhaps a world where entire civilizations lived in beauty they could not share with the mass of mankind. Perhaps where the ancient Anasazi still endured, living out the peace they wanted a millennium ago.

She got out and checked the few tracks. He walked with her. "Someone, we're guessing Wayne, drove in, came out, headed up-canyon. I can't figure out what's going on."

They climbed back in and bumped into the side canyon. After ten minutes it ended in a sheer wall. As they looked around, sitting still, a raven landed on the hood and peered in at them. When Zahnie touched the gas, it flew.

"Winsonfred ever mention Ed to you?"

She looked at Red cockeyed.

"You know, Ed the buzzard?"

"Oh, Ed. Grandfather doesn't talk to me about that. He knows better."

"You do know about Ed, though."

"Tony talks about him."

"You don't believe?"

She sighed. "I grew up with a lot of stuff, and I don't know what to think. I do know there's more to the world than the scientists and white folks generally include in their way of looking at things."

"I don't know anything about Navajo spirituality."

"I can tell you one thing. It doesn't include Ed. Winsonfred came back talking about reincarnation after he went to Taos."

Red gave her a quizzical look.

"About, mmm, thirty years ago, Winsonfred's wives kicked him out for fooling around."

Winsonfred fooling around at seventy-three? This was good.

"So he upped and went to Taos with a hippie girlfriend. Lived in a commune that summer, and they treated him like a guru, a fountainhead of Native wisdom. When it got cold, though, Winsonfred came back to the hogan, begging to be let in." She snorted. "He brought some new ideas as souvenirs, including his belief in reincarnation. Anyway, that part's not Navajo."

For a moment she just drove. "I walked away from traditional Navajo stuff. I walked away from my family. That was after Roqui left me."

Red looked at Zahnie. Her face was set hard.

"About Ed. Do you believe Grandfather?"

"I don't know," Red said. "Winsonfred said Ed watched me come into town, described what I did, said he got the info from Ed. Don't know how else Winsonfred could have known."

"He comes up with those things."

"Wonder if Ed will report to Winsonfred about us out here. Maybe if Wayne caught us, Ed would tell Winsonfred to send the cops."

"You can hope," she said with a smile.

She stopped suddenly. Here was the mouth of another canyon, and more ATV tracks going in and out. They followed these, too, this time for maybe an hour. Twice Zahnie pointed out ruins on the north wall of the canyon. "I'm only showing you the best ones," she said.

Red wanted to go exploring—to touch—but this was not the day.

Finally, they came to a wall about fifteen feet high across the canyon. End of the line. They got out. The heat almost made Red itch. A little trickle ran down the wall, and a pool collected at the bottom, a couple of inches deep. She stooped beside the pool, took off her baseball cap, filled it with water, and slapped it on her head. The water soaked her hair and ran down her cheeks. She gave him a beguiling smile.

Red followed suit.

She glanced warily at him and took off her shirt. Her bra was a no-nonsense type, and her delicate cleavage was more alluring than she could have guessed. She soaked the shirt in the pool and put it back on.

Red followed suit.

She studied the pool. He could see what was on her mind, but she wasn't about to do it. At last she turned and sat down, shorts and all, in the two inches of water.

He did the same.

Merriment played on her face. They smiled at each other, aware of what was happening to the other's nether regions, which were similar but interestingly different. And aware of how very good it felt. And all conspired to make Little Turtle Without a Shell look pretty pert. Red did not say one word that might break the spell.

26

CANNONBALLS

Don't bathe in rainwater. The male rain will mate with you.
—Navajo saying

The rest of the day was just what Red wanted. A spanking-hot sun. The most spectacular red-rock scenery on the planet. A glorious, cool-shadowed twilight. Nary a sign of any bad guys. And the play of words and eyes of two people who were soon to be lovers, and knew it, and loved life, and the air, and the way they inhabited the world. The coming of evening felt savory.

They drove out of that canyon, then up and back through other canyons, like a yo-yo. They laughed a lot. They noticed the orange blossoms of the globe mallow, the feathery lavender blossoms of the tamarisks, the outrageous fuchsia blooms on the prickly pear. Occasionally they saw rainbows of rock on the skyline, the miracles of the stone arches of this country, and a true-blue arc of sky within. They saw ruins they promised themselves they'd visit someday. They laughed at each other's every line or smiled wide, deep, love-drunk smiles. They drank the heady wine of the first hours of new romance.

Red started some words to a nice tune he made up as he went, and Zahnie pitched in a couple of good lines:

> *"Running on stones,*
> *Jumping them wide,*
> *Waterfalls down,*
> *Laughing we try.*
>
> *"[chorus]*
> *So long to the past.*
> *It's gone at last,*
> *Birds circling high.*
> *Come hold my hand.*
> *It's warm by your side.*
>
> *"Bring me your story,*
> *I'll give you mine,*
> *Water and fire*
> *Burning back time.*
>
> *"[chorus]*
> *So long to the past.*
> *It's gone at last,*
> *Birds circling high.*
> *Come hold my hand.*
> *It's warm by your side."*

In one side canyon a little water flowed. Zahnie chugged the SUV a quarter mile up, and they walked another quarter along a sluice no wider than a thigh, carrying the food and sleeping bags. There they found the prize they hoped for, a clear, deep pool. It collected at the foot of a lip ten or twelve feet high. Zahnie climbed the lip first, stood silhouetted against the pearly evening sky, and piece by piece removed all her clothing. She came to the edge and looked down at Red, who was gazing up at her marvelous brown-red body. Then she leapt in the air, shrieked like a kid, doubled up, and cannonballed into the pool. She stood up grinning wildly. The water trickled around the nipples of her lovely breasts and covered with a cool blanket the mysteries below. God, she was something out in the wild. This was her true home.

As fast as he could, Red jimmy-jammed out of his shirt, shorts, and shoes, clambered up the rock, and cannonballed down beside her.

Except she was gone, running back up the rock, hooting as she went. He followed. They roared like savages or like small water gods. In this series of jumps Red was never able to catch up with her. Always she ran half a lap ahead of him, glistening with drops and the blue twilight and with the glow of the love in his eyes following her.

Then he didn't even look, just cannonballed off with his eyes closed. He came up snorting and spouting, and before he could clear his eyes to see, she grabbed him, encircled him in her arms, wrapped his lips in hers, and wrapped her wet thighs around his hips.

After a precious and private hour or two they napped without remembering to eat. Much later they woke up intermittently to watch the Big Dipper circle the North Star and speak thus of great wheels of time and the dance of galaxies. Then they made love again in the time known to human beings, dozed awhile, and repeated verse and chorus.

Zahnie's love that night felt like the first drops of rain on Red's parched heart after a long drought. His heart beat with utter surprise. He had spent his life more turtle-shelled than he had ever known.

27

THE HUNT

Don't yell when it is raining. You'll be struck by lightning.
—Navajo saying

Unfortunately, the next morning there were still looters to chase down. Zahnie was keen to hunt, and Red was half-willing. He was more willing after she got up and packed and he was sure she wasn't going to slip back down next to him.

More leisurely now, or at least with less intensity, they drove back down the narrow little side canyon (Honeymoon Canyon, he called it in his mind). Lukas Gulch looked roomy beside it. The peculiarity was, as soon as they turned up the canyon he said, "Stop the car." He turned one ear toward something.

"You hear it?"

"Nothing," she said.

"A high-pitched buzz."

"My God," she said, "another damned ATV."

She looked around furiously, slammed the Bronco into reverse, bounced them backward past the turn, and rammed them back into Honeymoon Canyon. One curve and they were mostly out of sight.

"I wonder if he hears us as clear as we hear him?"

"Not over that hornet engine of his," Red said, hoping he was right.

Red hated the idea of a showdown with the angry redneck Wayne Kravin. He got out Wayne's service automatic.

She gave Red a look, bombed out the door, crashed it shut, and cringed at the noise.

The high-wound engine kept whining. She ran up a little slope, whipped the binoculars out of her fanny pack, and got them trained on the intersection. Red kept up, ready.

The engine revved its whine higher.

Long moments passed.

Then the ATV came into view. It looked for sure like Kravin's, purple and white. Wayne wore the same helmet he was wearing at the ruin the other day.

Zahnie brought her hands down and stared without the binocs, gape mouthed. The ATV passed the turn without even a hesitation and boiled its way down-canyon. Wayne was sure in a hell of a hurry. A blue feather flapped wildly in the wind behind his helmet.

Suddenly Zahnie yelled, "Jesus H. Christ!" and started running for the Bronco.

Red hotfooted along behind.

The chase that followed made Red's skull of permanent potential interest to phrenologists. Zahnie charged over rocks, slalomed through sand, and did takeoffs and landings bumpier than a student pilot. Real quick, Red rammed his arms against the ceiling, trying to hold his body down. It did no good. His noggin felt like a battered grapefruit.

He didn't see how they'd catch Wayne Kravin once he saw the pursuit, and he couldn't figure why they would want to crack their own heads instead of Wayne's.

They were in luck. Wayne's engine kept him from hearing

them until the Bronco was reasonably close. Then they were in for bad luck. When Wayne did see and hear them, it put a booster up his ass. He put the pedal to the metal. So did Zahnie.

The next several minutes, or several lifetimes, were indescribable. Red tumbled through an overwhelming assault on all senses slashed with random, savage pain, and fear roaring in his ears like a hurricane.

Suddenly Wayne zoomed into a washout and hit something that brought the ATV to a sudden stop—and his body flew without benefit of wings, sailing above the sagebrush like a Frisbee.

Zahnie dodged whatever the ATV hit. Their rear fender brushed the machine aside with a clang. They careened out of the washout, caught a little air, and whumpffed to the earth.

Before Red could catch his breath, Zahnie was out of the Bronco, running and hollering, "Are you okay? Are you okay?"

Red gave up on making sense of life. He held the .45 ready. Something to restore order.

She darted around sagebrushes and pounced on the body. "Are you all right?" She was screaming and bawling at the same time.

The body sat up. It was brown, black-haired, and young-faced, not Wayne Kravin at all. From the single braid in back a big feather, painted blue, dangled from a thong.

"Yeah, yeah, I'm okay," an irritable male voice said.

He rolled onto his knees, stood up, and nearly fell down.

She grabbed him by the shoulders. She hugged him. She held him at arm's length. She shook him. She hugged him some more.

"What's going on?" Red said, half-voiced.

The stranger flexed arms and legs, making sure they still worked. He looked at Zahnie angrily and then warily at Red.

"Damon," said Zahnie, "this is Red Stuart. Red, this is my son, Damon."

Now Red understood the hugging followed by shaking followed by hugging followed by cussing. The usual response of every parent to every teenage kid.

Damon's response was simpler. He clammed up. Young fellow couldn't have shut his mouth tighter if his mother had read him his rights. He sat in the shade of the Bronco, drank their water, and ate their trail mix, but he wouldn't say a word. Even "yes" and "no" for water and food were so soft and sullen Red saw the words instead of hearing them.

Zahnie went to work, whipsawing from Zahnie the cop to Zahnie the mom.

"Why aren't you in Santa Fe?"

A flat, bored look.

"Dope easier to get here?"

More flat and bored. *Sheesh.* Red remembered feeling just like that once.

Zahnie reached out and thumbed an eyelid up. *It's illegal search and seizure for a cop,* Red thought, *but not for a mom.* "You're stoned out of your mind right now. Your pupils are blown up like black balloons." He was a stoner, all right, body covered with tattoos. Red had never seen a tattoo on a Navajo before.

Damon shook Zahnie's hand off. Red knew exactly where the boy was coming from. He ached for both son and mother.

Zahnie snatched in a breath and held it, and for an instant Red felt her grief and fear. But her voice came out hard. "Damon, what are you doing in Lukas Gulch?"

No answer.

Yeah, if Red were Damon, he'd stonewall her, too.

"How'd you get Wayne Kravin's ATV?"

A scared look flitted across Damon's face right then, but he shook his head and said nothing.

"You working with Wayne?"

The kid shook his head no, which was an improvement.

"You steal the ATV?"

The kid shrugged. Red didn't know what that meant.

"What are you doing in Lukas Gulch? I think Wayne Kravin is looting somewhere around here. I pray it isn't something worse. You said you'd never come back to Moonlight Water. What are you doing here?"

Bored silence. An act, but a good one.

Now her tone softened. "Damon, I try to put you out of my mind. Every day I'm scared what trouble you're going to get into. You're going to get busted. You're going to OD. You're going to end up dead. If I dwelled on it, it would kill me."

The kid just hung his head.

"Now it looks like you're in big trouble. If you don't tell me, I can't help you."

Damon tried to hide his face and wagged his head no.

"Damon?" A big tear slid down from one of his eyes. Then another went wavery down from the other eye. "Damon?"

The kid's chest heaved upward, a sob burst out, and he collapsed forward onto Zahnie's shoulder. She held him with both arms and rocked him. The sobs came loud and hard and racking, with a worrisome undertone of panic.

"Damon, what's going on?"

He raised his face to hers and, half-blinded by tears, said, "I'll take you there."

"There" was about half an hour up the gulch, bumping along at a pace a cripple could have walked. Red sat in the back to put Damon and his mother together. Not that Damon seemed to notice his mother, or Red, or anything else except the dread and fear he was floating in.

Red stuck his head out the window to dry the sweat off his face and neck, and for some reason he looked up. Overhead a buzzard circled. For no reason at all, he thought, *Ed. If Damon climbs further inside himself, Ed will lead us where we need to go*. Red kept watching Ed. In many circles, with great patience as he waited for the slow human beings, Ed was arcing up the canyon with them. Red drew his head in for the sake of the shade. Ed was on the job. That fantasy actually made Red feel better.

Suddenly, without a word, Damon pointed off to the right (with his finger, Red noticed, not his lips in the usual Navajo way). Zahnie frowned slightly and forced the SUV cross-country in that direction.

"Stop."

She obeyed. They sat in front of a huge red boulder that seemed to be mirroring heat at them. Damon got out, slammed the door loudly enough to cause rockfall, slithered to the side of the boulder, and again pointed with his finger.

Zahnie and Red got there at the same instant. She sucked in air so hard she made a little shriek.

Red had never seen a body ripped open by gunfire. The hole in Dr. Nielsen's chest was huge, red, and hot, like a volcanic crater. His life's blood had blasted away, lava from a living heart, now splattered on his clothes and in the dust, desiccated.

By clamping down, Red kept his breakfast.

"What happened?" said Zahnie softly.

"They killed him," said Damon, his voice squeezing out of a throat tight with fear. "He . . . Never mind. They killed him. They're looking for me. They'll be back soon, and if we're still here, they'll kill all of us."

Zahnie said this was a crime scene, so they couldn't touch the body, much less bury it, or even cover it with rocks—had to be left as-is for the investigating officers. But Red knew it wouldn't stay the way it was. He looked into the sky for Ed. There the buzzard was, riding a thermal in big circles around their little group. Ed might hold off, but his colleagues and other critters wouldn't.

Zahnie tried to get a GPS reading and cursed. Without hope, she tried the radio. "The canyon walls are blocking our angle on the satellite," she said. "Can't report the crime."

Damon pleaded, "Crime scene, my ass, it's a murder scene, and we're the ones gonna get murdered. Please, let's get the *fuck* out of here."

That gave Red's brain a good kick in the tail, and instinctively he felt for the .45. Zahnie frowned but jumped into the Bronco and gunned away, leaving James Nielsen's body behind. Half an hour later they passed the ATV. Zahnie spoke her determination through her foot on the gas. She also read Red's mind, for she said, "Hell, we left all sorts of tracks. The bad guys will know someone was there."

She paused and looked across the bench seat at her son. "Damon, who exactly are *they?*"

The boy just stared out the window.

Lonely. Alone. Miserable about it.

Thought Red, *Like me, a lot of times.*

Damon made refusal into a palpable force. Once in a while, Zahnie would demand, "Damon, exactly who are they?" Damon would answer with stone-heavy silence. Zahnie would hold her breath in anger, glare at Damon, and then sigh. Five minutes would pass, and Zahnie would ask, "Damon, *exactly* who are they?" Again the teenager would whack her upside the head with the rock of muteness.

It went this way until Zahnie suddenly said, "This is far enough." She didn't let Damon protest. "I'll radio in the crime, we'll have lunch, and we won't go back until we've got some cops on the scene." She punched some buttons and gave the sheriff their present location. Then she got the cooler out, pretending not to notice how antsy Damon was.

"Okay, they are looting in Lukas Gulch. Are you part of them?"

No answer.

The kid concentrated fiercely on opening his cellophane package of crackers.

For the first time Red really scoped out the kid physically. First glance you'd think he was older than seventeen, slender, and with a handsome, sculpted face. Second glance said he was truly a kid, wanted to pull attitude but couldn't. The only incongruity was that he wore a necklace with some polished inlaid stones in a setting of silver (Red later found out it was Zuni, and way expensive). He wore his shorts and tank top in a nonchalant way, but he made them look good. With his build, style, and sultry expression, he might have been a very masculine male model.

"What were you doing up there?"

He was stonewalling his mother, hard.

"Are you looting too?"

Stonewall, stonewall.

She handed out peanut butter and jelly sandwiches and said what had to come next, trying to conceal the hint of quiver in her voice. "Do you know you're headed for a murder rap? Accessory, at least."

Damon looked at her with stony eyes. "Goddamn you," he said, quiet and hard.

Then he hid his expression by staring down at his sandwich.

Zahnie glared at him.

"Be right back," he said. He rose smoothly and walked the twenty steps to the SUV, opened the passenger door, and slipped in.

Suddenly, Red realized what was happening. He jumped and ran for the Bronco. Damon cranked the engine and made it roar. The Bronco threw up dust and jerked forward.

Red hurled himself at the passenger door, caught both arms in the open window, and clamped on.

The Bronco shot ahead. Damon looked at Red and yelled, "I can't go to jail!" He wiggle-waggled the Bronco. Red held on, but he was going to need his teeth to keep it up. "She has her radio," Damon hollered, "and I'll radio in your location."

He wiggle-waggled the Bronco harder, left and right and then hard left.

Red lost it and sailed for the sagebrush. He slid and rolled through branches that scraped and poked him. He got his breath back and sat up.

Zahnie was standing in the middle of the road, screaming at Damon.

The Bronco stopped a hundred yards away. The driver's door opened. Damon got out, opened a rear door, set their packs and a big water container on the ground, looked toward his mother for a long moment, got back in, and drove off in a spurt of dust.

28

UGLY BUSINESS

Don't eat from a pot that is still cooking. You'll starve to death someday.

—Navajo saying

This wasn't Red's big fantasy.

She looked at him and said stonily, "They'll get right out here."

She led the way to the shadow side of a tall boulder. He wanted to take her hand, but it wasn't the time.

Red's mind was on what had happened between them the night before. His heart was playing in keys he hadn't remembered in years. Maybe she felt the same. Maybe not all the tears in her eyes were bitter or angry or grieving. He sought her gaze, but it was turned inward.

Murder will do that, Red said to himself. Especially when your own kid is implicated.

After a few minutes she relaxed. "Look here," she said. She sketched with a finger in the air and he saw. A drawing of a horse was incised into the boulder. She reached higher. "And another." She pointed to the lower left corner of the rock with a boot. "And one more. They're horses," she said. "What does that mean to you?"

Red shrugged. "Don't know."

"They're Navajo, and after the Spanish came. No horses in the Four Corners until Europeans brought them."

"No whirlybirds, either."

He'd heard the copter an instant before she did.

She kissed his cheek lightly. "Now it's all business."

Damon was wearing cuffs. "Sorry, Zahnie," said Sheriff Rulon Rule. "He was easy to spot, and he knows enough not to run from a gun."

Circling, the copter managed to trail the SUV to the crime scene, landing at the junction of the two tracks, so the wind from the rotors wouldn't disturb any evidence. Two deputies scouted, one armed with an automatic rifle, the other with a shotgun.

Rulon Rule's voice was hard. "What's going on, Zahnie?"

She led the way behind the boulder.

Rule's voice was tinged with emotion now. "James Nielsen shot to death."

Finally, Rule huffed his breath out and looked around. "What's Damon got to do with it?"

"Nothing, except he found the body."

Being hopeful, thought Red.

"That man?" Rule inclined his head toward Red.

"Nothing at all. This is Red Stuart. He was camping with me." She walked over and took his hand.

The sheriff gimlet-eyed Red.

"In fact, please let Red take the Bronco back to Tony's."

"You sure he was camping with you at the time of the shooting?"

"Beyond sure." She added a look that clued the sheriff in.

The sheriff nodded. "Okay."

Zahnie leaned her head against the front of Red's shoulder. "Take the Bronco home. Don't know when I'll be back, maybe half the night. I'll meet you in the Granary. In bed." Red eased out the air he was holding in his chest.

"Let's do what we have to do," the sheriff graveled at the coroner. To the copter pilot he hollered, "Take this boy in and put him in Holding."

"Mom!" Damon's voice was sharp. Zahnie and Red turned to him.

Damon drew both of them aside and spoke softly, pleadingly. "If I go to jail, they'll kill me."

"Tell what you know and I'll do everything I can." Compassion and toughness knit oddly in her face.

"Just keep me out."

"Probably nothing I can do when you're a murder suspect."

"Mom, don't you get it? *They will shoot me, too.*"

She wrapped her arms around him. "I'll be with you this evening. I'll get a guard put on you the rest of the night. And see you again first thing in the morning. With a lawyer."

Damon looked like a deer caught in headlights.

"Let's get down to business, Zahnie!" called the sheriff, and she had to let go of Damon.

The pilot pushed him roughly toward the whirlybird.

Red got out of the car and looked at the front door of Harmony House. A thought struck him. If he still had money, he could save the old folks' home and would.

Tired, he trudged through the darkness around the main house to Zahnie's little place. It was cluttered with outdoor gear but clean. In the fridge she had nothing but milk (past its date), cheese with blue-green blossoms of mold, and white bread. Red cut the mold off, made a sandwich, carried it to the loft, and got into her bed, a single-width mattress on a hard board. Felt good because it was hers.

He turned out the lights and lay there maybe half an hour, unable to sleep.

Zahnie's kid in jail.

James Nielsen's chest caved in. Blood splashed all over the clothes, on the boulder, in the dust.

Red switched the lights back on. First he stared at the ceiling, then the walls. Before long he started noticing things. He studied a picture of a group of schoolkids, about ten Navajos and two Anglos, with Damon sitting right in front, grinning. Cute kid. Red thought of the tenderness, and sadness, Zahnie must feel when she looked at the picture.

Then he checked out some handwritten sheets pushpinned into the wall. They were poems in an attractive, flowing penmanship. Hey, they were good, too:

> *So soon the dawn*
> *comes tumbling on the heels of night*
> *I stand and watch*
> *your shadow melt in light*
> *Roses bloom across the western sky*
> *The yellow moon descends behind the pines*
> *And for a moment you and I*
> *Always parting*
> *Stand as friends.*

Feeling guilty, he read them all. Loved them. Damn, this woman was fine.

She came with the first light, her face stiff with fatigue. Faking sleep, Red watched her undress. She was beautiful and her movements graceful in a way only a lover would appreciate viscerally. She was also racked by the effort of staying up all night, hours spent near the stink of a decaying human body, and terrible fear about what would happen to Damon. Red could smell the fatigue and fear on her.

Naked, she slipped in next to him. Red snored once and then threw his arms around her—she smiled. She started kissing him. Her lips were weary but hungry. Later, in her moment of pleasure, her face finally relaxed, and in a breath she was asleep.

29

THE BAR OF JUSTICE

Don't eat with your left hand. Ghosts do that.

—Navajo saying

They slept only a couple of hours. Zahnie made a phone call, negotiated, and got the public defender she wanted. They pointed Red's van toward the county seat, Montezuma City, twenty-five miles up the highway.

When they got to the old-style county courthouse, the lawyer was walking up the sidewalk. "Rose Sanchez, Red Stuart." They shook.

"Call me Rose," she said. She was a hefty woman of middle age, her hair red-gold without a hint of gray, a face that said, *Don't get in my way.* She didn't look in the slightest Hispanic. Later Zahnie told him the Mormons had picked up some Hispanic names when they had polygamous colonies south of the border. Even on a hot summer day Rose Sanchez wore a suit coat with shoulder pads wide enough to make the NFL.

Rose strode down the basement stairs, under the sign that said: SHERIFF'S OFFICE, and strutted past the front desk like she owned the place. Zahnie and Red followed wearily. The interrogation room was halfway down the hall. Rose opened the door like she had a right, which she did.

The sight jolted Red. Damon was seated at the middle of a long table. Four cops crowded around him, in uniform, sidearms at their hips, cuffs dangling from their belts. Damon seemed small and scared, and the cops looked big and mean. Every anti-authoritarian hair on Red's spine stood up.

"This stops right now," said Rose. She glared at the cops. "You know better than this. A minor, no parent, no attorney? Guns and handcuffs? Where's the sheriff?"

"Back in a minute," said a cop as stretch-necked as a vulture.

"Has his potty break been long enough for you to rough Damon up?"

Red liked Rose.

At that moment Sheriff Rule materialized behind them in the hall. "Zahnie, Mr. Stuart, you can't be here."

Rose slashed Rule with her words. "Neither can these officers, nor the weapons nor the cuffs. What's going on, Rulon? You know better than this."

For a moment Rule almost lost the kindly good humor of his face. "Now, Rose, let's all just calm down and work this out."

He nodded at the cops to leave, then slid past Zahnie and Red and started closing the door on them. The last words they heard were angry-sounding ones from Rose. "Anything you got from my client will be inadmissible."

A moment later, Rulon Rule lumbered out and closed the door behind him. Lawyer–client talk, apparently, and privileged. In twenty minutes Rose invited Rulon Rule back in and Zahnie began to weep. Red held her.

They waited a long time on two hard chairs up front while Damon was grilled. The words *murder one, murder two* beat in Red's head like a pulse. In an hour the sheriff took a break and Rose walked back up front. "I think it's going to work out okay," she said. "At least no murder charges. Damon will have to stay custody until we talk to the judge. Why don't you two go eat and come back in an hour?"

They did, and discovered the little Mormon town had a tiny, unfashionable, very good Mexican restaurant. Zahnie ordered nothing, fidgeted, and pushed them back to the sheriff's office in half an hour. More time on hard-backed chairs, staring at their fingernails.

Rose led the way out of the interrogation room. "Let's get some coffee." Red was willing to bet that meant coffee and doughnuts for sizable Rose.

"I want to talk to Damon," said Zahnie.

"After we're done talking."

She hesitated. "Okay." Then Zahnie called, "Sheriff, what are you doing to protect him?"

Rule padded out of the room and spoke softly. "He'll be in an inside cell, no windows. No one but officers can see him, and whoever you say."

"Me, Rose, and Mr. Stuart. No one else, period."

"Fine, Zahnie."

Coffee and a gigantic cinnamon roll for Rose, it turned out. "They'll let him out on bail. Talking to the judge, doing the paperwork, it'll take a couple of hours." She looked each of them in the eyes to make sure she had their attention. "The charge against Damon right now is stealing the ATV. It's baloney, and they'll drop it. No jury would convict him. We would say he used the ATV to get out of the wilderness and report a crime."

All three of them knew better.

"It's possible other charges will be filed. Obstruction, perhaps, if his story isn't true. I think it is. They scared him good."

"What was that bullshit intimidation?" Red's tongue was running loose.

"Actually," said Rose, "the sheriff was doing us a favor. He would never tell you this. He talked Damon into a test, the up-to-date version of a paraffin test, early this morning. It showed Damon hadn't fired a gun, which means he couldn't be the killer."

Zahnie's breath gushed out.

"Once the sheriff knew that, he squeezed Damon hard. Too many officers, weapons, cuffs, intimidation—whatever he got would have no chance in a court of law. He knew that. He was after the killer, not Damon.

"The boy's not out of the woods," Rose hastened to add. "He may have been one of them. If you're committing a crime and someone is killed, even though you didn't pull the trigger, you can be convicted of murder. That's still possible. If he's not telling the truth."

Rose picked a raisin off the cinnamon roll, dabbed up some icing with it, and poked it into her mouth with a blunt finger.

"We have other problems. Damon won't say what he was doing in Lukas Gulch. Everybody's guess is looting. Eventually they'll find the site, get evidence, and the feds will bring charges."

She switched her eyes back and forth between them. "The biggest problem is that he admits he saw the murder but won't say who the murderer was. Or murderers. That could lead to an obstruction of justice charge. Will lead, unless Damon changes his mind fast."

"So why is the sheriff letting Damon out, if he isn't coming clean?" This was Zahnie.

"Sheriff Rule likes to solve crimes fast, real fast. Particularly when the crime is against a respected member of an old LDS family like the Nielsens." Red cocked an eyebrow at *respected*, but no one noticed. "To get things done he goes by his gut a lot. He has a remarkable record for intuiting right.

"In this case he believes Damon. He used a lot of juice to force the truth out. If he's wrong and Damon could be charged with murder, Rule has screwed up big-time. He knows that, and he took a chance. Which is a lucky break for Damon."

"Does the sheriff believe the murderers will come after Damon?" This was Mom being scared.

"Yes. That's one of the reasons he's making it a bailable offense. If this works, and you agree, Damon will be out this afternoon."

"Thank God."

"He could be back in jail real quick. They want the names of the killers, and the sheriff will put the pressure on. However, he can't make an obstruction charge stick yet. He's taking a calculated risk. He hopes you'll help Damon see the way."

"What do you mean, *if this works*?" Red asked.

"We go back over to the courthouse, all of us, walk with Damon upstairs to Judge Johnson's chambers, and discuss it with him. The sheriff will ask for bail of ten thousand." She studied Zahnie. "There are no bail bondsmen in Redrock County."

"I don't have that kind of money," she said.

To Red's surprise, he quickly put in, "But I do."

30

SURPRISE!

Don't waste any part of an animal when you butcher. Your
flock will diminish.

—Navajo saying

It was accomplished snappily. Red unscrewed a rear panel of
the van, dug into his stash, handed the county clerk a stack of
hundreds, and got a receipt for ten grand. As he did it, Zahnie
watched him oddly, and Red's fingers moved stiffly, uncom-
fortably. Both of them were surely wondering what it meant
between the two of them, Red playing papa.

No matter what she wondered, though, a mother can't say
no to anyone willing to spring her child from the hoosegow,
especially when being in a jail is a setup to be killed. All she
can do is what Zahnie did: squeeze Red's hand, look deep into
his eyes, flick back a tear, and say, "Thank you."

Which was more than Damon said. Somehow the kid managed to look rabbity and sullen at the same time. Instead of
thank you, he muttered, "I'm hungry."

Back to the Mexican restaurant, where Damon kept his face
in his plate and scarfed up a sopaipilla stuffed with green chile

and pork without saying a word. His mother watched him, ate nothing, and held her tongue and her emotions.

On the way to Moonlight Water, on a glaring, hot desert afternoon, Red drove and Zahnie sat turned around in the front seat of the van so she could grill Damon. "We can't protect you if you don't tell us who to protect you against."

In the rearview mirror Red could see the kid staring blankly at the passing sagebrush.

"Damon, if you don't cooperate, the sheriff will charge you with obstruction of justice."

More stare. Damon picked up the old newspaper Red had left in the backseat and pretended to read the sports section.

"Since when do you read the newspaper? Tell us what you were doing up there."

Silence.

"It's looting. All right, pot hunting. It's got to be pot hunting."

Silence.

"For Christ's sake, tell us *who* will try to kill you. And why."

Silence, with eau de moroseness.

After a few more questions, Zahnie matched Damon with her own silence. Attitude hung like a stinking fart in the closed car. Everybody wanted to open the window and no one knew how.

Finally, Red pitched in, "Hey, Damon, say something."

"Okay. Who are you, besides the guy who's boning my mom and bailed me out to impress her? You look like somebody."

Zahnie actually smiled. "It's a long story."

Damon shrugged like, *What else have we got to do?*

"You remember," said Zahnie, "when you were a kid, Leeja had those albums around, and a big poster, a group called Elegant Demons?"

"Yeah."

"You like them?" *Why can't I keep my mouth shut?* Red wondered.

"Not my kind of music."

"You really remember?" Zahnie sounded tickled.

"Sure. Leeja and Roqui raised me much as you. Great dad, Roqui."

Old resentments died hard. Red remembered that Zahnie had told him in the Navajo way your mother's sisters are also your mother. So Leeja was Damon's mother, too.

"Back to the posters. Red is Rob Roy, the guy who did the wild dancing."

"No shit?"

Red could hear in his voice that Damon liked it. "Was Rob Roy," Red put in.

"That's cool, that's really cool." Pause. "Whaddya mean, *was*?"

"I'm out of the band. Long story, tell it later. Rob Roy was my stage name. Call me Red."

"Cool." Damon gave him a thumbs-up.

They drove in silence for a few minutes. In the rearview Red saw that Damon was asleep. He may have been a tough guy and he may have been a pothead, but he was mostly a super-stressed seventeen-year-old kid. A tired, uneducated, third-world seventeen-year-old kid with few prospects and little hope and pissed off about it.

When they stopped in Tony's driveway, Damon sat up, wide awake and antsy.

"How about some sleep in a bed?" asked Zahnie.

"Yeah."

"Use Grandpa Winsonfred's room. Pay your respects to him first."

"Okay." Damon jacked the door open and went along the flagstone steps toward the big stone house.

Red followed him.

Zahnie put her arms around Red from behind. He turned and kissed her. "We have a couple of hours to ourselves," she said.

It twisted Red's heart to say it: "He's bad scared. He's going to run rabbit the minute we take our eyes off him. I left my former life with enough cash to live on for maybe, probably, one year. Can't afford to lose that bail money. I'm going to sit at the foot of the stairs while he's up there."

She gave Red a light kiss. "After I shower, we'll sit together."

Tony took a break from work and getting ready to go to jail while Red told him everything about Damon, ending with the bail.

"The Harmony House family and the Redrock County justice system, quite a duo, huh?"

Red had something niggling at him, and he decided to try Tony on it. "Tony, you know what's going on with Damon. I mean, he's fooling around with drugs, yeah. At his age, what's different about that? But is there something else?"

Tony made a face. "Yes. Two years ago his best friend, Alan Etcitty, got killed. The famous one-car accident on the reservation, newspaper-talk for *drunk driver*. Which it was." Tony breathed in and out. "Hard on a kid Damon's age."

"Yeah."

"Big surprise," Tony said. "You think you're immortal, and your best buddy the same age is suddenly dead. That's when he ran off to Santa Fe. Has hardly been around since."

"Thanks," said Red.

Virgil held up a box and called, "Tony, will you play checkers with me?"

Tony grinned and nodded. "At least it's legal."

"Where's Winsonfred?" Red asked.

"Still across at Leeja's. You know, if we go out of business, at least most of them have relations—they'll take them in even if they're not that crazy about doing it."

They set up the checkerboard on the coffee table. Red sat next to Virgil and started in on a stray *National Geographic*. Clarita was reading again, this time Charlotte Brontë. During the checkers game, from time to time Virgil would take one of Tony's checkers, lift it, inspect it, and pop it in his mouth. Red never did see Virgil put one back, but figured he must have. Or else that was how he won.

Zahnie slipped onto the arm of the sofa and rested an arm around Red's shoulders.

He cupped her cheek with one hand. They moved to a big overstuffed chair. She sat on his lap and gave him a long kiss.

Then Red moved to assuage another guilt, so the weight wouldn't get too overwhelming. "Hey, maybe I intruded. If so, I'm sorry. But I read your poems posted on the walls of the bedroom, and they're great."

Zahnie pulled a thoughtful look. "Oh. You mean the songs. They're not mine, they're Damon's."

"Damon's? And they're lyrics, not poems?" Red had trouble putting together the sullen-looking kid and the beautiful words.

"Yeah, his songs. He went to Santa Fe to get discovered."

"The kid might deserve it." And for the first time in a long while Red thought about playing music with someone.

Zahnie put her head on Red's shoulder, and he leaned his cheek on her head.

When Damon came down, Zahnie caught him by the forearm and looked up into his eyes. "Red thinks you're going to split as soon as our eyes aren't on you. This true?"

The boy said nothing and made a point of staring in another direction.

"Damon, you have to make your court date. Or you'll be a fugitive."

Feeling small, Red added, "And I can't afford to lose the ten grand. Sorry, but that's no shit."

Damon looked at Red. "Dude, I can't hang around. They'll peel the hide off me and leave me to dry in the sun. For real."

"Maybe you're exaggerating," said Zahnie. "Maybe you have a few days. Nobody even knows you got caught. Maybe we can find some wiggle room."

Damon shrugged.

"If you tell us who they are," said Zahnie.

"Right," he said sardonically. "The ultra-cool alternative, suicide."

Just then Jolo called dinner, and the tubular walker-soldier started the one-foot-per-minute trundle toward the dining room. More food for those without teeth or taste buds.

Now Red saw the scene with new eyes. Tony and Jolo cared about these old folks and actually enjoyed taking care of them. In a short while, Harmony House would probably be derelict, some people would suffer, lots of people would worry, and the community would not hold its head quite as high.

After dinner Red said to Damon, "You write songs?"

In two minutes Damon had an old Martin D-18 out from under his mother's bed and a hard-backed chair from the kitchen.

"Damn nice guitar," said Red.

"I better not tell you how I got it." He tuned the instrument. A teenage glare made Tony mute the TV.

'What you doin'?" Virgil whined, "*I Love Lucy* is on." Clarita put down her Brontë to give full attention to Damon, who was probably her great-grandnephew twice removed or some such relation. Virgil whacked in again in his nasal voice, "Lucy, you got some 'splaining to do." Red wondered if the attention would throw the kid off.

Damon strummed the strings hard once, a big, attention-getting chord, teased it into perfect tune, and launched into, *"Raven, raven, craven demon."* It was an exquisite young male voice, high, sweet, throbbing, innocent. The way he phrased things was full of nuance and delicious hints. Lots of people have good voices, but few are terrific singers. Damon had a gift, something that couldn't be taught.

When Damon got to the final chord Tony, Zahnie, Clarita, and Red applauded vigorously. Red thought it embarrassed the kid, but he just started strumming in a new key for the next one. Just then Virgil nasaled in loudly, "He ain't no Desi

Arnaz." Damon rolled his eyes. Red knew the feeling. *Everybody's a critic.*

Damon kept going, and he got on a roll. He sang and sang and everyone listened, except for Virgil, who watched Lucy and Ricky, apparently forgetting the sound was off. Soon Red could hear what Damon's musical strengths and weaknesses were. His rhythm guitar playing was ordinary, probably because his skills were basic and he used nothing but open tuning. Sometimes he sounded like a young musician imitating other acts, especially James Taylor, without even knowing he was borrowing.

Red had an idea. "Hey, Damon, let me back you?"

The kid hesitated. Then a grin spread over his face. Red could see him thinking, *I'm gonna jam with Rob Roy of the Elegant Demons.*

Red sat at Clarita's piano and gave Damon a wink. "How about that one about looking in the windows of the rich people's houses at night? What key's it in?"

They did half a dozen of the songs again. Red laid down a rich, full backup with some nice harmonic nuances and brought off a couple of bluesy bridges that surprised even him.

When Damon just sang, and as he got into it deeper, he was even better. Red would have told any producer that the kid was a hugely talented singer-songwriter, sensitive, unusual, very much himself. Compare him to? Maybe a Navajo Leonard Cohen, not the lyricist—who was?—but good-looking, with a better, more expressive voice and a feel for human emotion. Yes, Damon was far from polished, but Red heard something pure and real in his music that would touch a lot of hearts. It touched Red's.

As the last chord of his song "After the Squaw Dance" faded, Red said, "Damon, you're incredible."

"I went to Santa Fe, Mom thought I just wanted to stay stoned all the time. I wanted to make it in the music scene. Course, it—"

"Did you stay stoned?"

"Got a problem with that?"

"Can't talk, I did it for years. I will tell you that it makes it hard to focus on a career, and I did quit getting loaded."

Damon squinched his eyes at Red in a way he probably intended as hostile.

At that moment the front door eased open without a knock, and Rulon Rule stood in the doorway. The sheriff's face fit a Good Humor ice-cream man better than a law-enforcement officer. Nevertheless, he growled, "I need to talk to Damon."

Damon shot angry eyes at his mother.

"I didn't know this was coming," she said. Then, to the sheriff, "Not without a lawyer."

"I took the liberty," said the sheriff, and opened the door wider to reveal Rose Sanchez and, behind her, Yazzie Goldman.

They all stepped inside. Rose said, "Nobody says a word until we establish the rules. Sheriff, are you treating Damon as a suspect in the murder of James Nielsen?"

"I believe him to have information about the crime. He is not a suspect for committing that crime, or as an accessory, or in any other charges relating to James Nielsen's death. Okay, Rose?"

The lawyer nodded yes.

"I want to sit in."

"Now, Zahnie."

Rose said firmly, "If we're looking for a deal, Rulon, the parent has to be in on it. You know that."

The sheriff nodded. "And for the record, Mr. Goldman?"

"We may get information about the theft of ancient artifacts from BLM lands. As head of the BLM here, I should hear that."

The sheriff nodded.

"Okay," Rose went on, "let's start with just lawyer and clients."

31

IS IT A DEAL?

Don't draw in the sand with your fingers. Snakes will crawl
to it.

—Navajo saying

Walking behind her son and his lawyer, Zahnie felt her heart
pull tight, like it was hefting a big load.

The three arranged themselves in Winsonfred's room, Damon on the little bed, Rose and Zahnie on hard-backed chairs.

Rose started the conversation. "Damon, Sheriff Rule believes you and unknown others were hunting pots up in Lukas
Gulch. But there was a more serious crime committed there,
murder. The way the sheriff sees it, he'll forego bringing pot-
hunting charges against a minor to get information leading to
murder charges against unknown persons in the death of Dr.
James Nielsen. So he's offering you immunity on everything to
do with the crime of looting archeological sites in Lukas Gulch
in return for information on all the illegal activities there, and
on the murder. Information now, testimony in court later. I
advise you to take this deal. The charges for looting are serious, and the penalties include time in federal prison." Pause.
"Does this deal suit you?"

"I talk about who killed Nielsen, I'm dead."

Zahnie regarded her little boy. Sometimes he seemed grown-up. Now he looked pinched and old.

"The sheriff understands that. He wants to ask you about the background of what's going on up there. He's not going to ask you for any names. I'll be sitting there to make sure he doesn't."

Damon just stared at the floor.

"Young man, you'd best take this deal."

Damon shrugged. "Okay."

Zahnie thought, *He's convinced the only safe thing is for him to skip.*

"Damon, the sheriff asks you a question, you have to answer. To earn the immunity. If it's something you don't have to answer under our agreement, I'll step in."

Damon shrugged and grimaced. "Okay."

When the sheriff came in, he looked at Damon ruefully, like a kindly school principal correcting a wayward youngster. He sat down on the bed and waited for Damon to look him in the eye. Yazzie Goldman stood, his arms folded. Zahnie supposed he would always look powerful and imposing, whatever his age.

"Damon, you boys finished digging in Lukas Gulch?"

"A couple more days."

The sheriff and Zahnie looked at each other. Two hours was a typical time for pot hunters to excavate and do their dirty work. Several days meant lots and lots of good stuff.

"Lots of sites, or just one?"

"A big one. Alan Etcitty and I found it."

Zahnie had a rolling tumbleweed of feelings. A huge discovery, potentially historic and life-changing. Alan was dead now two years, rolled his pickup, drunk. Since then Damon was often sour and remote.

Now, though, Zahnie heard the pride in his voice. Understandable—this sounded like a find to compare with the huge ones of the early days.

"How many of you?"

Zahnie expected Rose to object, but she didn't.

"Three. Up in the gulch, three, plus me. Living in the boonies."

"More somewhere else?"

"The guy with the connections to sell."

Zahnie and the sheriff traded thoughtful looks.

"You aren't selling the artifacts yourselves?"

"There's a lot of it. You know . . ."

More thoughtful looks between Zahnie and the sheriff. Maybe *oh-shit* looks.

Zahnie said, "Okay, who's the seller?"

Rose jumped in. "Sheriff, could this person be charged with murder? Killing during the commission of a crime, though he didn't pull the trigger?"

Rose and the sheriff both thought. Rose asked, "Damon, was the seller ever at the site?"

"He was the first person I showed it to. Hasn't been there since then."

"Anywhere near?"

"No."

"Then, Sheriff, do you believe he could be charged?"

"No."

"Answer the question, Damon."

Damon hesitated.

"Who's the seller?"

With a twisty smile, Damon said, "Johnny Cash."

Everybody chuckled but Zahnie.

"Does he wear black and play the guitar?" Gi-*tar*, the sheriff pronounced it.

"You know him?"

"Yeah."

"Johnny Cash?"

"Yeah, him and me got the deal rolling."

Zahnie said, "Damon, if you don't tell the truth, you lose your immunity."

"Yeah. Like I said, Johnny Cash. I never figured it was his real name."

She looked at Yazzie. He gave a shake of his head too small to disturb the air.

"How'd you meet this guy?"

Damon named an expensive hotel bar on the plaza in Santa Fe, one with live music.

"So what's his place in this operation?"

"Fronts dough for expenses. He has buyers for the goods, he says. Must—he's paying good money for it. Says from Santa Fe you can sell worldwide, on the Internet."

Zahnie felt bile in her throat.

"What expenses you talking about?"

"Food and water, stake-bed truck, advances against what we're supposed to get later. He bought us a backhoe, which quit the first afternoon, but he had the cash to go out and get us another one."

Yazzie managed to radiate violence without a flicker. Rule grinned like a pig in shit and reached up to clap Yazzie on the shoulder. Yazzie sidestepped.

"Well, ain't we hit the jackpot?" Rule said. "The feds come in and arrest one dozen small-time dealers. Right smack at the same time the biggest theft in county history was going down under their noses, and the sons of bitches missed it clean."

"Or they were set up to miss it," said Yazzie. "A distraction."

"What's good is, local law found it," said Rule.

The county lawmen would have the smell of meat in their nostrils now. *Me too,* thought Zahnie. The only reason for a backhoe was to dig deep, probably excavating kivas, probably knocking down walls.

"Butchers," said Yazzie.

"Mr. Goldman," said Rose, "you are here as an observer only."

Zahnie was an observer who wanted to throw up.

"Damon," said Rule, his voice like a rasp, "you're damn lucky your lawyer got you broad immunity. They'd throw all the books in the law library at you."

"Back off, Rulon," said Rose. "Gloat about what you got."

The sheriff leaned back, apparently relaxing, wiped his hands on his thighs. "Damon, of the three other men up there in Lukas Gulch, did one or more of them participate in the killing of Dr. Nielsen?"

"Yes." Pause. "One. Pretty sure the older one gave the order."

"Why'd they get rid of him?"

"They brought him in to give them some idea what the stuff was worth. They didn't trust Johnny Cash, not all the way, wanted a knowledgeable local person. When he finished his estimate—he didn't even try to pry a bigger fee out of them—they saved themselves paying him a dime."

Damon mouthed but seemed to be unable to get something out. The second time he managed. "They're a family. In fact, they call themselves a Corps, like soldiers or something. They tried not to let me hear that stuff. Now I think . . . I think they planned to get rid of me, too." He sounded like his mouth was full of tart persimmons. "I'm not a good ol' boy."

Rose said, "Damon, you're getting too close to names here. Back away."

Rule pushed back his chair. "Counselor, I believe I have what I need."

"And Red gets his bail money back?"

"When we get before the judge, which is nine o'clock sharp," said Rule. "It's set." He got to his feet. "And it's getting toward my bedtime."

Zahnie said good night and nodded them out the door. She squeezed Red's hand. To Damon—"Everything okay?"

Damon shrugged. "I'm okay with the deal."

"You feel safe?"

"Maybe I better hang in Santa Fe until the trial. They don't know where I live."

Zahnie hesitated. "You'll show up for court."

"It's jail if I don't."

She nodded to herself. "Then take my car. Tomorrow if you want to go. Right after breakfast."

"Sounds good."

She put both arms around him and kissed him on the cheek. Something about it seemed daring to Red, not something she did a lot. "Sleep in Grandpa Winsonfred's room."

Damon went upstairs without looking back.

To Red—"Let's go to bed."

Behind her through the darkness, Red said, "Gianni came in while you guys were talking."

"He can go to breakfast with us. Run back and tell him the Squash Blossom Café at seven o'clock. You, me, Damon, and Gianni. For some reason Damon likes that place."

In the Granary she made them tea and told Red the whole story of the interrogation. He got a laugh out of "Johnny Cash." At that point she yawned and said, "Time for bed."

She led him up to the loft, unbuttoning her blouse as she went. "*Damn* that stupid kid." She threw the blouse at her clothes hamper, and it fluttered short. Her face said she was still turning something about Damon over in her mind.

She nipped out of her jeans and underwear, put everything in the hamper, and stretched out on the narrow bed under the sheet, which came up to just below her small, perfect breasts. She looked at him in a way that said her mood had changed for the better.

Red started undressing, hesitantly.

"I like it," she said, "that you undress like it's new and special."

He sat down on the edge of the bed and smiled.

She lifted the sheet wide. "Let's get this show on the road. Tomorrow I've got bad guys to chase."

32

LICKETY-SPLIT

Don't have tattoos. Only a medicine man, during a ceremony, can write or draw on the body.

—Navajo saying

"Gianni went to meet someone," Jolo told Red. "He'll meet you there." Now he was late, big-city style.

The Squash Blossom Café was a bare-bones eatery. The mustard and ketchup came in slick plastic packets, and so did the syrup.

"I'm hungry," said Damon.

"Let's not wait to order," said Zahnie. "Got to be in court, seal the deal, and get the money back."

A middle-aged woman with a face like a chipped sandstone boulder cooked and ran the register. A Navajo waitress worked the tables. Zahnie showed Red an article on the wall, framed and displayed like it was an enthusiastic review or award. Turned out to be a page from the AAA guidebook declaring that this restaurant offered the worst food and worst service in the entire Southwest. The Boulder didn't look to Red like she had enough sense of humor to brag about it, yet she'd framed it and hung it.

He looked around for Gianni, but no luck yet.

All of a sudden the Boulder came rolling out from the back. A young couple were seating themselves, apparently tourists, the man Japanese from his appearance and the woman a perky blonde. She carried a tiny baby in the crook of one arm.

"You'll have to leave," the Boulder said. She threw them the bossy look of an overseer.

The Asian man, a mild-mannered guy with wire-rim glasses, stood up. "What's the problem?" he said, puzzled. He had no trace of an accent, and their clothes were pure California.

"You'll have to leave," the Boulder repeated. She pointed at the baby. "No shirt, no shoes, no service."

The baby had bare feet, not that anyone puts shoes on a one-month-old infant.

The blonde wife's mouth dropped open. "What did you say?"

The Boulder spoke like spelling it out for a moron. "No shirt, no shoes, no service." She pointed to the door, like they needed help finding it.

"Get real," said the mother. Her eyes were wide, her skin turning red.

The Boulder's words were like the handle of a bullwhip being slapped into a hand. "No shirt, no shoes, no service."

"This is racial bullshit," said the mother.

"Darlene!" said her husband.

"The rules are the same for everybody," barked the Boulder. "Get out."

"Screw you," said the tourist woman.

She and her husband stalked toward the front door. As they passed, Zahnie said, "Excuse me." The woman stopped and looked at Zahnie wildly. "It's stupid," said Zahnie, "and it's mean. But it's not racial. She did it to me. She does it to everyone. She does it to people she's known twenty years. She's just crazy."

The blonde woman stomped out, trailed limply by her husband.

As the waitress slid out platters of pancakes like a weary blackjack dealer, Gianni wheeled up in one of those white rental compacts under a big leafy cottonwood tree, which was unloading clouds of white fluff from its branches. As Gianni stepped out of the car, Red caught a drop of sweat falling from his nose and said, "*He-e-re's Johnny*, arriving in a snowstorm."

Red met Gianni at the door and accepted his air kisses. "*Abrazos, abrazos*," Gianni said. "Sorry I'm late." It had taken years for Red to find out that *abrazos* were Mexican hugs, not Italian, but it didn't matter.

As he led Gianni back to the table, intending to introduce Gianni to his hot new musical discovery, Damon, Red saw the young man was gone.

"Men's room," said Zahnie, and nodded toward a pantry-width door that bore a label in glue-on glittery letters: MEN.

Gianni waved at the waitress and called, "Two headlights, three little pigs on the side." He grinned at Red. "Eggs sunny-side up with links. The only good thing about this place is she speaks real, old-time diner lingo. What a day. Look at that sky."

Red looked outside. What he noticed was a lithe figure half a block away running up the dirt street like a speedboat. Red did a double take and hollered, "Damon! He's taking off!"

Zahnie swore.

They all ran for the exit. Red sprinted for all he was worth. A moment later the door banged again and he heard the waitress shout something about the check.

As Red hit the road, Damon looked back and saw him. He cut left onto a path or track or something. When Red got there and looked left, the kid was out of sight.

Zahnie came huffing up beside Red.

"He was on that two-track, but I lost him."

The track split off into a couple of driveways and led to a dirt road at the end of the block.

"Let's get the van!" she urged, and they ran back, clinging to each other's hands for solace.

At mid-block Gianni came up and said, panting, "You two drive the roads near the bluffs. I'll drive the ones on the river side of the highway."

They jumped into vehicles and kicked up dust on the way out of the parking lot.

It didn't work. No Damon. Twenty minutes later Red and Zahnie sat in the restaurant again. The Boulder refused to make new pancakes, even after getting paid and being offered another round of full pay. But she said she'd microwave the cold ones. They drank lemonade made of lemon flavoring and corn syrup and eyed each other glumly.

Gianni joined them. "No fleeing Damon I could see. Asked everywhere, but no-go."

Zahnie was crying softly. "Red, I've got to call the sheriff."

"He hasn't jumped bail yet. We don't know that he will."

"I'd like law enforcement to be on the lookout for him."

Red looked at her and supposed that if you're a cop, you believe in that system. "Okay."

"And I'm going over to the office now. I've got to talk to Yazzie about what we're going to do."

"Okay."

"Meet me there when you're done."

When she was gone, tear tracks hardly dry on her face, Gianni said, "What gives, bro?"

Red told Gianni, "It doesn't matter. Leeja recognized me from a poster and blew my cover to Zahnie and everyone. Which is okay here."

"So where are we now?"

Red gave him a short version of the story, how Damon was hunting pots, Dr. Nielsen got murdered, Damon got caught and made a deal with the cops but wouldn't give any names, Red bailed him out, and now the kid was gone.

All the way through Gianni looked at Red like he'd always thought his friend was a few bricks shy, but now he'd lost the whole load.

Red was absorbed in remembering the tears on Zahnie's face.

"Hell, you don't have enough to blow ten grand."

Red murmured, "No kidding."

Gianni blew breath out big. "You can't imagine how lucky you are. This deal I've got going, sorry it's been taking up my time, it's a copper mine. In a couple of days I can take you out there. And the money will come steady, some every month, but the picture is pretty clear. We're going to double our money— every one of the investors, including you. Which you deserve. We needed the capital. One to two years, double your money, and more to come. Is that sweet or what?"

Red tried to tell himself it was sweet, but he couldn't stop fretting about Zahnie and Damon.

Gianni said, "So I got to do some finishing up, huh? See you guys at home for supper."

"Yeah." Red tried to say *sounds good,* but it came out garbled.

Zahnie and Red drove around town that afternoon to talk to Navajo families, who lived mostly on the west side in trailers.

Now, driving around, Red saw Moonlight Water more intimately. The little town was a crazy jumble, Victorian homes cheek by jowl with trailers and a very occasional modern house in the Santa Fe style. The citizens had planted thousands of shrubs and trees, making an oasis. There were several galleries selling arts and crafts. Front yards sported homemade life-sized metal sculptures, the artistic impulse alive and well. For himself, Red had met no artists except Clarita and Jolo. The streets were empty of everything but heat. A dog snapped at a dust devil, attacking and attacking the air again, but eerily, without a single sound. Quiet waited like an open door. Red felt an urge to sing, to howl.

Damon's songs. Hell, probably an oddball community like this encouraged Damon and gave him plenty of room to explore his music. Like they seemed to encourage Jolo.

Red and Zahnie made stop after stop in search of Damon. They'd pull into a dirt drive, steer around a half-dozen cars being used as parts warehouses, and sit. A man or woman would soon come out of the trailer, and Zahnie would speak with them in Navajo, saying that Damon was running from the law and she was afraid it would make his trouble worse, so if they saw him, would they call her or tell him to come home?

Each time Zahnie plopped back into the van and slammed the door, her face was frustration. Red wondered if this was a waste of time. Since Zahnie was a federal agent herself and was with a white guy, would the Navajos hide Damon even from her? He didn't know.

Red's stomach felt sour. He liked Damon and loved his music, and he saw all that talent doing the Big Flush.

They glummed their way through supper at Tony's. For some reason Gianni didn't show up. What more? Damon on the lam and in danger, Red losing ten grand, Tony headed to jail, Harmony House going downhill, even Virgil's chocolate pudding routine didn't cheer anyone up. Tony stayed at his desk.

"Not even time to eat with us?" Red asked.

"I've got to get Harmony House's finances straightened out," Tony said, "as much as I can." He sighed. "Everything shipshape for when I'm gone."

Red had no words.

He saw that the bill Tony was paying was Mutual of Omaha. "Life insurance on me," he said, "to tide the business over in case of my demise." He snorted. "Harmony House would be better off if they sent me to the electric chair. Which they would dearly love to do. Marijuana is spawn of the devil."

"What's next?"

"Preliminary hearing." Red watched Tony's body language. He was a deflated balloon.

Red put a hand on his shoulder.

Tony let his arms sag onto the desk and looked up. "Do you know what my lawyer's talking about? A plea. Dismiss the two smaller charges, plead on possession with intent. Maximum sentence fifteen years, minimum one. Then it's up to the parole board. Judge can't give you less than the one." He made a sardonic *hmmph!* "Do you know what they do to gay men in Utah State Prison? A year of getting cornholed."

Tony looked into Red's eyes. Red wanted to run away screaming.

"How will I stand it?" Tony said softly.

Then he gave a wicked cackle. Red couldn't look into his face. "Maybe I'll get AIDS. That'll slow them down." He let out a wild riff of snicker. "Saved by AIDS!"

Gianni walked in on this last line and gave Tony a screwy look.

Zahnie said loudly, "All right, no more hanging our heads. Time to drive out to Leeja's and pick up Winsonfred."

33

VENTURING FORTH

Don't cross the path of a coyote. You'll be in danger.

—Navajo saying

Leeja started to greet them with a shriek and stopped. Zahnie clasped Red's hand briefly, which felt to him like a way of staking her claim in front of her sister the poacher. "Nothing new on Damon," Zahnie said flatly.

Leeja embraced her sister. "I'm so sorry."

Leeja's sad eyes lit up when she looked Gianni in the face. "It is so great to see you. Wondering what's going on, no one to talk to—forget that!" She pantomimed tearing her hair out.

The teenagers Sallyfene and Wandafene had a different complaint. "We're rezzed out," they groaned.

Leeja got that lightbulb-coming-on look. Red wondered if it was dangerous. "You know what? Could be Damon's meeting up with a friend at Delgado's."

"Give me a break," said Zahnie.

"Seriously. There might be a girl he promised to meet up with if the shit hit the fan, or whatever."

Zahnie started to wonder. It was true. Damon without a girl

following him around was unusual. And there might be one or two willing to help him hide his tracks. Still, she was dubious.

"Listen to me—I know Damon," Leeja said. "He's partly mine. Plus, at a time like this we gotta do something or we're gonna go nuts. He likes Delgado's."

"We wanna go!" cried Sallyfene and Wandafene.

Leeja whirled on her daughters. "You're babysitting your brothers," she snapped. "And your father." Roqui was passed out with his feet under the kitchen table and his head curved against the refrigerator door like he was a crookneck squash.

"Aw-w-w-w!" moaned the girls.

"Leeja, it's getting late," said Zahnie.

"All right, we're hustling," Leeja told Zahnie. Then Leeja bumped her belly against Gianni, a bright smile in her eyes. "You wanna go dancing? Few beers? Some fun? Make a little music, compadre?"

"Sure," said Gianni, turning lightly pink behind his ears.

"Leeja . . . ," said Zahnie with hands on both hips.

"We'll find Damon and celebrate with music and dancing!"

Red liked Leeja just fine, but he had a hard time believing the woman he loved was the sister of this woman, slightly nuts, transparent, and somehow not hard to forgive.

"I want to go out," said Winsonfred. Red hadn't even noticed him until then, sitting in front of Leeja's tube watching MTV with the sound off.

Zahnie's face sagged. Then she pulled him up and along.

Leeja called on the way out the door, "You kids can have Pop-Tarts, but do not knock down all the ice cream!"

The joint called Delgado's was just off the rez in yet another new direction. No Damon.

"We'll wait," said Zahnie. *She's in a take-no-nonsense mode,* observed Red.

They slid onto stools at the bar next to the pool table and listened to the jukebox, waiting, hoping, out of ideas. The second song was a Hank Williams, Jr., tune, sung in Navajo. Red and Gianni relaxed and got silly slapping each other on the back at the weird-sounding lyrics.

The third beer got Gianni started on one of his favorite stories of the musical wars, the tale of his own exit from the music biz.

"Red and I got a gig to play this wedding, a big deal for us then—somebody was going to pay us actual money. The bride-to-be heard the band in a neighborhood club and hired us. We drive to the address, Atherton, pull into the circular drive of a stone house that is at least twenty thousand square feet of conspicuous consumption. Money oozed from the mortar. I figure pretty quick this is not gonna be any piece of cake.

"We were wearing tie-dyed shirts and torn jeans. I had an American flag sewn on my ass. We drive around back and there's an enormous white tent, caterers running around like crazy, florists breaking out in cold sweats over the tilt of their bird-of-paradise centerpieces. Then from the van's rear window we see the Red Queen, the one who's obviously causing all this crazy-making."

Red put in, "This would be the bride's mother."

The fourth beer started going down. Even Zahnie was drinking, everyone but Red.

Back to Gianni. "She's scaring the living shit out of everyone, me included, and we haven't even been introduced yet. And now I am certain that the daughter hired us as an act of rebellion against the mother, with us caught in the middle.

"In the van we decide that before meeting the Red Queen we need all the fortification we can get. We roll a fat joint and start toking. The van fills with smoke. Surprise entrance by the Red Queen.

"She's alarmed, pissed, horrified, and hyperventilating like crazy. Of course, what she's sucking up is Maui Zowie. The guys stumble out of the van to set up. I stay to chat up the Red

Queen. She reclines on the cushions in the van stoned out of her gourd on secondhand smoke. She notices the flag on my ass, touches my buns, makes some off-color patriotic comment. I'm laughing, and she pulls me to her.

"We spend the next hour giving the caterers a break and the band time to set up.

"And the band"—here he threw a mock-hostile look at Red—"not knowing if I was going to emerge alive or dead or at all, found a more rocking vocalist than me right in the wedding party, the bride's brother. He was more than happy to play my Fender Stratocaster. Charming the hosiery off that middle-aged woman was the *real* end of my rock-and-roll career!"

Gianni laughed and clapped and everyone joined in. Red thought they were all so wound up about Damon that they were blowing off tension. Red tossed in, "*However,* this was the start of a brand-new career."

"Yep, she was my first client and in the middle of a big divorce. A really nice lady. She just had trouble being fun while hidden behind a strand of cultured pearls."

Red looked up at the ceiling, trying not to laugh. "I give you this, Gianni. She was the most radiant mother of the bride I've ever seen."

Leeja listened to the whole story with a big grin. When Gianni finished, she spoke to the bartender, pulled the plug on the jukebox, and strutted to a battered upright piano. Some ivories were even missing. The bench was a folding chair. "You guys wanna hear some music?" she called. "Real music?"

Zahnie looked at Red. "It just runs in the family." When Leeja's hands hit the keys, he knew what she was talking about.

Leeja's honky-tonk was brassy, loud, and proud. Perfect for the mood, despite the instrument and no matter the wrong notes. She grinned back at Red, Gianni, Winsonfred, and her sister. The left hand made a strong beat to shake your booty by, and the right hand clamored strong as any man's.

Soon she switched to a Jerry Lee Lewis tune, raucous as a

bar fight. It was so much fun Red grabbed Zahnie and began
to swing her by the hands. Gianni walked over, pulled a chair
next to Leeja's, and gave her a sexy grin. Winsonfred sent up a
fine little whoop. Zahnie spun away from Red and danced up
a storm. He had never seen her so loosey-goosey. Little Turtle
comes out to play.

Zahnie passed a table where two women sat and into a door
that read: BULLS and COWS. The two shook their heads, jumped
up, and started dancing with each other. The big one might have
been a Navajo or a Mexican or anything. Shaped like a Buddha,
dressed in a lot of layers of cloth, a shawl, full skirts, and the
like. Later Red picked up that her name was Briz.

The other, the one Briz called Pinky Lee, was built like a stray
cat that foraged in garbage cans. Her hair was white-blonde,
and she showed off her slinky body with ultra-tight clothes.
Red had a soft spot for strays, being one himself.

The two women danced without touching, or even looking
at each other, Briz a mountain whose grasses blew gently in
the wind, Pinky Lee wound tight, quick and lithe. Gianni eyed
them nervously.

Pinky Lee was eyeing two white cowboys in big hats playing pool. The game felt intense. When they bent into the light
to shoot, all you saw was blue-jeaned butts, back ends of
pool cues, and big hats. Tens and twenties ornamented the
rail.

All of a sudden Pinky Lee pranced over to the pool table,
waggling her ass. Some word or grunt came from behind the
bar. Pinky Lee stilettoed a look at the barman. She held up some
quarters and smacked them down on the wooden rail. Then she
flashed a bright, brittle smile at the cowboys, pranced back to
Briz, and danced.

Declaration: *I wanna break into your private game.*

Finished in the bathroom, Zahnie leaned across the bar to
order more beer. The bar keep was staring at Pinky Lee too

hard to notice. Gianni and Leeja joined Zahnie and hijacked the barman's attention for another round.

"You're the life of the party," Red told Leeja.

Just then the hats started cussing up a storm.

Whatever was wrong, Pinky Lee moved right in, took a cue stick from the hat who looked long and thin and hard as a folding knife. Red could see by the pool table that he'd scratched when he was five balls ahead. He glared while his opponent picked up the wad of bills and stuck them away. Hat number two looked like he was auditioning for one of those slick ads where a male model flashes five days of beard.

"You want to put something on the game, little lady?" asked Five-Day. His voice was melting butter on corn bread.

"Nope, I'm not very good," she said. Red could see that. Pinky hadn't even checked to see if her cue stick was straight.

Folding Knife made an exaggerated sigh, but Five-Day smiled at her like a cat smiles at a canary. "You start us off, then."

"Oh, you break," said Pinky Lee. "I never have any luck at that."

He hit the cue ball ferociously hard but didn't drop any balls.

Pinky Lee's first shot showed her skill. The tip glanced off the cue ball, and it barely moved.

Swiftly, Five-Day started sinking the striped balls. He ran seven and then missed a table-length bank shot on the cue ball because the table wasn't level. He was showing off.

Pinky Lee shot with a bit of pink tongue caught between her lips and by accident put the five ball in a side pocket. She let out a little shriek of delight, stuck out her tongue again, and on the next shot missed everything with the cue ball.

The eight ball, though, was behind the six on the rail. Unable to run the table on her, Five-Day got the eight ball halfway out of its bad spot.

Red noticed that the bartender was edgy.

Pinky Lee made another miserable shot, half-missing the cue

ball and nudging three of her own balls around. Thing of it was, though, that the eight ball was now surrounded by all her solids. In fact, there wasn't any way for Five-Day to touch the eight ball.

Folding Knife barked a laugh. "Damned if the bitch ain't gonna win on a scratch."

"Win? Me?!" Pinky Lee cocked her hips and fluttered her eyelashes at him.

"Damn!" said Five-Day.

"Little lady wins on a scratch," said Folding Knife. "Them's the rules."

Five-Day explained to Pinky what a scratch was.

Red grinned at Gianni and heard the barman grunt.

"It ain't over yet," said Five-Day. He lined up and tried a trick shot where you shoot down on the cue ball hard and it jumps over other balls and bumps its target. World champions do it well. Five-Day poked the cue ball clear off the table.

Pinky Lee flashed out a hand and caught it. She looked around at everybody like a dumb blonde. "What happened?" she asked in kind of a dazed way.

The barkeep half-smothered a laugh behind the back of his hand.

Five-Day slammed the butt of his cue stick on the floor.

Folding Knife crowed, "The 'little lady' won." He swaggered to the table. "Wanna try your luck again?"

Five-Day slammed his butt into a chair.

"Why, uh, sure!"

"How about putting something on it this time? Ten bucks." He fingered a sawbuck flat on the wooden rail.

She looked at Briz. No help in that inscrutable face.

"I guess that'd be okay!" she said brightly. She fished in her pocket and came up with a sawbuck.

This time Red was not a bit surprised when she brought off a similar trick. Knife was not mentally quick, but he was plenty pissed off.

She took the two bills and fluttered them in the air like pom-poms. She high-fived Briz, who raised one impassive hand.

"I think the little lady's shuckin' us." This came from Five-Day, who was stroking his cue stick almost lecherously. "I think she's takin' us for a ride."

Pinky Lee turned on him and put an edge in her voice. "You backin' that up, or you just talkin'?"

"Pinky Lee!" said the barman.

"A girl's gotta have some fun," she said in a lah-de-dah tone.

"Backin' it up." Five-Day put a twenty on the rail.

"You call that backin'?" Pinky Lee laid down two twenties and a ten.

Five-Day studied her, then matched Pinky Lee's bills.

"My break, I believe," said Pinky Lee.

All of a sudden she had a nice stroke. She nodded to herself with satisfaction when the fourteen ball dropped. Then she ran the entire table. Five-Day never even had a chance to get his cue stick out.

Pinky Lee put the hundred bucks in her rear jeans pocket quick. The air was thick with cowboy snortin'.

A quick sixty bucks and as neat a job as I've ever seen, thought Red.

The two hats eyed Pinky Lee's form and considered the possibilities. Knife advanced on her. She backed off, but he pinned her against the bar. Red saw the barman reach for whatever fight-stopper he had, probably a baseball bat. Then he treated himself to a lopsided smile and put it back.

Zahnie grabbed Red's arm and squeezed.

"I think we done been flimflammed," said Knife.

Five-Day stalked up beside Knife. "Yeah. Flimflammed."

Together the two hats made about four of Pinky Lee. Red considered evening up the odds, but Zahnie's hold on his arm tightened.

Knife leaned into Pinky Lee's face now, forcing her to bend back. She was trying to keep her cue stick between herself and them. "I bet you come here every night. I bet you play this table every night. I bet you know every hair on that felt. And you sucker newcomers."

Pinky Lee glanced back at the barman. He just grinned at her and put his hands flat on the bar.

Five-Day reached out and cupped her cheek with one big hand. "Since I missed a coupla pockets, think I'll try for the hole with hair around it." He grabbed one breast roughly.

She flashed a foot into Five-Day's belly and shoved him into Knife. Right quick, Five-Day got his balance and grabbed the cue stick out of her hand. With a look of slow malice, he raised the stick, brought it down, and splintered it on the bar. Now he held a truly nasty weapon, a wooden pole about four feet long with a jagged point.

Pinky Lee looked nearly as scared as she should have been.

Enough. Thanks to the U.S. military, Red was an old hand at just such bar fights. He grabbed fast and hard and got both ends of the cue stick. One quick spin twisted it out of Five-Day's hands. Holding Five-Day's eyes hard, Red hurled it against the back bar.

Pinky Lee screamed.

Knife was waving a switchblade in her face.

Red grabbed a jar of hot sausages and broke it over Knife's head.

At the same time, Briz raised the eight ball and with a roundhouse swing coldcocked Knife right behind the ear. He slithered to the floor.

Five-Day was trying to head-butt Pinky Lee. Red lowered a shoulder and rammed him clear across the pool table and off the other side.

Unluckily, they rolled and Red landed on the bottom. He had a bad moment getting his breath while Five-Day clobbered his gut with a massive fist.

Briz broke a wooden chair over Five-Day's head.

While he was dazed, Red hit him hard with the base of his palm on the base of the nose.

Blood gushed like Red had clipped a fire hydrant with a truck. He pushed the bleeder off quick. Five-Day's eyes rolled up in his head, and he zonked out. The barman came out with bar towels to stop the bleeding.

Red creaked to his feet. They looked at one another, Pinky Lee, Briz, and Red, triumphant. "Think I owe you, Superman," said Pinky Lee. "Big-time."

Red and Pinky Lee stumbled to the bar, leaving their enemies snoozing. Zahnie threw her arms around Red. Gianni clapped his friend on the back.

All of a sudden Red remembered Winsonfred. The old man sat on a bar stool, drinking a Coke, quiet as a boiled egg. Though he was thin and dry as a wisp of straw, his eyes were enormous. He was watching Gianni. Then Winsonfred beckoned to Red with a finger. "Gianni didn't fight for you," he said.

"I taught him way back in the army to stay out of my fights."

Winsonfred seemed to sip and swallow these words. "You don't see," he said.

Pinky Lee ripped Red's attention away. "Randy," she said to the bartender, "you're fired." She looked at Red. "You and your friends, the rest of the evening's on the house."

Leeja said, "That's okay, Pinky, we'll pass." She grabbed Red's sleeve and they all headed for the door.

Pinky hollered at their backs, "I'll keep an eye out for the kid."

Red said over his shoulder, "You own this place?"

"Yeah," called Pinky Lee. "Like I said—a girl has to have a little fun."

"Night," said Red.

The deep, dark air was deliciously cool. "Not the first time I've seen the whole thing," said Leeja, "including Randy getting fired."

Gianni and Red looked at each other and chuckled.

As they got to the car, Leeja nodded at Red and whispered to Zahnie, "This guy is a keeper. Don't blow it."

34

CONFESSION

Don't kill a deer without leaving part of it. You'll never get another one.

—Navajo saying

When they left Leeja's place, with nowhere to wait for news of Damon other than home, the night was very black and the stars unnaturally bright. Red and Zahnie lay on the bed built into the back of his van so they could cuddle. Red wrapped his arms around her and kissed her lightly. She buried her face in the crook of his neck, and he pictured the vast, empty spaces beyond the moon, where there are no human beings to love each other. Some stars glimmered a tinge of mystical blue, and he wondered if there was some sort of love out there anyway, maybe the stars loving one another. How else could it be so beautiful, even in the middle of pain and worry?

From the front passenger seat, Winsonfred gave driver Gianni the eye, as if to say, *Get with it, buster.*

Gianni said, "Hey, don't look—"

Winsonfred stopped him with a soft hand on the shoulder. "That is not," said the Ancient One, "what you are feeling guilty about."

Silence. Cold, rigid silence.

Red and Zahnie didn't know how long the silence lasted, because they wrapped up in each other and fell asleep.

When Gianni stopped in Tony's driveway, Winsonfred said to him, "Now's the time. Own up. Tell everyone why your face is that color." This was a high, quavery old man's version of a command.

Gianni gave him a stricken look.

Then, to Red's amazement, Gianni turned around shame-faced and hangdog and said in a cobbly voice, "Buddy, let's stay up awhile. I got some things to say."

Long after midnight, then, they assembled around the coffee table, Red feeling very wobbly. Tony came over from his end-less stack of bills, looked blearily from face to face, and col-lapsed onto the sofa. Winsonfred looked at Gianni with the forbearance of a confessor.

Gianni fished a little plastic holder out of his wallet and, with the look of the guilty, he gave each of them a business card. It said, "Gianni Cash."

"Damon just didn't know the clever way I spell my DBA."

The rest of the card said "Indian trader" and gave an 800 number. Red looked up in Gianni's eyes. With Internet print-ing miracles, anybody could be anybody.

Gianni laid out two more statements, like a stud dealer turning over cards that the player wants to see but dreads. "At breakfast? Damon ran away because he saw me." Pause. "The seller is me."

Red's stomach squirted something nasty up his gullet.

He looked his old army buddy in the eye, and Gianni gave him back a squirmy smile. Maybe the smiles had been squirmy for years now, and Red had paid no attention.

"Looks like I'm involved in a big problem. Very big. I just want you to know that I haven't done anything wrong, not the way I see things, and I haven't encouraged or hired any wrong-doing."

Gianni smiled and took a shot at looking each of them in the eye. When he got to Winsonfred, Gianni dropped his gaze and coughed.

Zahnie's voice was a blackjack. "You listen to me and listen good. I want to know where Damon is."

"I gave him a wad of cash and told him to get his ass to Santa Fe. The others in this deal, they don't know where he lives or who with. *I* don't know. He's out of it. Safe."

Zahnie took a long moment to breathe. "All right, now tell us what the hell is going on," she said in a hard voice. "All the details. We'll be the judge of wrongdoing."

Gianni was caught between the confessor and the cop.

The cop's attack was relentless.

"You know James Nielsen has been murdered."

"I had nothing to do with that. I've known Dr. Nielsen all my life. It's awful." His mouth wiggled. In a formal tone he added, "I don't condone it."

"You could be implicated."

"Well, according to you, the sheriff said the seller couldn't be."

Zahnie gave Red an angry look. *Damn. I trusted Gianni and spilled the beans to him.*

She gave Gianni her cop stare, which would have boiled a glacier. She noticed Gianni looking into Winsonfred's face for something. The old man was having some sort of effect on him.

"What's going on out there in Lukas Gulch?"

Gianni worked his mouth. Winsonfred nodded, as though to say, *Tell the truth.*

"If you're the one who tells us, it will go easier for you."

Pause, then, "Okay, we're Moqui digging." The old Mormon term for unearthing Anasazi artifacts.

"Where?"

Gianni considered. "You use this stuff in a court of law?"

"Absolutely. And you're headed right there."

"Then I'd better keep my own counsel."

"Let's call the sheriff."

"I'd have to head out for California. Now."

"You can be extradited. You will be. This is a federal and state crime."

Gianni considered. Winsonfred waited, his eyes saying, *Just the truth.*

"I can tell you what I know."

"Well, bravo." Zahnie's voice had snap in it. "Where is the site *exactly*?"

"Halfway up Lucky Dog Canyon from Lukas Gulch."

"How'd you connect with Damon?"

"Sat in with a band in Santa Fe, played a couple of tunes, shared a toke. Turned out we grew up in the same town. I told him, like I tell everybody in the Four Corners, I'm an Indian trader. Which I am. Next day he comes to me at La Fonda saying he'll show me something unbelievable."

When Gianni paused to consider, Zahnie pushed him. "The something was?"

"A big ruin. Nothing's going to be Chaco Canyon or Mesa Verde again, but a great find. Untouched. A bonanza. Blind luck, just a couple of kids wandering in the outback." He shook his head and smiled ruefully.

"On public land."

He had a little trouble letting go of the next words. "I guess so."

"How are you getting around the law?"

He shrugged. "The old way was to go through Christie's or Sotheby's. Then you'd have to get certificates telling where the artifacts came from."

"You mean you'd have to fake certificates."

He shook his head. "None of that matters anymore. There's a new world out there, created by the Internet. I've got Arab collectors, Iranian collectors, Taiwanese collectors, a couple of really good Australian guys, a South African collector, even a collector in Argentina. These buyers don't care about certificates—U.S. law doesn't apply in their countries."

"Oh, shit." Taking in this information, Zahnie wilted.

Winsonfred waited patiently, expectantly.

Then Zahnie put her cop stare back on. "So, there's a bonanza. What did you do?"

"I'm a trader, not a Moqui hunter. I needed someone experienced."

"Who?"

"We won't talk names yet. I found someone I'd known a long, long time. We made a deal. I supplied the money, they supplied the labor. Damon was the guide. A team."

"Of crooks. Thieves."

"You'd best be grateful I'm no killer. Otherwise . . ." He sighed. "I guess Damon's share is wind and sand now anyway. The whole deal is."

Red's stomach lurched.

"How much money, grand sum total?"

"At the end, when I've peddled it all, up probably close to two million. That's gross, less expenses, equipment, everything."

"You ass." Her voice cut like a knife. "That's the heavy equipment Damon mentioned, backhoes with bulldozer blades. Your partners are tearing the hell out of a major archeological site, destroying all the knowledge in it. A man is dead. Not a good man, but he didn't deserve a shotgun blast in the chest."

Gianni opened his mouth, but Zahnie blocked it with a hand. "I know, you didn't kill him. And I know you wouldn't have."

"It's cost us a fortune."

"Back to the point. You deliberately destroyed a major site, a huge find, for pure greed."

"Get off your high horse," said Gianni. "What I do, the artifacts end up out in the world, and the knowledge is available to people. It's not buried under dirt by some ostrich archeologists. Who made you the policeman of what the public gets to see?"

That did it. They flew at each other like fighting cocks. The gist of the argument was 1) Zahnie blasted Gianni for preventing the archeologists from getting lots of information layered in the ground, and 2) Gianni mocked the archeological policy of excavating sites and putting everything back under dirt, out of sight.

Zahnie finished with, "You destroy public sites for money. You're scum!"

Gianni gave a theatrical shrug. "If I am," he said, "Red is, too."

Red blurted, "What?"

Gianni smiled with his knowledge. "You're a partner."

"What?"

"The joint venture I said I'd put you in? Double your money in a short time?"

Lightning bolted in Red's head, and thunder shook his soul.

"We were short of capital right then, and that's where your money went."

"You son of a bitch!"

Gianni laughed. "Hey, it was a great deal. If nobody had caught wind of it, your investment would have turned a fancy dime."

Red launched himself at Gianni, a windmill falling on a small human being.

"No, no," sang Winsonfred.

Gianni got inside Red's big fists, and the punches only thumped his back.

Tony pulled them apart, catching a blow on the back of the head as he shoved Red away.

Gianni was purple-faced and breathing hard.

"Idiot!" Red shouted. "You idiot!"

Now Gianni recovered his slick charm and pulled off a lopsided grin. "One comfort," he said. "You won't make a dime off of evil. We'll both lose every penny now."

Red fell to his hands and knees and did dry heaves. *All of it gone. Who was this man he'd trusted with his life?*

"You'd *better* not make one stinking cent," snarled Zahnie.
Red's emotional boat heaved up and down the heavy seas.

Now her voice changed to theatrical sweetness. "Gianni,
you've skirted the real issue here. You are very good at creating
diversions. Back to the big picture. A man has been murdered.
Undoubtedly by your partners. Who are they?"

Gianni showed how a man can squirm without moving. His
eyes wandered up and down and left to right. He met Red's
gaze, no help, and then looked for a long moment at Winsonfred. Gianni muttered, "The Kravins. The dad, Travis. Wayne.
And his brother, Emery."

"No way!" Zahnie shouted.

Everyone shuddered. She looked sideways at Red. "Wayne,
that bastard, he's a political dinosaur. Why the hell did you
pick him?"

"We played on the basketball team together. We hung out,
the only non-Mormons on the team." Gianni paused. "The real
deal is this. Travis has had a mad-on for fifty years. He figures
he got done out of a big mine, the Bounty of the Lord, back
during the first uranium boom, about 1955. One hundred fifty
million dollars of uranium ore came out of that mine.

"He got done out of it real stinky. That's a school section,
where the mine is. A school section, unlike federal land, you
have to pay per-acre rent annually to the state. He and a bunch
of other local boys, all Mormons but Travis, staked all the law
allowed, but agreed not to file the claims with the county, so
they wouldn't have to pay the rent. Nobody was to file until
they got some big company interested in developing it.

"Somehow, they all got into a pissing contest, I don't know
what about. When they found a developer, the nine Mormons
went in and made their claims legal and put another claimant
in Travis's place. They sold jointly. He was out in the cold, not
a thing he could do. Except get bitter and mean. Touchy to get

anywhere near that old man, and Wayne is still riding the same mean bull."

"No shit. Shows how dumb greed will make you." Zahnie screwed a hard look at Gianni. He gave back a lame smile.

"All right, Gianni, out with it. What are the coordinates for the site? Lucky Dog is miles of sand and slickrock."

Gianni stared into space, weighing his options.

Ri-i-i-ng!

Tony half-ran to the desk and answered the phone. Then he held the receiver out to Zahnie. "It's Damon."

She listened. Her face contorted in a terrible way. She hung the phone up. In a strangled voice she said, "The Kravins have got him. If the cops or anyone comes near the site, they'll kill him."

35

NOW WHAT?

Don't talk about snakes. They will come around.

—Navajo saying

Red held Zahnie while she sobbed.

After a long time Gianni said, "I know something that may fix this. Part of it."

Zahnie wrapped herself tighter into Red.

"I know something."

Red mouthed, *Not yet.*

They waited. Finally Zahnie pulled her head a little way up from Red's wet shirt.

"War conference," said Gianni. "I know something."

Zahnie shook her head no.

Winsonfred said, "Let this man redeem himself."

Zahnie looked at her grandfather.

"Let him."

Gianni said, "I know something important, maybe. Damon said 'come anywhere near the site,' right?"

Zahnie nodded yes.

"They're faking you out. Old man Kravin called me today

and told me they were closed out at the site and had moved everything to the mine."

Red remembered some lie Gianni had told about the investment being a mine.

"The looted stuff needs good truck access, safe storage, weatherproof, completely secret, to let us take a couple of years to sell it for what it's really worth. The country's full of mine shafts, left over from uranium on the cranium. Kravin's using one."

Red looked into Gianni's eyes hard. *How can we possibly trust this man?*

In a meek voice Zahnie said, "Which mine?"

"He wouldn't say. That way I can't do a thing without him, just like he can't do a thing without my connections. But they're at the mine right now, packing things away very carefully in crates and storing the crates in a shaft, or a couple of shafts."

Zahnie's shoulders shook with more sobbing. "You have no idea how many mines there are. We'll never find him. Even with an airplane we couldn't find him."

Gianni said, "They're supposed to come back day after tomorrow and Wayne is gonna take me out there with him, show me the stuff, let me take some artifacts to start peddling. For sure he'll blindfold me, but you could track him somehow."

Red said, "When they come back, I don't think Damon will be with them."

Zahnie hurled her face into Red's lap.

Gianni said slowly, "I guess I think the same."

They froze, Red, Gianni, and Winsonfred gazing at one another, Zahnie crying softly.

"I have an idea," said Winsonfred. "The sun will be up in two or three hours. Let's get a little sleep and come back at it fresh."

They did.

———

Zahnie and Red woke up at the same moment and with the same thought. She looked at him hard and spoke it. "Let's go find Damon."

In ten minutes they had another war council around the coffee table, Red and Zahnie, Gianni, Tony, Clarita, and Winsonfred. "Okay," said Zahnie, "here it is. What mine would Travis use to hide the artifacts? In this goddamn big, goddamn wild country? It has to be hard to spot, remote, and secure."

"Good point," said Red. He studied Gianni's face, wanting to be sure of him.

"We have to figure this quick and figure it right." Zahnie's voice was steady, betraying none of a mother's fear.

No one spoke.

Still no one spoke. "Maybe his own mine," Clarita said evenly.

Several voices said "What?" at once.

"His good claim. When Travis got cheated out of the Bounty of the Lord Mine, he located another claim he thought was great. Road to Glory, he called it. Staked it, did discovery work, bragged all over the country, made a deal to have it developed. I'm remembering now, it was in the newspaper—the Road to Glory Mine, and a contract with the Atlas Corporation. He got some advance money, which he used to buy his family a house. Travis was about to be rich.

"That was when, before any more digging got done, the AEC announced the government was over-supplied with uranium and was suspending purchases. Travis went from rich to busted in a sentence from a microphone in Washington, D.C., him and a thousand other local prospectors. But he did a lot of work at the mine first, put in some shafts or drifts. . . ." Her face showed how far back her mind had gone. "Travis believed in that mine. Got some advance money, but no ore came out, and he lost a lifetime of royalties."

"Where is it?" This was Zahnie.

"No idea, dear."

"The county courthouse will have a record!" Tony exclaimed. "The clerk records all claims."

They grinned at one another.

"It doesn't open until Monday morning," said Gianni.

Oh, shit. This was early Saturday morning.

Said Red, "Damon can't wait."

"Come on, Grandma!" urged Tony. "It's in there." He tapped her head lightly with his finger. "Bring it out. Shake it loose." He was her cheerleader. "Jiggle your hair!"

Clarita did.

"Harder. Shake it loose."

Clarita stared at the ceiling, at the floor, wrung her hands, tapped her head, and did a little finger dance in her hair. She froze. She whispered, "I got something. It's somewhere in Shaughnessy. . . ."

Red's heart jumped up until he saw Zahnie shaking her head. Everyone waited for her bad news. "It drains into Lake Powell," Zahnie said, "and it's huge. We'd need a week to search that place."

They made miserable eyes at one another.

"I have an idea," said Winsonfred.

Everyone waited.

"I'm going with you," he warned.

"Whatever!" snapped Zahnie.

He smiled beatifically at her. "I'll ask Ed to find them for us."

36

THE BIRD LEADING THE BLIND

Don't sleep while you're herding sheep. A crow will peck your eyes out.

—Navajo saying

They were gone in half an hour.

"This is looney tunes," said Red. From his tone he could have been excited about this, or scared shitless, or both.

"Looniest we ever sang," said Gianni.

"Totally insane," said Zahnie.

"But it's the only song we've got," said Red.

"We have no choice," said Zahnie.

Gianni said, "Unless we just want to wring our hands. It's better than giving the Kravins all the time they want to hide the goodies—"

He stopped short. They all knew the rest, and no one wanted it said. *To kill Damon and dump his body down a shaft where not even the buzzards could get to it.*

"What's that white-man saying?" asked Winsonfred. "'Oh, ye of little faith.'"

They laughed like madmen, and no one could think why.

They had camping gear, two coolers full of ice and food,

lots of water, pissant weapons, the .45 Red confiscated from Wayne and an aged double-barrel borrowed from Clarita. Red gave a wry grin inside. Was their most powerful weapon the intuition of a cheerful 103-year-old man in the backseat?

Clarita reminded them that the mine would be up toward the canyon rim, not out on the flat. The upshot of this was that they weren't driving into the canyon. They were going to check out the mesas above, as directed by Ed, yes, by Ed, find the road to it, and make a guerilla attack.

Some Scots warriors, according to Grandpa's stories, turned into berserkers. Red quietly decided that, when the time came, he would do exactly that.

Before noon they got within distant sight of what both the map and GPS said was Shaughnessy. *Anonymous Source, let that be the one with the Kravins, the loot, and Damon.*

They found a small piece of shade for lunch. No one cared as much about the food as the gallon bottles of water Jolo had provided, still half-frozen.

Zahnie went back to her maps and GPS. Gianni sat off to himself. Winsonfred asked for a hand up a boulder, saying he needed to commune with Ed. He didn't say whether their two-way reception was good. Red paced, kept a wary eye on Gianni, watched the old man, and scanned the skies for buzzards. He saw dozens, but not one made wigwag signals, or whatever passed for language with Ed.

In a few minutes Winsonfred said, "Ed's found them. He's ready to go." Zahnie took the wheel.

If he was really there, Ed did not flap along in front of the Bronco. Winsonfred kept his eyes mostly closed and paid hot attention to something no one else could see or hear. Red stopped watching the buzzards. *No offense, Ed, but you all look alike to me.*

From time to time Winsonfred would say to Zahnie, "Over there," or, "Toward that knob," or, "The other side of that wash and follow it." Once he said, "Ed is really frustrated with us. The ground is such an awkward way to travel."

And then, lo and behold, they came to a dirt track. It was not on any map, just one of the thousands scratched across this wild country, made by someone who simply went back and forth. It was pretty decent, looked well used. Later they would see that it had been worked on recently. "This is the way," Winsonfred said.

"Then why the hell didn't he put us on the road to start with?" snapped Zahnie.

Winsonfred shrugged. "Maybe it comes in from the north, in Canyonlands."

Zahnie braked to a stop in the middle of it. Everyone got out for no reason Red could see and peered around. "It leads over the rim to the mine," said Winsonfred.

Without a word, unanimously, they jumped back in and got the hell off that road. Zahnie slid them to a stop behind some giant boulders and everyone piled out again.

"Sheesh." Winsonfred wiped his forehead with his sleeve.

They heaved breath in and out. They'd had a hairy escape.

Sure, there had to be a scratched-out road. When Kravin was developing the claim, he had to get men and equipment in there. Now he had to get the stake-bed truck in and out with the artifacts.

"Wouldn't that be an ugly finale?" said Zahnie. "Meet them bumper to bumper on the road and shoot it out?"

"A blue-painted heliwheeler," Gianni said, smiling. Red wondered what was behind that smile that could be trusted.

"What now?" asked Zahnie.

Gianni said, "See where the road goes."

"Terminates," Red put in.

Winsonfred shook his head and grinned.

"What's so funny?" Red challenged him.

"All of you," he enunciated, "want to live. I'm kind of hoping to die today."

"Not a chance," Red growled.

"I wish there was," Winsonfred said. "But I probably can't do the dangerous stuff."

"You're right, no chance," said Zahnie.

After consultation they followed parallel to the road from as far away as they could and still keep an eye on it, creeping cross-country over some very rough ground and being careful not to get stuck in the sand. Finding a route was tricky. Sometimes they got out and glassed ahead, then glassed the road. Through the binoculars they got a sense of where they were going. With the GPS Zahnie pinpointed them on a large topo map. The rim of Shaughnessy was still over a mile away. And from there on?

"Ed have any more ideas?" Red asked Winsonfred.

"He gave us the road," said the old man. "He probably figures we're smart enough to follow it. He's got buzzard things to do."

"Wait!" exclaimed Zahnie. She was glassing the road. She thrust the binoculars at Red. "Tell me exactly what you see."

He spotted it immediately. A stake-bed truck, crawling along the road, headed out. "Same thing as you see. I can't tell . . ." He handed the binocs back to Zahnie. "How many people you see inside it?"

She studied the silhouettes. "Old man driver, passenger, and another passenger, looks like big Emery, riding on the back of the truck with a few crates."

"Damon?"

Big, beefy guys, no skinny teenagers. "They'll never let him leave. But maybe they're not done using him yet. We gotta go!" She jumped into the Bronco and gunned the engine.

"After we make sure they're gone," Red said, walking away. He climbed a boulder and fixed on the vehicle. It drew even and eventually sputtered out of sight.

Red breathed to himself, *The time is now.*

He leapt down off the boulder, jumped into the car, and gave Zahnie a quick squeeze. "Let's move!"

The road wound across slickrock and through red sand to the rim of a huge, gaping gouge in the earth. Zahnie checked her GPS and confirmed, "Shaughnessy."

Red wanted to get in and out of the monster's mouth very quickly—with Damon in the backseat.

Not that anyone said a word about Damon. Was he left to guard the site? Left trussed up? Or left like James Nielsen? Or stuck into a shallow grave?

Zahnie drove grim faced.

If Damon was still there, surely he would come back with them. Surely he wouldn't hold them at gunpoint until his accomplices came back? Surely he wouldn't help the Kravins kill his mother and friends? Surely there were no certainties. Red's skin puckered.

He glanced back over his shoulder, uneasy about Giannni.

They bumped down a steep section, crawling over rocks at a speed slower than walking. Then the road swung onto a narrow shelf, maybe a couple of hundred feet below the rim and a couple of thousand stomach-clenching feet above the canyon floor. Down there, green-gray sagebrush and a dry streambed. Up here, a steep, boulder-strewn track. All around, an open door to air, and to death.

Red was not crazy about being in the shotgun seat. In a couple of places he thought one of the right-side wheels was spinning in space, but he damn well didn't want to know for sure.

Suddenly the shelf widened, the road turned toward the wall, and there it crouched, dark and low. ROAD TO GLORY MINE, said the crudely painted sign. A jeep was parked in front, no ATV.

They got out and Zahnie yelled, "Damon! Damon!" over and over. Seven openings faced them in the rock wall like cannon barrels. Their eyes were drawn to each of the ugly little darknesses. Each person's mind speculated on what was in those shadows. The Road to Glory looked small and mean.

Gianni grabbed the double-barrel. Red started to reach for it.

Winsonfred said, "Give the man a chance."

Red looked into Gianni's eyes. *Scared,* he thought he saw, *like me.*

He turned his attention back to the mine. They could see all of four holes from the outside, penetrating only twenty or thirty feet. Zahnie called these gopher holes, exploratory digs yielding little or nothing. Two other holes pushed into the mountain maybe twice that far, maybe still not yielding much. The seventh, on the far right, angled down into the rock a long way. This one Zahnie called an incline. It was clearly an avenue of transport, and fresh tire tracks were visible going in and out.

Red's skin prickled with the anticipation of a sniper's shot with his name on it.

Whose shot? Travis? Wayne? Emery? Damon? All the same. Death is indifferent.

Zahnie and Gianni stood there, unsure. Winsonfred mounted the bumper and sat on the hood looking up. Far above their heads Red saw a buzzard riding a thermal. Everyone on their team was here, except Damon.

Red surveyed the area. In front of him the shelf ended against high crags. Above the holes stretched a broken wall too steep for even a mountain goat to climb. Back to the left stretched the road, the single path to salvation. Behind them, two thousand feet to fall, head over heels and over and over and over.

"Damon!" Red was surprised to hear his own voice. "Damon!"

Red saw Gianni looking all around, like they were on army exercises twenty years ago, eyeballing for enemies, in those days pretend ones. In his right hand he carried the side-by-side casually. Red had the willies.

A dozen steps from the entrance, at the foot of the incline, sat an old wooden box. It was full of tubes, like huge cigars, wrapped in red, waxy paper. Red knew what it was before Zahnie spoke.

"Dynamite. Don't get near it. May have been here for years. Unstable as hell. Can go off with a nudge. Kids have gotten killed just picking a stick up."

Suddenly Red got smart about standing there in the open. Even the dark shaft would be safer. He walked inside a dozen steps, and the narrow tunnel widened into a small, dank room with a low ceiling. Here, neatly stacked, stood crate on wooden crate. The lids weren't nailed shut, and Red found pots inside. He walked back to the entrance. "There are boxes of artifacts in here," he called.

No one cheered, their minds on Damon.

"I'm going to look further back."

After less than fifty yards the light was dim and the ground changed. Red stood in front of a series of scooped-out areas, like small vestibules. He wondered if that was where Kravin removed ore.

Beyond this point Red would need his flashlight, and he got it out of his fanny pack.

Wait.

In the dark, two boxy shapes covered by tarps. He reached for the canvas on one.

Whirrr!

Red jumped way back. *Damn!* A rattler slithered through a slatted crate. The thing oozed away as fast as it could go.

Very gingerly, Red tapped the wooden crate with a foot. Then he shook it hard. No more rattles.

Gently, he lifted the lid. Jerry cans of water, cans of food, sacks of pinto beans, and so on. They were prepared to camp here for a long time, if need be. He flicked on the flashlight and saw that the incline extended a lot farther back.

Suddenly Red's mind shrieked, *Get out of here!*

He hurried back up the shaft, his mind a-spin.

Twenty yards from the entrance he heard:

Wheels on gravel outside.

Shouts.

Zahnie and Gianni scuffling into the shaft!

Where was Winsonfred and what . . . ?

From the shadows of the entrance Red peered out into the blinding brightness. Zahnie and Gianni huddled near him.

The stake-bed truck was parked right behind the Bronco and Jeep, and a silver-haired driver was getting out.

Under the front end of the Bronco lay Winsonfred, wriggling to get all the way under. Red hoped they hadn't seen him.

The silver-haired man, apparently Travis, stood behind the SUV, shouting. "C'mon out, assholes! C'mon out!" In one hand he had some sort of lever-action rifle, maybe a .30-.30. "You think you seen us and we ain't seen you? Come out! You didn't fool nobody!"

Two other men clambered down from the truck. Wayne was holding a 9mm semi-automatic pistol, Emery an automatic rifle. They leveled the guns at the mine entrance where Zahnie, Red, and Gianni crouched in the shadows.

So it's now.

37

APOCALYPSE

Don't wear your blanket with the stripes sideways. You'll go crazy.

—Navajo saying

The wide-bodied young one, Emery, lumbered behind a rock just big enough to hide a dog and threw himself down. He stuck out on both sides. Using the stone as a rest, he held his rifle on the mine opening.

Up in the crags there might have been something to duck behind. Down here, nothing.

"C'mon out, goddamn it!" Travis bellowed a couple more times. His voice grated like a chain saw.

Gianni started forward. Red grabbed his elbow.

"Damn it, they'll shoot you."

"I'm their partner! They might think I'm alone."

Red seized him by both shoulders.

Gianni rasped, "They know someone's in here. Let me play this out."

Red put a hand on the double-barrel, but Gianni wrenched it away and stumbled into the sunlight.

Gianni was backlit by the sun. Red's feelings dropped into a dry well and split open. Half of them said his friend was going to get killed. The other half said the traitor was going to sell them out.

" 'Lo, Travis."

"Lordy," said the old man, "look who it ain't."

Old Kravin looked like a crazy redneck. Standing next to him, Wayne was black stone slate. No sentiment there, no decency, no humanity, a void.

"Why's Emery behind that rock?" said Gianni.

"Didn't know it was you, Gianni," said Kravin. "Tell you what, though, been doing good work." The old man's smile was a leer. "We're ready for those big bucks you promised."

Gianni ignored that and kept walking toward them, steady and slow. He was close now, where the shotgun was a far better weapon than a rifle or pistol. "Thought I'd check out the goods before I signed any checks."

"How'd you know where we was? Kid give you GPS readings? He had some money. He get it from you?"

"Just wanted to know I was paying for something real. We can go to town, exchange goodies for dollars right now, you want to."

"Why not? You see that kid when you get here?"

"No sign."

"Guess he got scared and run. He won't get far." Travis cackled. "Got no water." Something shrewd came into his voice now. "Ask you again. You pay that kid to rat us out?"

"Travis," said Wayne sharply, "quit the b.s."

Red put the sights of the .45 on Emery. Too far. The sights of the lummox were trained on Gianni. Red shifted to Wayne, though the range was still a little long. He wished he knew if Emery had the rifle on full auto or on single shot.

Gianni stopped in front of the stake-bed truck. Travis and Wayne stood between it and the Jeep, no doubt ready to drop down.

Winsonfred lay very still under the front bumper of the Bronco.

Wayne eyed Gianni, appraising. "Everything's cool here, Gianni. I don't see no trouble." He let his grin broaden slowly, then shouted, "Fire!"

Gianni hit the ground to roll under the jeep.

Emery fired a single shot. Gianni swung the shotgun toward the big man and blasted. Emery shot again. Gianni bellowed, and the second barrel of the shotgun tore up the front end of the jeep.

Red shot at Wayne but missed—he and his dark energy ducked behind the jeep.

Covered with red-rock dust and sweat and blood, Gianni scooted farther under the front bumper and fumbled in a shirt pocket for more shells. Looked like he was hit high in the chest, near the collarbone.

"*Berserker,*" Red hissed at himself. He roared, "*John-ny!*" and sprinted for the front of the Bronco. Emery got off three fast shots at Red, one close enough that he dived and slid to cover on his belly underneath the Bronco. Winsonfred lizarded sideways to make more room.

Emery jumped up, sprinted to the back of the jeep, and rummaged in the rear. *Christ,* Red thought, *don't let him get at more firepower!*

Red looked under the Bronco over to the jeep and saw Emery's overalls. He leveled his.45 and fired at the shinbone.

Emery howled and one leg disappeared.

Got no second clip, Red shouted in his head. *Save your shots!* He rolled out from underneath the Bronco, jumped up, and sighted right on the big son of a bitch's head.

Pain blasted Red's skull and bolted down his spine.

Red dropped the .45, grabbed his head, staggered to his knees. *No sound,* he realized dimly. *Pistol-whipped.*

The next thing he felt was the muzzle of a pistol against his temple, cold and deadly. Wayne jumped down from the top of the Bronco and snatched back his .45.

"You're lucky you're too big to carry off." Wayne switched

hands on the pistols and held his .45 by the barrel. He yelled, "No more shooting! That's an order!"

Travis padded out from behind the truck, looking like a man cheated out of a tavern brawl.

Emery stood behind the jeep and limped forward like an idiot. Red guessed his shot had missed the bone.

"Get up," Wayne snapped.

Red heaved himself to his feet.

Wayne dragged Gianni out from under the Jeep, then looked under the Bronco and said, "Well, look what we have here." Winsonfred scooched out sheepishly. "The old Navajo, what's-his-name? Hey, you're the kid's grandfather, aren't you, probably great-grandfather."

Winsonfred looked deeply, deeply ashamed.

"Come to save your boy?" Wayne cackled.

Travis turned in Red's direction and grated, "I don't know who you are, but you won't need no headstone."

Wayne snapped out words in command: "Emery, shoot out the radio in the Bronco."

Emery did.

"Now, you're all going to the back of the incline, the far back, you and this asshole and that sweet old man, ain't it a shame? After we blast, you'll have a ton of stones to mark your bones for all eternity."

"Don't worry," added Emery. "One bullet, and you won't feel the rocks fall."

"Shut up, both of you!" ordered Wayne. "No need to shoot. They deserve to suffer." He pointed his pistol at Red's head. "Let's get going, boys. Fate is waiting for you down that dark hole."

Gianni got slowly to his knees and then to his feet. Red put his arm around his old friend to steady him. Or maybe himself.

Travis picked up Gianni's shotgun from the dust, but Red could see the other two shells in Gianni's hand.

Heliwheeler of a situation. Only weapon left is an unarmed woman hidden in a mine.

A mourning dove called. Red snorted.

The three let themselves get herded toward the mine entrance, two injured, disarmed, middle-aged sad sacks and a 103-year-old man. Red couldn't see Zahnie, which was a good sign. He acted woozy. No harm in a little fakery. It didn't take much.

The mourning dove sounded again. Red wished he had one shot at that damn bird, wherever it was.

They piddled, limped, and stumbled forward. Red thought, *These guys are miners. They know how to set a blast to close a shaft just so.*

Then from inside Red's mind spoke the thunder-deep voice of Moses. *Enter that mine, walk into the darkness, and you'll never come out.*

He kept staggering forward, prodded by Wayne.

Enter that mine, walk into the darkness, and you'll never come out.

He took another couple of steps, right to the line of shadow and sunlight. He stopped.

Okay, Red said to himself, *live or die.*

Red elbowed Wayne in the gut, whirled, and grabbed the arm with the gun.

Blam! A shot grazed Red's boot.

Someone shouted, "Now!"

At that moment two dark blurs charged. Red didn't know which blur came first. Zahnie barreled out of the mine, screaming like a kamikaze. And something dropped like a big sandbag from about twenty feet straight over their heads.

Red kneed Wayne in the balls as hard as he could.

"Ah-a-a-a-ah!"

Zahnie gave Wayne a clean block and knocked him into Red. All three went down in a tangle.

Red grabbed Wayne to squeeze the breath out of him and keep the gun down. *Fight for your fucking life! And hers.*

The overhead surprise landed butt first on Emery's shoulder. *It's Damon!*

Red and Damon and Gianni and Travis and Emery got into a flurry of fists and kicks.

Wayne smashed Red's nose with a club fist and squirmed away. Zahnie had the .45, and Wayne was grabbing at her arm.

Emery was fighting one-handed—that shoulder was dislocated or broken. Gianni grabbed Emery's rifle and swung it like a club, but the barrel glanced off his head.

Red hurled himself into Wayne's midsection, but Wayne was ready and shoved back.

Zahnie fired a shot that turned the bastard's ear into a bloody, mashed cauliflower.

Wayne grabbed his ear and hollered, "The incline!"

Red shook his head, trying to get set right.

Oh. Wayne and crew weren't whipped, they were just heading for the better cover. Emery grabbed at Zahnie from behind. She threw the .45 toward Red. Emery yanked her radio off her belt and threw it over the cliff. She spun away. Then he, Wayne, and Travis zigzagged into the mine entrance with most of the guns.

At the same time, Red and the others ran like hell the other way, behind the vehicles. The shotgun was back in Gianni's left hand. *Praise be!* thought Red. He had the .45 back in hand.

Winsonfred lay in no-man's-land, between the antagonists, probably hurt, maybe dead.

Zahnie and Damon were hugging like mad. "I was hid up there the whole time," Damon jabbered. He pointed to the steep rocks above the mine entrance. "I saw it all, I—"

"Damon," Red said seriously, "thank you for saving my life."

The pride in the boy's eyes could have electric-powered a small town.

"Zahnie," Red said with equal seriousness, "I thank you for my life."

She squeezed him. "You were a hero."

"The mourning dove call, right?" he said to her.

She nodded. "Mother–son signal."

Gianni said, "Let's shoot the box of dynamite and seal them in."

Red looked at the box of red cigars. *Unpredictable.* "No, might blow the whole face of this mountain off."

Travis's voice graveled out of the mine's interior: "Looks like a Chinaman's standoff. You best get in that Bronco and get outta here. We don't wanna have to kill you."

That was worth a couple of grins. "You could have fooled us," Gianni shouted toward the mine shaft.

"I've got an idea," Gianni said. "Let's see if the keys are in the truck." He crept to the open window, reached in, and held them up. His shirt was soaked with blood—apparently he was operating on adrenaline.

He handed Red the shotgun. "I'm going to attack them with the truck," he said. "I'll drive the sucker right into the shaft and run the bastards down."

Red snapped, "Don't be stupid!"

Damon was checking the jeep. "No keys here. Let's push it off the cliff, take the truck and Bronco, and just leave the bastards stuck here."

Red snatched the shells out of Gianni's shirt pocket, loaded, and shot the jeep in the radiator. "Let's go," Red said. He told Gianni, "Take the keys to the truck."

Just then Red saw Winsonfred struggle to his feet, right out in the open.

"Get over here!"

"I got something to do," the old man said softly.

Red couldn't figure out where Winsonfred was headed.

Wayne and Emery stuck their weapons out from behind shad-owed corners at the old man but didn't shoot. The Kravins evi-dently considered the old guy a waste of ammo.

After about ten steps Winsonfred leaned over, reached into the wooden box, picked up a handful of dynamite sticks, and tucked them into the crook of his left arm.

"Don't shoot!" yelled Wayne.

Then Winsonfred started the short shuffle to the mine en-trance.

Red stared wild-eyed. *The Kravins can't believe it.*

"Let's go!" Red shouted. He ran behind the vehicles and threw himself flat. Zahnie, Gianni, and Damon flopped beside him.

When Winsonfred was halfway there, Travis stuck out the barrel of the lever-action.

"Dad!" shouted Wayne. "No shots!" He clubbed his father over the head.

Travis collapsed.

When Winsonfred was ten feet from the entrance, he threw a stick in.

Emery bellowed.

Miraculously, the stick rolled to a quiet stop.

Emery dived for it.

Winsonfred threw another one.

Second miracle. The stick just rolled.

Roaring like a banshee, Emery dived for it.

"Don't touch it!" screamed Wayne.

Winsonfred looked at the two sticks in Emery's hands, then at the bunch in his arm. He threw all of them in at once.

Apocalypse!

Darkness, darkness, the blackness Red always knew waited for him somewhere.

Then slowly, blearily, gray light. Consciousness.

Zahnie, Damon, Gianni, and Red were in a ragged pile.

When he could look, Red saw an incredible rage of sand and pebbles, whirling in every direction, a DuPont dust devil.

Through the whirlwind he saw the lump that must be Winsonfred's body, knocked halfway back toward them. *The old man found a way.*

Zahnie said something, but Red was stone deaf. He wasn't the only one. No one heard Zahnie. She shrugged at the sky.

They stood up slowly, brushing off dust and rock fragments, shaking their heads, clearing their brains, wiggling their fingers in their ears, waiting for their hearing to come back.

They looked around. They inspected themselves. Inspected each other. Looked at Winsonfred's body. The mine was a blocked tomb now.

Red saw Zahnie say something to Damon but heard nothing. She came to Red and embraced him, they rocked, they held each other. None of them could rouse the desire to go anywhere.

Slowly, hearing returned. He could hear Damon murmuring softly, "My God, my God . . ."

Suddenly Red thought of what he heard, what he saw, and what he didn't see.

"My God . . ."

The cloud in front of them hovered in the air, drifted to earth, its energy leeching away.

Within it a shape assembled itself and rose above the ground. It seemed to move, though Red didn't let himself think so.

It did move.

Waving its arms, it emerged from millions of particles toward them.

It appeared to be Winsonfred.

It was Winsonfred.

Zahnie ran toward him.

He took a couple of steps into her arms.

Red ran up and flung his arms around both of them.

The Ancient One pulled his battered head back, looked into their faces, and saw their tears.

"Why were you afraid?" he said. "I told you, I have trouble dying!"

They stumbled, an awkward, six-legged creature, toward Damon and Gianni.

"Look!" cried the old man, sweeping an arm toward where the incline used to be. The entrance was shattered, pulverized, blown to smithereens. Half a mountain had crashed down upon Wayne, Travis, and Emery. Red hoped they died instantly. A piece by piece death in the blackness, buried by tons of rock, knowing—Red didn't wish that on anyone.

"You did it!" all but Winsonfred began to shout. "You did it!" They slapped the old man on the back until they nearly knocked him down again.

Red looked up into the pure-blue sky, thinking he wanted to thank the Anonymous Source.

Instead a buzzard hung above the mesa, circling.

Red waved.

He knew buzzards don't wave back. This one, though, circled away from the summit and let itself angle down. They all watched, transfixed. After a few moments it perched on the roof of the Bronco.

They stared. Except for Winsonfred, who seemed to be listening. Before long the buzzard launched himself into the air and winged away to the west.

"Ed's going to the lake," said Winsonfred. "Sometimes he and his friends roost for the night in some cottonwoods there." Pause. "I thanked him, and he said he was glad to help. But he wants us to remember something. He hung around because he was hungry. Next time he does us a favor, we shouldn't leave a mountain of rubble on top of all that good meat."

They laughed. At first it was an edgy-in-the-face-of-death laugh. Then it got free, it came from the belly, it sprayed happily into the air. Maybe it was different for each one of them. Gianni from his satisfaction at doing right. Damon from a sense of belonging. Winsonfred from his delight and pride in Ed. Zahnie from a mother's blessed relief. Red sent his laugh to roll all around heaven with hers. They'd found their rhythm, together.

38

BUZZARDS AND DANCING

Changing Woman, she who is old every winter and young every spring, she got pregnant by Sun when a ray of sunlight passed through the drops of a waterfall.

—Navajo creation story

On the way back to Moonlight Water, Damon told his long story. How he ran away from the Squash Blossom Café, got picked up by Gianni and accepted a roll of bills and a ride ten miles out of town, and then started hitchhiking to Santa Fe. And who should pick him up but Travis Kravin!

Damon faked eagerness, jumped into Travis's cab, and fed him a line about how he was escaping to keep from being questioned by the cops and how he sure was glad to see Travis.

Damon didn't know if Travis was on to him. Then they made him call Zahnie. So he knew, knew absolutely and fatally, and lay in wait for his chance.

While they were stacking all the crates of artifacts in the incline, Damon stepped aside to relieve himself. Out of sight, he rock-climbed up the canyon wall and hid. He was hoping they would search for him thoroughly—that would give him a good chance to push someone off the edge. But they were too cagey for that. Knowing he couldn't carry enough food and water to get to the highway, they drove off and left him to the buzzards.

Damon decided to wait for dark, determined to walk out thirsty for however many days it took, knowing he probably wouldn't make it.

He climbed up and watched the Kravins go outward bound and saw his mom's gang come rolling along in the Bronco like a miracle. He watched the good guys try to sneak by and the bad guys follow the Bronco back to the mine.

He scrambled down to the best position he could to help them, behind a boulder above the entrance to the incline, waited, and at the right moment leapt in to save everyone's lives.

Deciding to jump onto Wayne from twenty feet up, "That was totally easy. I loved it."

Red said, "It might have stumped me."

And so Damon basked in the glow of his deeds. In Red's opinion he deserved every bit of it.

Then for miles through the twilight they whooped it up. They had to stop at the hospital in Montezuma City, where Gianni got his shoulder patched up but refused to be admitted.

From the hospital they went to the only convenience store open late and bought soda pop and snacks. Driving on, they played My Botticelli Is, with Damon winning every game. They sang old folk songs, and Red supplied new lyrics that everyone found hilarious.

Winsonfred said, "We're driving, but it feels like we're flying."

"No more root beer for you, old man," teased Zahnie. Winsonfred hadn't touched alcohol in years.

They partied their way south on the highway, straight through Moonlight Water and up the canyon to Harmony House.

Everyone made up for lost sleep.

———

After breakfast, Red said to Zahnie, "You want to take a walk?"

She heard something in his voice.

Red and Zahnie walked in silence down the canyon road. A changeling moon was sinking behind the bluffs to the west, its face mottled and ambiguous. They held hands. Sometimes Red stopped and kissed Zahnie, but she was hesitant. Finally they got all the way to town, and at the gas station Red bought them each a Phish Stick. Halfway back, when the ice cream was gone, he jumped up onto a boulder and patted the rock. She hesitated and then sat next to him.

"Zahnie," he said, "this is a crazy time to ask this, but . . ." He heaved breath in and out. "Maybe any time would be crazy." He locked eyes with her. "Zahnie Kee, will you marry me?"

She inched away from him.

He started to reach for her and held back.

"We're too different," she said.

"I love you," he said, the first time he'd spoken those words to her.

"We're too different."

She looked as deep into his eyes as he had into hers. She said, "Let's keep it simple. We're good together now. That's enough."

She slid off the boulder and they walked home in silence. There she said, "Let's go up to the Granary."

She sat him down in her small kitchen and got out two beers. She danced over to him and handed him one. "Celebrate with me," she said. She knew he didn't drink. They clinked bottles and she watched him take an obligatory sip.

"What are we celebrating?"

"I learned something up there at the mine." She danced a couple of steps away. "'Tain't what you do," she sang. She clinked his glass again, but this time he didn't sip.

She drained her bottle, took his, and sat across from him. Her voice went serious. "How come I didn't get a dream to teach me like you did?"

"Maybe you didn't have as much to learn as me."

"I've gotten something from our time together. Something big. I remembered to cut loose and dance sometimes, like that paper inside your van says, even if no one else hears the music."

He considered at length. "You want to dance?"

She took his hand.

"Lying down?"

"Absolutely," she said.

39

STRUGGLES

Don't sleep with your wife when you just come back from hunting. It will cause bad luck to your wife.

—Navajo saying

They climbed down the stairs inside the Granary and enjoyed the peace of safety. As they walked toward Harmony House, Gianni jumped in front of them, threw up his one good arm in a stop sign, and said, "Wait. You are about to see something special, a grand presentation of Gianni Productions, Unlimited."

He walked them into the dining room. "Ta-da!"

Tony, Clarita, Damon, Jolo, and Eric were gathered around a woman who had them hooting with laughter.

Her back was to Red, so he walked around front to make sure.

It was her. *Oh, jeez, what now?*

"Hello, Georgia."

"Hello, Rob. Or Red."

"You look like the cat that got the canary."

"Yep. Caught the disappearing man." She made a fang-biting motion and chuckled.

Red looked down and shuffled his feet. Zahnie took his hand and squeezed.

"Hello, Zahnie," said Georgia, "I've heard a lot about you already, all good." Red couldn't help noticing how good Georgia looked. Not just pretty, but healthy and alive.

"Zahnie," mumbled Red, "this is—"

"I'm his wife, Georgia. But you don't have to let go of his hand. I already did that."

Zahnie squeezed Red's harder.

"Georgia, I . . ."

"You what?" She looked like she was about to cackle.

"Red," said Clarita, "act like a gentleman."

"I don't know what to say."

"I have a question," said Georgia. They all waited. Her body language was a grin. "Yo, dude," she said, "how does it feel to be dead?"

They moved outside to a picnic table under the trees. The day was pleasant under the shade of the century-old cottonwoods. Winsonfred, Tony, and Damon played horseshoes. They could see Red, Zahnie, Georgia, and Gianni sitting at a table but could not hear them. Gianni had a stack of papers in front of him the size of a Webster's. Jolo kept the pitchers of lemonade full.

"Who else knows?" asked Red.

"No one," said Georgia. "Yet. Gianni said not to tell."

Gianni gave his buddy a grin.

"His phone call came at a good time. I was in the middle of throwing Nora out of the house."

"Throwing her out?"

"Let's just say it was something I tried that didn't work out."

Red nodded and almost let himself smile.

"Zahnie," said Georgia, "you don't need all that *he's-mine* body language. I don't want him back, and I hope you two do great together."

Zahnie blinked at her.

"Really, I do," said Georgia.

Zahnie gave Red's hand another squeeze and let go.

"Gianni spilled it all to me, your fake death and your version of a spiritual quest. He also told me to get my ass up here."

"I thought I'd done enough that was fake, I oughta to do something real. And good."

Eyes lanced from face to face.

"The question," said Red to Georgia, "is what do you want?"

Gianni spoke up. "She wants good things for everybody, herself, you, and Harmony House."

"No," said a voice behind them, "the question is: What does the law want?"

It was Rulon Rule, all chesty with uniform-bearing authority. Red was amazed that Georgia's appearance had shocked him so much that he hadn't heard Rule coming. "I've heard some stories about you folks today, quite some. So I'm going to ask the questions now, and I'm gonna do it in my office. But let's start with this. Johnny Montella, you're under arrest."

The charges the sheriff wanted to bring against Gianni were bad. Looting was a crime that could send you to county court, tribal court, and federal court, giving them three chances to crucify you. And Gianni was guilty as hell. He had planned to loot, he had executed his plan, he had helped destroy an archeological site and archeological knowledge, and he had tried to make a bundle doing it. Make Red a bundle, too. The sheriff didn't give a damn that Gianni had lost every penny.

True, Gianni had put himself in the line of fire to undo some of the damage—this mattered plenty to Red. Zahnie had mixed feelings. But not Sheriff Rule, who was a by-the-Rule-book cop.

Gianni made a quick call to Rosie Sanchez, knowing that a local lawyer, and a Mormon, was needed. She proved to be a fighting Saint.

Gianni presented Rose with a contract he'd written out months before and that Kravin had signed. It laid out the workings of a partnership. And in it Travis claimed he had found the site on private land. If Gianni had been deceived into thinking the excavation was legal, he wasn't culpable.

Rosie wielded that piece of paper like an ax. She told the sheriff the only culprits he had were the ones buried under tons of rock at the Road to Glory Mine, all guilty as sin. And considering what they had done, the county should be grateful as hell they were taken care of, with Gianni's help. What's more, she could point out after a few days that most of the artifacts were in good shape, crated up a couple of hundred feet from the explosion, of considerable value, and could be used to educate the public.

Rose told the sheriff that if he charged Gianni in the face of that contract, she would be delighted to bring suit against the county for malicious prosecution. About that time Gianni seemed to be falling in love with her.

Still, Sheriff Rule might have looked around hard and come up with cause enough for a grand jury to bring an indictment. And a jury might have used its common sense and figured the piece of paper was strictly Cover Your Ass. Therefore, Rose paraded her client's generosity in front of the sheriff. Gianni volunteered to help curate all the saved artifacts for the Museum of the Four Corners in Montezuma City, an act that would increase the museum's prestige, demonstrate the community's wise treatment of artifacts, and bring more tourists to town. He further volunteered to pay the museum's costs in creating a display that would put the artifacts in proper context and explain their meaning to the public.

So, if Gianni had lost a hundred thousand bucks on his grab for a bonanza, he now got to chip in tens of thousands more. Red's friend would be burning the midnight oil at the law firm for quite a while to get back to square one.

That didn't seem unjust to Red.

Several days later, when her shift started at noon, Zahnie drove to Montezuma City and bought a certain something at the drugstore that she would never mention to Red. Not that she really needed to run the test. She already knew.

Later, in her own bathroom, she did the test. She sat there and watched the stick turn blue. She was terrified.

Red had troubles.

His emotions bounced around like the Ping-Pong balls used to pick the winning lottery number. The balls whooshed around a glass cage, blew against the walls, and went crazy. Then the air was turned off and the balls fell down the hole, the first one bearing the lucky number.

In that whirlwind Red's brain didn't have a chance to pick a winner.

Georgia had gone off to see the Grand Canyon for a couple of days while Gianni duked it out with Sheriff Rule. Red was half-crazy wondering what Georgia had in mind. She didn't seem vengeful, but . . .

The fantasy of waking up every morning next to Zahnie Kee, preferably a naked Zahnie Kee, spun him to the sky.

She was apparently saying no, and that squished his Ping-Pong ball flat.

Zahnie wore a uniform, she had duties to perform, and she had a living to earn—these were her assertions. So every morning she kissed him good-bye and marched off. Every evening she came back home and took him to her bed. But she had an air about her. He could tell that she was waiting for him to ask her again to marry him and she was keeping *no* on the tip of her tongue.

He didn't know why—he didn't see any huge issues between them—and he didn't ask.

He needed to get a clear view of the situation, but his insides were a dust devil.

On one of Zahnie's days off, at the dining table, Red said, "Let's find a place where we can spend the morning at the river and skinny-dip."

She stood up and took their breakfast plates and silverware away. She couldn't stand it. She had to push him back. *Had* to.

"I spend every day at the river."

"Let's walk up the canyon then." He took their coffee cups to the sink.

"Damon and I are going to Montezuma City." Red would know this usually meant grocery shopping. She began running the dishwater.

"I'll come along and buy us all lunch." He squirted some liquid soap in.

"I want this one just to be Damon and me."

Zahnie and Red did the dishes, you wash, I'll dry. She kept her head turned away and expressionless.

Suddenly he took her shoulders and looked in her eyes. "What's going on?"

She looked out the window over his shoulder, pursed her mouth, and slid away from him a bit. "Just thinking about us. Differences. Things I can't get around."

She put her hands back in the hot dishwater and made a face. She was determined to say it and have him believe her. She had to. "I have family here. I don't mean the Navajo people, or even the people of Moonlight Water. The people around the table in this house."

She turned to Red and put it to him. "You're alone in the world. Not just recently, because you ran off. I don't think you ever had a family—a duo with your grandpa barely counts, and he's been gone a long time. If you ever knew how to be in a family, you've forgotten."

She saw puzzlement and doubt in his face.

She reached for an iron skillet and started scrubbing, searching for the right words. "But that's not all of it." She stared into the bottom of the skillet like ultimate reality was in the black iron. "You say you love me. You wait, but I don't say, 'I love you.'" She looked right at him to say the hard part. "Because it doesn't matter. Whether I love you or not. This is fact. You dance to one beat, I dance to another."

He stopped drying. "Again. Zahnie, what's going on?"

She looked into his face. "We're where we need to be, you and me. Let's keep it there." *You have to leave, you're going to leave, but not yet, please.*

He waited for about three beats. "You think I'm going to split, don't you? Run off, as you put it."

"I know you are."

"My choice or yours?"

"Ours."

"This is so frustrating."

"Red, it's good, what we have for this short time. Don't mess it up."

She kissed him, made it warm, felt it get too warm. She turned her back, crossed her hands on her chest, and let her head fall forward. After a moment she made up her mind.

When they finished cleaning the kitchen, she led Red to the Granary, took him to bed, and made love with him lingeringly. For her, every gesture was an emotional good-bye.

"Let's doze a little," she said.

They spooned together, her in front, his arm across her.

"Do you understand?" she said.

"No," he said. Long pause. "I don't believe it's what you want."

Now, silently, came the tears. She wiped them away with one hand so he wouldn't know.

40

IT'S BEEN WAITING FOR YOU

Don't talk while the medicine man is singing. It will spoil the ceremony.

—Navajo saying

As Red walked back toward the main house the next day, Winsonfred popped out the back door. "Red," he called, "let's go down to the water!"

The river spot turned out to be a big eddy accessed by a two-track. Red shed his clothes zippety-quick, stood on the edge, and plopped in backward. Winsonfred sat under a big cottonwood well back from the water. Red thought Zahnie had said something about traditional Navajos staying away from Water Boy, and he wondered about that.

Ten minutes later Red was stretched out in his boxers next to Winsonfred. They didn't speak, and that felt good to Red. He closed his eyes and paid attention to the breeze cooling his body.

After a while Winsonfred said, "There's something for you to see over there. I picked it out special."

Red stirred and put his clothes on. They walked through tammies to the cliff that lined the river, and Winsonfred led the way up a short slope to a huge rock slab that leaned against the wall and created a shadowed alcove. As they slipped into it, Red felt like he was being led into a secret hiding place.

Winsonfred flung an arm out. "Behold!"

Red was surprised Winsonfred knew that word.

What Red beheld was . . . nothing. Or rather a big, blank rock wall.

He looked at Winsonfred with question marks in his eyes.

"A long time ago there was a breakout, right here where we're standing. A big hunk of stone came off. You can see the pieces laying down there, broken." Winsonfred gestured to the slope.

"Before this space of rock—I call it The Canvas—before it could get weathered, this big slab fell down from above and took the leaning position you see, which protected The Canvas from rain, wind, and sun. So it doesn't have the signs of time that most rock around here does, the ones that grow on an old human face, for instance, like mine. It looks youthful. Open. Ready.

"I told you to pay attention to the stories the rocks tell. How about the ones they may yet tell?"

Winsonfred took a long moment to run his eyes over the pristine stone. "You see, it's virgin. To me, it cries out for a petroglyph. It's waiting to be carved or painted, waiting for someone to make something on it that speaks to all of us."

He stopped and looked for a while.

"I always thought I might do a carving here. No reason we modern people shouldn't do what the ancients did, as long as we do it in a good spirit. But I'm not the one it's been waiting for—you are."

He turned and looked into Red's eyes full on. "It's what you came here to Moonlight Water to do."

Red was overwhelmed, still. Finally he said, "What would I say?"

Winsonfred said, "First think of how to come at it. The ancients, pecking a figure in rock, it took them a long time. You see a big carving, maybe fifteen-twenty figures, that took a big bunch of time. What that tells me is, the carver had something important inside needing to come out. Something sacred, I think. It took a big effort to birth it.

"So you have to look inside you and see what wants out. Then you'll know what to do."

Winsonfred waited.

"But what would I carve? Or paint?"

"You already know," said Winsonfred.

Red's heart swelled up. "Kokopelli."

"What else? You came to this country from other villages. You're a musician. You're also a trader. You have some things to give us. Your goodwill. Your friendship. Help with fighting some enemies. And seeds in the sack on your back, the seed gives women babies."

Red felt a cold splash in the face.

"That's what Kokopellis do, plant seeds in women." Winsonfred gave Red the sweetest of smiles. "Now, you are getting what you came here for, renewal, wholeness, a path of beauty and harmony. Here's your chance to pay a tribute to that."

Winsonfred paused.

"Seeds. Are you telling me . . . ?" said Red.

"Yes. And you already knew.

"Now let me suggest some things to you. Take your time. It might take you a week, a month, a year, I have no idea, and you mustn't give that a thought. Also, don't worry about whether it's beautiful. If you bring a good spirit to it, a kind of sacred attitude, that will make it beautiful."

"Zahnie's pregnant?"

"I know."

"I ask her to marry me. She says no."

"Sure."

"Why?"

"Have you forgotten? Little Turtle Without a Shell. She's too vulnerable. She's scared."

"I want her like I've never wanted anything. And I don't know what she'll decide."

"Let that be part of the song you sing on the rock."

Red looked for a while at the rock, without seeing it. He said, "Okay. I will." He let the surface of the stone soak into his mind. He said, "I want to paint."

Winsonfred lit up. "Grand. Anything else?"

"Yeah. Water-soluble paint. Better on this rock, a more matte look." He paused. "It won't last forever."

"Here it will last and last, my friend. No sun, no water, no wind."

"Don't care. Let it go, let it stay. Either way. Me doing it, that's what counts."

"You got it."

Painting it and . . . He couldn't think about her.

"The basement at Harmony House has gallons and gallons of that kind of paint, and brushes," said Winsonfred. "Go as the spirit moves you."

The old man took Red's arm gingerly. He stopped. He looked back at The Canvas. Then he looked into Red's eyes.

"I have one saying that's even better. You remember I told you about my Lakota brother-in-law? This comes from him. 'When you paint, do not look with the two eyes of your head, but the single eye of your heart.'"

41

GIANNI PRODUCTIONS, UNLIMITED

Don't point your fingers at a rainbow. It will break them.
—Navajo saying

The next morning Red, Gianni, and Georgia sat over coffee at the dining table.

"Me first," said Georgia. She got up and walked to a clump of shapes stacked beneath a window. She threw the blanket off like a bullfighter's cape. All three saw a display of cases and trunks with musical instruments.

Red jumped up, ran to them, and touched.

"Your whole collection," said Georgia.

"Which I abandoned . . . Hey, even my steel drums." He grinned. He was thinking of a particular use for those. He gave Georgia a hug and sat down next to her.

Gianni jumped in. "Now to business. This plan is mine. The idea is to get good things for Red, good things for Georgia, and good things for Harmony House. I promise you.

"The legal situation, California being a community property state, is that both of you still own everything but the house. That's Rob Macgregor's."

"Who's dead," said Red.

"The right thing, emotionally," said Georgia. "But—"

"Okay, I know, you need a divorce."

"Otherwise I can't touch a thing for seven years."

Georgia smiled at Red.

Now Gianni pushed on in his chairman-of-the-board manner, manifestly pleased with himself. "I am acting not as a lawyer representing either of you, but as a mediator helping you reach an agreement. Believing I have a good idea what each of you wants, I have some suggestions to offer."

He handed out several sheets of paper, a copy to each. "I had to do *something* in jail."

Red was to give Georgia half of his liquid assets, entirely stocks and bonds, which were estimated at a value of a little over $6 million.

Red nodded. *I have three million dollars and a house worth more*—it was a discombobulating thought.

"Basically, okay?" asked Georgia.

"I don't want the house," said Red. "Done with that life."

"We'll work that out," said Gianni. "Now we need the rest of the gang." He called, "Come on in."

Tony, Clarita, Winsonfred, and Damon filed in and pulled chairs up. Jolo and Eric sat on the sofa playing with the baby and listening in. Zahnie was at work.

"Now everyone be quiet," said Georgia, "and listen to the plan of a legal genius."

Gianni grinned and said, "This is going to sound strange, but it will work. I did something like it years ago.

"Right now your problem is that Harmony House is licensed by the state of Utah as an assisted living facility. Tony is right. When he enters his plea bargain, the state will revoke the license.

"As an aside, Rose Sanchez and I already negotiated a plea bargain for Tony. One to fifteen years, with the judge's recommendation of leniency from the parole board." Gianni smiled at Tony. "That should keep it to one."

"I'm really grateful," said Tony. He rolled his eyes. "I guess."

"From here the question is a practical one: How do you continue to take care of elderly people without a license?

"It's not such a trick. It involves a concept that sounds weird. Get past that and a lot of good things happen. Here it is: You make Harmony House a commune."

"Commune?" All of them said the word at the same time, in tones ranging from disbelief to dismay.

"All right, I'm having a little fun with you. Call it an intentional living community. Either way, what you do is let Harmony House go out of business. Re-incorporate with a new name, as a non-profit, with a new 501(c)(3). And call yourselves, maybe, Nizhoni Living Center."

Grumbling was still audible. "Commune."

"Legally, this is how it works. Intentional communities are not subject to state control. There is no body of regulations stipulating how you must operate. So you get the bureaucrats out of your hair. Your legal position is that you're a group of people who live together voluntarily. If some of you take care of the others, that's your business. The same way that if the commune hires a director and employees, that's its business. In fact, it's the same way a family operates.

"Extra-legally, this also works. The press usually defends people who follow alternate lifestyles, intentional living centers and communes included. Even use of marijuana has been winked at most of the time." He spread his arms broadly. "That's it. Believe me, this will cut the mustard."

They all looked at one another.

Tony broke the silence. "I'm waiting for the other shoe."

"Is the shoe called money? Okay, here's a biggie. If they take my suggestion, Red and Georgia will provide the money now. Red, you have over a million bucks in equity in a house you don't want. You'll give Georgia the house, and with the equity she'll create an endowment of one million dollars for Nizhoni Living Center."

Georgia squeezed Red's hand. He thought, *This is good.*

"A million is not a fortune, but managed conservatively, it should provide about fifty thousand dollars a year for expenses and repairs. Okay, Georgia? Red, you in?"

"Sure." *Hell of a deal.*

"To expand, and there are always more old folks, you'll have to raise money somehow."

"I'll donate another half million to be used for expansion, at the discretion of the board of directors," said Red. He hadn't known he could sound so legal.

"Bravo!" said Tony.

"My friend," said Gianni, "you are in the spirit."

"Next consideration—the board of directors. If we add in Zahnie, seems to me the people in this room are the keys. Get together and decide who will be on the board. I've suggested Tony, Clarita, and Zahnie. If you want to add Red or Georgia, and they're willing, that's up to you. Later you could add a tribal politician for influence. Or someone with big bucks."

Everyone nodded.

"Well, that's it. Sounds like we're basically agreed."

He stood up, stopped himself, and tapped another stack of papers. Gianni said, "I've prepared copies of the legal work for you to study at your leisure. Tony, Clarita, and Zahnie will need to sign statements of acceptance of board positions. Get them back to me. By the way, my firm is doing all legal work for you *pro bono.*"

"Hooray!" said Tony. He beat a *rat-a-tat-tat* on his thighs with his hands.

"Georgia," said Clarita, "you're a good woman."

"Thank you," said Georgia.

"And, Red, we love you."

42

WHEN THE SPIRIT DANCES

Don't try to count the stars. You'll have too many children.
— Navajo saying

Red made three trips from the van to get his guitar and the cans of paint into the alcove. He set his guitar case well off and took a long look at The Canvas of stone. Then he made a trip to the river to fill his pail with water.

Carefully, he positioned five-gallon cans of paint on slabs and water for cleaning brushes nearby. He propped his stepladder on The Canvas, being careful not to leave a scratch. He pried the lids off, and considered. He had five colors: sky blue, corn yellow, forest green, black, and scarlet. Two cans of blue because he pictured the entire figure of his Kokopelli basically as sky blue. One by one he let his two brushes sink into the blue, taking color even above the bristles. Why? He didn't know. He breathed in and out. He thought, *The single eye of the heart.*

He picked up a brush and stuffed his pocket with paint rags. He'd decided not to do a chalk sketch. He wanted this painting to be like one of the breaks he used to improvise onstage in the early days, flying high, never knowing what would come next, taking wild risks in front of thousands of people and trusting himself, trusting *it*.

He steadied the ladder, set the paint can on the folding ladder shelf, climbed up, and quickly painted the figure of Koko in broad outline, two strokes wide. Red's arm and hand sailed over the rock without him, making huge lines, no detail, the shape of a man bent over, a hint of a skirt, arms supporting a clarinet-shaped instrument, and one foot kicking high in a dance. Done in a flurry and no time. *Time, what a silly idea.*

He heard dance music in his head, and he laughed.

Now he changed cans and painted Koko's instrument, which Red heard as a high-pitched recorder, piping like a fife. The music took over his strokes. Scarlet, it called for. To the tune in his head, he sang, "Fife rhymes with life." A half-dozen gestures and it was finished—he was a wild man—and Koko's music resounded through his head.

Now the headdress, which Red imagined as feathers curving up from Koko's hair. *Black,* the feathers must be like Ed's. One stroke with the brush turned sideways, one sideways stroke down, and each feather bristled.

Pipe, pipe, pipe, dance, dance, dance.

He moved the ladder to the opposite side of Koko. The sack Red imagined as the color of corn kernels. He outlined it on the rock against Koko's back without a thought.

He made a quick switch of paint cans and grabbed a smaller brush. Quickly, to the rhythm of Koko's melody he dabbed the sack full of green leaves, with Koko's fertility. *Play it, Koko.*

Painting in a fetus flashed into Red's mind. It seemed like such a dumb idea that he slapped himself in the face with his green paint several times.

Something felt good about that. He jumped off the ladder, seized each of the other brushes, one by one, and slapped his face with whatever color was on it. *I want to be part of the painting.*

He laughed ecstatically, stripped bare naked, and painted

his own body, covering himself with spirals and his own hand-prints from head to toe.

Then he got the Martin D-28 out of its case and started to give Kokopelli a fine, strong rhythm backup. Easy. He'd been hearing the music for long minutes—or hours, who cared? Jumping in was irresistible.

Soon dancing was irresistible. He moved like a maniac, strumming wildly, his strap holding the guitar tight. He threw himself into the air, spun, and twice nearly fell when he landed.

Another thought hit him. *Maybe Koko is dancing, too.* He looked up. Koko—*yes, Koko is dancing! No, maybe it's me that's moving, and that makes Koko appear to jump around.*

He tried to stop dancing to see for sure, and he thought, *Yes, Koko is dancing. The music carries us. Koko and I have sailed to far galaxies. Together.*

Later Red came to, stark naked, evening shadows reaching into the alcove. He was getting cold.

He wondered how long he'd been out. He wondered when and why he had passed out.

He looked up at Kokopelli. Perfectly still.

He listened. Perfectly quiet.

He gazed at Koko for a long while. He grinned. It was a very, very fine Kokopelli.

Later, in the river, it was quite a cleanup job. Red scrubbed himself with paint rags and biodegradable soap and abraded his skin with sand until it was half-raw. After a while, he couldn't find any more traces of paint, but he hated to think what Zahnie might find in spots where he couldn't see well.

He shampooed his hair a half-dozen times.

He decided to ship the Martin to an expert in Marin County for a cleanup. *Honor thy instrument.*

He put on his clothes, hauled his stuff to the van, and went back for a last look at Kokopelli.

Yes. Very fine.

He'd done what he came for. *Maybe I won't be back here again. Or maybe I'll come back a lot.*

He took a long look at Koko, now silent and still.

"Hell of a jam session, man," said Red. Sounds strummed distantly inside him, memories.

"Thanks."

He went back to the world.

43

STRUGGLES AND UNCERTAINTIES

Don't face your house any direction but east, toward the sunrise. Good luck won't find the door.

—Navajo saying

Red said, "Let me tell you why we should get married. Really tell you."

They were cuddled in Zahnie's small bed. She pulled back from him and gave him a look. She hoped it had oomph.

"Give a poor boy a chance."

"Okay," she said, putting on a half smile. She piled a couple of pillows up and leaned back. He did the same. "God, I wish I still smoked," he said.

"Look," he went on. "Out the window the sun is beginning to light the canyon."

Pause. *He's stalling,* she thought.

"Every day it rises over the eastern rim, floods the western side with light, and gives your beautiful red skin a gold tint. I'd like to get used to this."

Okay, get on with it.

"I want to stay forever," he said. "I've found a family," he said. "Like you said, I never had one, or not for twenty years."

She said, "Keep going."

"For ten years, I've been wanting children."

She turned away from him, toward the window. She pretended to look at the sunrise.

"I like Navajos. Funny, spunky, resilient. I like Moonlight Water. Oddball, artistic, real. Damon and I have some good music going. The country has something for me, like Winsonfred said. Even the petroglyphs do."

"Yada-yada-yada."

He said, "Listen, I like me here."

"Yeah, you need a home somewhere. Like playing music in Santa Fe."

He reached across her, took her hand, and held it between her breasts. She liked the feel of that. *It's not you, dummy, it's me.*

"My home is wherever you are."

"Why? Really, why?"

"You don't care about whatever I used to be. You don't care why Georgia found me not enough. You don't care what I accomplished or what I messed up. You want to do things that need doing, and you want to know if I'll pitch in. You want to work hard, play hard, *live.* Now. In that way, Zahnie, you have become my life."

I can't stand this.

She rolled over and looked at him. "I love it that you ask me to marry you." She looked into his eyes for a long moment. Then she gave him a quick buss and got up. "But really, we cannot make it work. Not in the long run."

She turned her back, stood up, and stepped away, so he couldn't see the feelings on her face.

Red went to the main house to play music with Damon. When he'd disappeared inside, Zahnie headed for the back door of Harmony House. She wanted one of Jolo's cinnamon rolls.

Georgia came out the door with two big wheeled suitcases. She left one and bumped the other down the steps toward her rental car.

"You leaving?" said Zahnie.

"It's time," said Georgia.

"For good?"

Georgia smiled broadly, held an arm to indicate the countryside, and sang to the old tune:

"The rez is not my home,
"I'm a California gal."

She pulled the suitcase to the car. Zahnie grabbed the other suitcase and followed her.

Georgia said, "Hey, thanks." She popped the trunk open. The two women lifted the big suitcases inside.

Zahnie said, "Thank you, Georgia. You saved Harmony House, my home."

"Me and Red," said Georgia, and threw both arms around her. "Good-bye, Zahnie."

Zahnie thought, *Well, she's Anglo—this is her way.*

Finally, Zahnie pulled back.

"It's been a pleasure, really." Georgia grinned hugely and said, "I wish you and Red happiness for as long as these skies are blue and the rivers flow to the ocean."

"Thank you," said Zahnie. "Do you think he's a good man?"

"As good as they come."

"But he ran off on you."

"I threw him out. We . . . His life was killing him, Zahnie. He had to go."

Finally Zahnie couldn't stand it any longer. "I don't think we're going to be together."

"Really?!" Georgia's astonishment sounded genuine.

Zahnie nodded.

"Tell me."

"He'll run off. I wish he'd get it over with."

"Zahnie!"

"Well, don't you think so?"

Georgia took her time breathing. "Zahnie, Red is at home here. I've never seen him so happy, so much at peace with himself. With or without you, he's staying."

Pause.

"Do you belong with him?" Georgia shrugged. "I can't say. Only you can."

"There are problems."

Georgia studied Zahnie's face for a moment, then opened the car door and slipped in. Thoughtfully, she started the car and then looked up into Zahnie's face. "Maybe there are. But I don't think Red is one of them."

She grinned and touched the accelerator. "Be happy, Zahnie!" she called out the window.

Red called it out to everyone at the dinner table. "Let's have a party. A big party—didn't you say parties here are for the whole town? A party to celebrate the grand opening of the Nizhoni Living Center."

They all thought that was a terrific idea.

Then Red went looking for Damon, who was in a corner picking guitar alone. Red followed the sounds. They'd been playing Damon's songs every day, working out arrangements and the breaks and shaping them into an act. Red hinted that they could get some gigs in Santa Fe and Albuquerque. Actually, he was confident. His secret was out—Georgia said the band guys knew and were doing fine without him—and he still had contacts. The kid's songs were good, his singing great, and his looks the kind that made girls go crazy. And Red had more in mind. He felt like writing music, creating new songs with this kid.

MOONLIGHT WATER • 309

Coming up, Red said, "Damon, let's rehearse, get it right, make it shine. We just got our first gig."

"What's the gig?" Damon was stoked.

"Tell you after we try some songs out."

So Red played his Fender Stratocaster and the two of them polished their performances of Damon's songs all afternoon. "Kid," said Red, "we got the stuff."

"I can't wait to get started. Let's move to Santa Fe."

"This is my place, buddy. Santa Fe, or anywhere else you dream of, belongs to you." Red told him about the big party. "It's important, and it's here. Now."

Damon nodded, his eyes full.

"Listen," said Red, "take the van and go to Montezuma City and get some stuff, will you? We'll need supplies."

Damon took the list and zipped out in Red's van.

In the last hour before supper Red sat alone at Clarita's piano and pecked out melodies and filled in harmonies and wrote down lyrics. He didn't let anyone hear the lyrics.

The next morning Red led Damon into Tony's house, where Zahnie wouldn't notice them if she passed by. They put down drop cloths, spread out the butcher paper Damon had brought back, and popped the lids off paint cans.

That evening the talk at Harmony House was of Georgia, Red, Gianni, and the forthcoming grants. Everyone was happy, Zahnie thought, except Tony. And her secret self, torn and yearning and feeling strange, out of kilter. *Why am I so stupid?*

While dessert was arriving—chocolate pudding, so Virgil wouldn't act up again—Clarita said, "Zahnie? Tony and I have agreed that he will be the director, with a salary of fifty thousand dollars plus room and board, when he gets back. In his absence I will act as director without pay. But I have a condition. That you pinch-hit as director as soon as the rafting season ends, and get paid half of Tony's salary for half a year."

Zahnie didn't work in the winter anyway. She said, "Count me in." She was surprised at the listlessness of her own voice.

As the group disbanded, Zahnie took Clarita aside and shared her difficult news. Clarita did not reveal that she already knew it. She also knew no Navajo woman would consider an abortion. It would be saying no to fate. To life.

Zahnie asked Clarita her questions, big questions. Clarita listened with an open heart and a painful sense of inadequacy.

They talked in whispers for a while. They weren't likely to be overheard anyway, because Red and Damon were making music at the grand piano. Clarita waited, her hand on Zahnie's arm, listening to the young woman circle and circle through the same uncertainties. Finally came the clear plea: "I don't want to raise a fatherless child again."

Clarita looked across at Red and Damon and hoped that Zahnie would follow her glance. But Zahnie didn't, as far as Clarita could tell.

When Zahnie stood up to go, Clarita said, "Granddaughter, I wish so much for your happiness. I can't tell you what to do, but I can tell you that there is no joy without taking risks."

Zahnie made a face, but they embraced, and Zahnie walked toward her small house, alone. Clarita whispered to herself, "Not another fatherless child."

Zahnie hoped Red would come to her soon. His presence each day was a growing wonderful-terrible combination. For these special days, one at a time, it was a joy. When he was gone, she told herself, it would be a great relief. No more suspense about when he'd take off and act out every man's fantasy, to start a new life. Again.

44

APOCALYPSO NOW

If you don't have a wife, don't wish for one. If you do, you'll never have one.

—Navajo saying

The grand opening of the Nizhoni Living Center was a blast. They had tubs of soda pop and beer and big coolers of lemonade. Tony grilled hamburgers, hot dogs, and bratwurst on the outdoor barbecue. Jolo whipped up every kind of fresh vegetable, salad, and dessert imaginable. Yazzie brought a dozen cases of beer. Which was good, because it was *hot* outside.

The guests stood or sat on hay bales that served as chairs for the makeshift stage. They were Moonlighters—every sort of human being—schoolteachers, archeologists, bluegrass musicians, cowboys, a sculptor who made his living as a river guide, a farmer who grew wine grapes, and a lot of traditional Mormons. A dozen of Clarita's Navajo progeny turned out, which Tony said was unusual, because they usually avoided big gatherings of white people. The Harmony House folks were bonding into a Nizhoni community and having fun doing it.

The occasion for the party was given due attention. Red

and Damon on one end, with Clarita and Yazzie on the other, put up a big sign of butcher paper and paint:

GRAND OPENING

NIZHONI LIVING CENTER

Naturally, the story of the great encounter at the Road to Glory Mine had to be told and re-told, each of the heroes entertaining small groups with his deeds. Winsonfred went to the microphone and made a whispery speech about giving Ed due credit, and everyone cheered, even Zahnie. Damon got the most slaps on the back for his role in the affair, and Red thought that was a fine thing. Exactly right.

Red had his four steel drums, called a boom, cellopan, guitar pan, and ping pong, and ranging from bass to treble, lined up against one wall of the main house. He and Damon made music right along, Damon singing beautifully. The people outpartied the music.

Red grinned and said, "Way of the world, kid. Give 'em a drink and they don't listen." Damon looked dubious. "Hear me now," said Red. "You make it beautiful. You sing your heart out. If the people don't notice, the gods of music will." Damon gave an ambiguous smile. Youth.

In a few minutes Zahnie, Yazzie, and Clarita sat on bales front and center and gave full attention to the playing. Winsonfred climbed on the stage with a drum that looked older than he was. Red gave him a look, and Winsonfred smiled back. Without rehearsal he added a light *tum*-tum, like a heartbeat. It was perfect. How could it be anything else?

The evening circled on. People got tipsy and then sobered up a little, or got tipsier. The temperature dropped toward ninety degrees. A little girl backed up against one of the soda pop tubs, now just a big bucket of ice and water, and fell in. Other people took her example by putting arms, legs, heads, or even shirts and hats into the tub. Men and women alike took off their

T-shirts, soaked them in the cold water, and pulled them back on. Though the Navajos turned away in embarrassment and the Mormons could only force smiles, about half the crowd half-stripped, dunked their clothes, and put them back on soaking and icy.

Tum-tum, the evening's heartbeat. Winsonfred.

Red was getting nervous. He told himself he knew how to do this. He'd learned it from a young woman who told him what one of his concerts did for her. Usually, she said, she was too self-conscious to dance. The first time she heard Red's band go wild on a jam, she went wild along with it. In a couple of months dancing was her favorite date.

The secret was that energy. With luck and practice, the performers got everyone's minds and hands and feet dancing to the same beat. When that got rolling, a miracle happened. Communal energy throbbed in everyone, performers and audience, angels and devils. Minds and hearts did a swing together and felt the fun. Energy throbbed in every heart.

Tonight he would persuade it to happen. He and Damon.

The moment the sun dropped behind the mesa to the west, Damon said, "It's time, boss."

Red whispered to Yazzie and Clarita to get ready. They disappeared into Tony's house.

Red lined up the steel drums behind the microphones. Damon unfolded his chair and stashed a pair of Red's maracas and a certain cloth-covered prop underneath it. By the time they took their seats onstage, people noticed and the hubbub died down.

Tum-tum.

"Ladies and gentlemen and," cried Red, taking his seat and getting out his rubber-tipped hammers, "white folks and red folks! Desert rats, lizards, and occasional buzzards. *Plunk your bottoms on bales. Open your ears and hearts.* We have arrived at this evening's entertainment.

"You may have read the story of the battle of the Road to Glory Mine in the newspaper, but it skirts the truth. You may have heard it this evening in bits and pieces from those of us who were there, but we stretch the truth. There is one supreme source for the story of this great victory, and you're about to hear it. Damon has told the story true in a song called 'Apocalypso Now.' "

The crowd moved closer to the stage. Zahnie slipped to the rear, uncertain. Winsonfred kept right on providing the evening's heartbeat.

"Now, before my friend Damon Kee sings the song and I accompany him, I must explain the title. This song is climaxed by a great explosion, as you probably know. 'And the Road to Glory . . . she came tumblin' down.' Sounds like an occasion for a brass fanfare or some such. But in the last month I've learned something. Which I'll say nothing about except that I've added to Damon's song the calypso beat. Here we give you the world premiere of Damon Kee's 'Apocalypso Now'!"

With those words Red whacked the highest-tuned steel drum and launched into a vigorous eight-bar intro. Damon stood and gave the maracas what for, right on the beat.

In the first stanza Damon sang of how the spirits of the Kravins were captured by the White Man Monster of Greed. With their minds taken over by this monster, they laid dark plans.

Red banged into the chorus. Damon donned a straw hat with plastic bananas sewn onto it and danced out in front, shaking those maracas like a madman, shuffling and gliding to the calypso bang.

The crowd laughed and applauded.

The chorus rocked along—

"They fooled the feds, that Kravin Korps,
Had the Road to Glory for their hidey-hole,
But they didn't figure on the fabulous five,
The powerful five from Harmony House.
Harmony rode against the Money Monster
And the Road to Glory . . .
She came tumblin' down."

In the second stanza Damon sang about how the Kravins captured him and made him work for them—there was a certain poetic license here. Maybe that's why, when the chorus came around, Damon bopped to the beat like one sexy Latin guy, hands twirling and elbows eloquent.

The third verse told how Ed the heroic buzzard led the fabulous five across the wild, lost lands to the Road to Glory Mine. Their mission—to rescue Damon.

The fourth told how the craven Kravins sneaked up on four of the fabulous five at the mine and got the drop on them. The four were saved by Damon's heroic leap through the empty air to land . . . right on top of the boss Kravin.

> *"They fooled the feds, that Kravin Korps,*
> *Had the Road to Glory for their hidey-hole,*
> *But they didn't figure on the fabulous five,*
> *The powerful five from Harmony House.*
> *Harmony rode forth against the Money Monster*
> *And the Road to Glory . . .*
> *She came tumblin' down."*

The last stanza was Winsonfred's turn for heroism. The young centenarian found the dynamite, walked up to the mine shaft, and threw it down the Kravins' throats.

"Apocalypse *now!*" Winsonfred mugged for the audience—*tum*-tum, *tum*-tum. And did those steel drums ever beat it out.

The crowd hooted and hollered. During the final chorus Winsonfred jumped up, grabbed the banana hat off Damon's head, and did a syncopated turn at geriatric speed. Luckily, the music made a grand *ritard*.

Cheering, stomping, and slapping of knees.

Red and Damon took their bows. Winsonfred beat *tum*-tum, *tum*-tum.

When the applause died down, Red picked up his guitar and said, "With your indulgence, we'll venture one more song, a new one of mine. It's called 'Dance Your Way to Glory,' and the ending is unwritten. For a good reason—no one knows how it will turn out. Here, this evening, you in the audience may help me write the ending. It's a love song."

Now he had them puzzled, but they waited eagerly.

Tum-tum, *tum*-tum.

Damon re-tuned his Martin. Yazzie and Clarita slipped behind a corner of Tony's house.

Zahnie wished she could get Ed to give her a ride right on out of there.

As Red played the intro, he allowed himself a passing glance at her. She was at the back of the crowd, face taut.

The first phrase was the haunting melody "Morning of Carnival" from *Black Orpheus*. Red wrenched out all of its poignance. Then, just before beginning to sing, he gave a big grin, and he and Damon banged out a bright and lively jig.

Everyone laughed with relief.

The comic first stanza told how life tossed Red off a bridge, hauled him out of the sea, and yelled at him to go looking, looking for something, he did not know what.

Though Damon sang the verses, he and Red sang the chorus together, Red on the melody, Damon in sweet harmony:

"I have searched the world, seeking all that is true.
I have walked the road, I have looked for glory.
In all of this world what I found was you.
Now everything waits—write an end to this story.

"Give me the word—write an end bright with glory.
Join your voice with mine—
Join your life with mine—
My love, write us for the end of this story."

The second verse told how Red came to Moonlight Water and got whisked down the river by the lady ranger. The red, white, and money, all of those silly differences, had been washed away by the river.

The third verse took them to Lukas Gulch and ended with the words: "And the sun blazed through the waterfall, and it struck your heart, and it filled you with mine."

Zahnie gasped loudly. Other Navajos put their hands over their mouths at this bit from the Creation Story, and what it meant.

The crowd grew very still, and no one looked at Zahnie.

During the next chorus Yazzie and Clarita paraded out and stood behind Red and Damon. On thick dowels they held up a fancy sign painted on butcher paper. It read:

ZAHNIE, YOU'RE GOING TO HAVE A BABY. WONDERFUL!

The next verse told how Red and Zahnie bound themselves in the adventure of rescuing Damon.

On the chorus, Yazzie and Clarita trotted out with another glorious sign:

RED IS GOING TO BE A DADDY. ECSTASY!

Then the elder duo hustled off.

The audience now was preternaturally hushed.

No one heard the next verse, for everyone's mind was on what sign Winsonfred and Clarita would come back with. It read:

LET'S RAISE OUR CHILD TOGETHER

The final run-through of the chorus brought the oldsters out with the climactic sign. They stood behind Red and Damon so that a huge painted arrow aimed directly down at Red.

ZAHNIE KEE
WILL YOU MARRY ME?

Red sang the last lines of the chorus directly to Zahnie—

"Waltz with me to a happy ending.
Lift my heart to glory.
Join your voice to this song.
Write joy for the end of this story.

"Now give me the word—write an end bright with glory.
Join your voice with mine—
Join your life with mine—
Write joy for the end of this story."

As with one pair of eyes, the members of the audience looked back at Zahnie. Her mouth was wide open, her hands covered her face, and she peered at Red through her fingers.

He rose, set down his guitar carefully, and walked to her. He eased her hands away and looked into her eyes. He said loud enough for all to hear, "Zahnie Kee, will you marry me?"

She flicked her eyes to Winsonfred onstage. The Ancient One smiled hugely and beat *tum*-tum.

Now she stood and took Red's face between her hands. Clearly, she spoke the most dangerous of all words.

"Yes."

ACKNOWLEDGMENTS

The teachings of the Blessing Way are real, and they're posted on a wall in the elementary school our grandkids go to. The Navajo proverbs at the heads of our chapters are real, too. They were brought by Navajo students, collected by their teacher Ernie Bulow, and published by Buffalo Medicine Books. *Big* thanks to Ernie for permission to use them.

Bountiful thanks also to Kristin Sevick Brown, our editor extraordinaire.

Jim Frenkel for reading and reading the manuscript and brainstorming with us.

Our agent, Bob Diforio, the white knight with shining armor and a big heart.

Tom Blevins and Leeds Davis for tips on how to blow up a boat, and for a lifetime of grand companionship.

Gil Bateman of Cosmic Coastline, the guy who got replaced by Jerry Garcia, for great info about Bay Area music in the '80s, great talks, and real friendship.

Gene and Mary Foushee for helping us settle into this red rock magic called home, and for inspiration, great conversation, and volumes of information.

And to the vibrant, wondrous neighbors who populate our village by the rez. Your lives inspired this book.